J.D. BARKER
RICHARD BAILEY

THE
LIES
WE
TELL

The Lies We Tell

Published by:
Hampton Creek Press
P.O. Box 177
New Castle, NH 03854

Worldwide Print, Sales, and Distribution by Simon & Schuster

This is a work of fiction. Names, characters, places and incidents either are products of the author's imagination or are used fictitiously. Any resemblance to actual events or locales or persons, living or dead, is entirely coincidental unless noted otherwise.

Copyright © 2025 by Jonathan Dylan Barker
Registration: 1-14221406061
All rights reserved, including the right of reproduction in whole or in part in any form.

Hampton Creek Press is a registered Trademark of Hampton Creek Publishing, LLC

For information about special discounts for bulk purchases, please contact Simon & Schuster Special Sales at 1-866-506-1949 or business@simonandschuster.com

Cover Design by Domanza
Book design and formatting by Domanza

Author photograph by Bill Peterson of Peterson Gallery

Manufactured in the United States of America

ISBN: 9798990746121 (HARDCOVER 6x9)
ISBN: 9798990746138 (PAPERBACK 5.25x8)
ISBN: 9798990746145 (EBOOK)

© **Copyright 2024 - All rights reserved.**

The content contained within this book may not be reproduced, duplicated or transmitted without direct written permission from the author or the publisher.

Under no circumstances will any blame or legal responsibility be held against the publisher, or author, for any damages, reparation, or monetary loss due to the information contained within this book, either directly or indirectly.

Legal Notice:
This book is copyright protected. It is only for personal use. You cannot amend, distribute, sell, use, quote or paraphrase any part, or the content within this book, without the consent of the author or publisher.

Disclaimer Notice:
Please note the information contained within this document is for educational and entertainment purposes only. All effort has been executed to present accurate, up to date, reliable, complete information. No warranties of any kind are declared or implied. Readers acknowledge that the author is not engaged in the rendering of legal, financial, medical or professional advice. The content within this book has been derived from various sources. Please consult a licensed professional before attempting any techniques outlined in this book.

By reading this document, the reader agrees that under no circumstances is the author responsible for any losses, direct or indirect, that are incurred as a result of the use of the information contained within this document, including, but not limited to, errors, omissions, or inaccuracies.

ALSO BY J.D. BARKER

Forsaken
She Has A Broken Thing Where Her Heart Should Be
A Caller's Game
Behind A Closed Door
Something I Keep Upstairs

4MK THRILLER SERIES
The Fourth Monkey
The Fifth To Die
The Sixth Wicked Child

WITH JAMES PATTERSON
The Coast to Coast Murders
The Noise
Death of the Black Widow
Confessions of the Dead
The Writer

WITH OTHERS
Dracul
Heavy Are The Stones
We Don't Talk About Emma

CHAPTER 1

COMA

LIGHT SO BRIGHT it stings. A flash of color. Terrible pain behind my eyes and in my skull. It's like somebody is trying to beat their way out of me. I'm nauseous. I gasp for air but recoil, my mouth as dry as ash and my throat lined with straight razors. I sense my fingers, my toes, but they feel disembodied somehow, as if my limbs are disconnected. Who do these limbs belong to? It's like I'm being pulled out of a dark hole on a thin string, my grasp on reality a tenuous link at best. I crave water, something cool on my brow. I want to slip back into the darkness, go back to wherever I've been. I'm not sure who or where I am.

Above me is a ceiling, white like chalk, bright lights embedded inside it like glowing embers. Shadow puppets move beyond a window inset into the door. I wonder who those people are. I wonder who is in here. I want to cry and scream at the same time. I'm desperate but I don't know why. Where is this? What's happened to me?

A tube protrudes from my arm like a long, sinuous vein. It's connected to a bag that's filled with clear liquid. What is it? Poison? Sugar water? Alcohol?

A machine beeps beside me, a jagged, flittering line leaping up and down as the tinny speaker lets out sharp, clipped cries. Flashing numbers blink rapidly at me. Digital, escalating. My heart is like an explosion in my chest, detonating repeatedly. My cavity could erupt at any minute, spewing me all over the walls and floor.

I want to get up, but it's like I'm nailed to the bed. Nothing is responding. Something bad has happened, I can sense it.

"Hey there, Supernova," somebody says. "Boy, have I missed seeing those beautiful, glittering eyes."

My head snaps to the source of this strange voice. A man is sitting on a stool. I hadn't noticed him before. How hadn't I noticed him? He's right in front of me. He's tall and bullish, athletic, wide shoulders—looks like he could handle himself. I'm a little afraid. His hair is tidy, light brown, brushed to one side. He has what looks like a few days growth on his chin and cheeks. He has dark, narrow eyes, dark. They widen when he looks at me. I can't figure out what's lurking behind them.

I try to speak but I emit a rasping, gurgling squeak as if I've been strangled. My chest hurts too, as though somebody has punched me. I start to become claustrophobic, hemmed in. I try to remember things, anything, but my mind is a sea of nothingness. My history is a vacuous void. I'm like a newborn, as if the world is a new and wondrous thing to me, except I understand things. I am aware of what a lamp is, what a bed is, the chair in the corner of the room, the ceiling tiles, the drapes. But I have no idea who this man is or why he's here.

"Don't try to speak," he says, approaching me with his

palms held out, a gesture of peace. "Don't move. You've been in a horrible accident."

Accident? What accident? I peer down at my body, afraid of what might be missing. I'm relieved my arms are where they should be, my hands, both legs. My feet are obscured by long white socks. I look mummified.

"You've been in here for almost four days. I was so worried about you. We all were."

His hand slips over mine. His fingers are warm but calloused. He is somebody who works with the land. I can tell from his strength, his hardened skin. I notice the curve of his biceps beneath his shirt, his thick chest. He could crush me if he wanted to, and there isn't a damn thing I could do about it.

I wonder if I'm paralyzed, if I'll ever be able to move again. I concentrate hard, and eventually, my toes wiggle beneath my socks and my fingers move. It's a victory, but a shallow one.

I want to cry, to let it all out. I feel so alone, so naked. It's like my skin is a stranger to me, my bones a hard frame of nothingness. I'm terrified of this man, of the shadows that lurk behind the door. The silence is interrupted by a noise in the corridor, and everything inside me urges me to get up and make a run for it, to leap out the window if I have to. I have no idea what floor I'm on—I might be at the top of a tall building, but I don't care. Anything is better than this. The not knowing. The not remembering.

Is this man going to take me away? Lock me in a room? Examine me? Is he why I'm in here? Have I been kidnapped? Are the people in the corridor just like him?

A white-gold ring glimmers on his wedding finger, engraved. I look down at my own. My fingers are bare.

"Your rings are all gone, Sierra," he says. "The doctors had to cut them off. Your hands were so swollen."

So that's my name. Sierra. I like it, but it doesn't spark anything in me. No memory, no recollection. I thought it might, but it doesn't. My memory is a white sheet of paper. Not even an inkblot.

"Who am I?" I manage, but it hurts to speak. My tongue, my throat, my chest, they all scream out in agony. My voice is weird to me, deeper than I imagined. I'm so hoarse.

"You're Sierra Coleman," he replies, his face a mask of anxiety. "And we're in St. Margaret's Hospital, Thousand Oaks, California."

"Why am I here?"

"As I said, you were in an accident. A car crash. You were the only one inside. Nobody else was hurt. You were knocked out cold, completely out of it. Man, I didn't know what to do when I saw you lying on the road. The car was a twisted, mangled wreck. I thought you were dead."

The way he says the last word makes me shrink within myself. I ask the question that's been plaguing me ever since I saw him, although I'm not sure I want the answer.

"And... who... who are you?"

A smile spreads across his lips. He has a handsome smile, a charming one, but I don't trust him. How can I? I have no memory of him. He is a stranger to me. Heck, I'm a stranger to myself.

"You don't remember," he says. "But that's okay. I can fill you in when you're well."

"I'm okay. Honestly, just tell me. Please."

He perches on the edge of the bed, leans toward me as if he's going to take a bite out of me. I pull away. He notices my reaction, but it doesn't appear to bother him.

"I'm Wesley, Sierra. The man you fell in love with a little over three years ago. The person you've spent every day with ever since that weekend in Cabo San Lucas, the most important, magical weekend of our lives."

"I don't understand," I say. "What are you saying?"

He takes my face in his hand and kisses me. I try to pull away, but he's so strong.

"I'm your husband."

CHAPTER 2

BLONDIE

I'M SO CONFUSED, so disorientated. How can this man be my husband? How can we be married? I have no memory of him, no feelings. My heart doesn't flutter when he gets close. If anything, it's pounding. My body screams out for me to retreat. I can't believe him. I won't. This is all one big mistake. A lie. I need to find out who I truly am. I'm not Sierra Coleman. I'm not. I refuse to believe it.

"You're surprised," he says, standing. "I can tell. It's understandable. The doctors explained the potential for memory loss, but this is far worse than I feared. Can you… can you remember anything at all?"

I focus, concentrating all my energy on the part of my brain where the past is stored. Finding nothing, I shake my head. The door to that particular chamber is locked, and I have no idea where the key is. A cloud of frustration covers me like a thick blanket. I'm so angry with myself. Why is this so difficult?

"I'll help you," he adds. "Don't worry. We can work on this together. You and I. I'll help you through it."

Something about his eyes unsettles me. They're like little glass discs, computer screens. His smile never makes it past his cheeks.

I try to sit up but little shards of electric current fizz across my temples. I gasp and squint.

"Water," I say. "I need water."

"Of course." He reaches across me and grabs a water jug, pouring some of it into a plastic cup. He places a paper straw inside it and holds it to my lips. I suck greedily. The cool liquid is like iced gold on my tongue and throat. I relish it as it slips down my gullet and spreads through my abdomen. I try to drink some more but he pulls it away.

"The doctor says to drink a little at a time. We don't want you throwing up, now do we?"

It's the first time I've felt anything other than fear, anxiety. Taking the cup away makes me dislike him. He isn't aware of what this sensation is like, to be nobody, to be nothing. I want to tell him, to explain, but I still haven't decided whether I trust him.

The door opens and my heart leaps in my chest. It's one of the people from the corridor. One of the shadow puppets. She's around 5'7", choppy red hair—recently dyed—pale skin like milk, little freckles, thin as a rake, slight breasts. Her eyes are on fire, her feet tapping on the floor. She looks so excited, I think she's going to faint.

"Oh, Sierra," she shrieks, dropping her bag on the floor and practically running at me. I find the ability to sit up, despite my pounding head, and I shrink against the bed, trying to escape her. I fail. Her hands find me, followed by her arms, her thin torso. I'm pinned beneath her like a wrestler. Something wet is on my face, warm. I realize she's crying, sobbing. Her emotions are too much, so over the top.

"I was so worried," she says through tears and trembling shoulders. "I thought you might never come back to us."

Wesley, the man who says he's my husband, gently ushers her away.

"Come on now, Mary Elisabeth," he says. "We need to give Sierra her space. She's only recently come back to us."

"Of course," Mary Elisabeth says, peering up at him, then back at me. She doesn't blink. "I'm sorry. I'm so happy."

"I can't remember who you are," I say, and then I realize how it sounds, as if I don't care. Perhaps I don't.

Mary Elisabeth looks hurt, offended. "I'm your best friend, Sierra. We've been joined at the hip since we were kids."

The way she reacts makes me think twice, second-guessing myself. The guilt burns in my stomach. "I'm sorry," I say, shaking my head. "I just… I can't remember anything at all."

"Oh, Sea," she says—I'm guessing it's her pet name for me. "It's okay. I understand. It's not your fault. You're sick, but don't worry. Wesley and I, we'll help you get well again. We'll be with you every step of the way."

She fetches her bag, reaches inside, and pulls out some grapes and a Pepsi. I've never wanted something so badly in my life.

"Woah," Wesley says as she brings the items to me. "I'm not sure that's a good idea."

Once more, I want to punch the man who claims to be my husband. Why does he keep trying to take things away from me?

"Sure it is," Mary Elisabeth replies. "She hasn't eaten in days and she must be so thirsty."

"You're right," I say. "On both counts."

I eat three grapes in quick succession, relishing the taste. I wash them down with a mouthful of fizzy drink. I can't recall whether I liked these things before the crash, but I do now.

I close my eyes, shut the light out, try to blot out the sounds around me. I want to remember. I want to recall who these people are. I want to trust them, but it's hard when there's nothing at all, merely an impenetrable wall of blackness.

An image flashes before my eyes. A little girl. Maybe ten or eleven years old. Blonde pigtails. Sad eyes. She's mouthing something but I can't read her lips. I remember her face. I think she was with me while I was unconscious. I know her. I'm sure I do, but can't remember how. She's pleading with me, tears glistening, her lips trembling. I reach out to her but she backs away from me, and then the darkness starts to take her, and though I run after her, she's gone before I can get close.

"Sierra," Wesley says, hand clasping my shoulders. "Are you okay?"

I open my eyes and I'm back in my hospital bed, back with my supposed husband and best friend.

The shadow puppets have returned behind the door. It opens a crack and somebody looks through. The clatter of a clipboard, the murmur of voices and movement. A man in a white coat walks in and looks me up and down. He smiles, toothy and white.

"Ah, Mrs. Coleman," he says. Although he has confirmed the name Wesley gave to me, doesn't mean it's true. "You're awake. That's good." He eyes the others. "I'm afraid we'll need to check Mrs. Coleman over, so perhaps you can leave us for a little while."

"Of course," Wesley says. "Don't worry, Supernova. We'll be right outside."

I can't decide whether I'm happy about their departure or

more afraid than I was before. I know this doctor even less than I know the two of them, and the thought is terrifying to me.

As the newcomer looms over me, clipboard in hand, stethoscope held out like a dagger, I think of the little girl and her sad eyes. It's like something has been taken from me, more than merely my memory and sense of self. The girl is important to me. I'm sure of it. I just need to figure out why.

CHAPTER 3

CRASH

THE NIGHT IS filled with hospital noises, discomfort, and crippling anxiety. It's like I'm in a cocoon, but unlike a butterfly, I don't expect to burst out of it with colorful wings and a sense of freedom. I'm in a prison cell, but I have no idea what crime I've committed. I lay awake, staring at the ceiling, trying to focus on memories, but they're so ethereal, they never show themselves to me.

My newly declared husband and best friend departed together a little after 8 p.m. I wasn't sad when they left, but I wasn't happy about it either. Although I can't remember them, they're obviously close to me, which makes them the only link to a life that's painfully out of reach. I want to put the pieces of the jigsaw back together again. I need it more than anything else. I cling to the little snippets they've given to me like driftwood in the ocean. I want to nurture them, make them grow. Perhaps if I learn more, understand more, then my memory will slowly return like somebody pulling the curtains back from the stage.

I'm able to sit up fully now. The doctor gave me some painkillers for my headache and bruises. When he lifted my gown up, I saw the black and purple on my abdomen, my chest, and legs. I look like I've been in a fight.

I swing my feet over the edge of the bed and stand for the first time. Wooziness hits me like a hammer, so I sit back down again. I fight the urge to vomit. I'm fully aware it's merely the lingering effects of concussion. I give myself a few beats, wait for the feelings of sickness to subside, and try again. This time the wooziness is only half as bad, but it's sickening enough to force me back down on my backside. I have no idea if I'm the quitting type—I haven't introduced myself to myself yet—but I decide that's not the kind of person I want to be.

I stand again, slower this time, waiting for the hammer blow to come again, but this time I barely sense it. I'm up. My feet and legs are strong enough to hold me. I suppress a little cry of jubilation but I'm elated all the same.

Approaching the window to the corridor, I pull back the blinds. It's a bustle of activity. It's still early in the morning so the lights are dimmed, but I study the other rooms: an old man with a bandage over one eye, a young woman with a busted leg, a middle-aged guy with heavy strapping across his chest. It's a hospital. What did I expect? The head nurse looks up from her desk, sees me standing in the doorway, and raises a hand. I hold up my own and wiggle my fingers back at her. She smiles.

I think of the girl in my vision. I didn't ask Wesley or Mary Elisabeth about her. I didn't want to seem like I'm losing what remains of my mind. It's possible she's a figment of a thousand different memories, glued together like a broken plate. She could be one person or a hundred people. I'm yet to fully appreciate what's left of me, so how can I truly understand whether my brain is functioning properly?

I decide I need some air so I approach the window. It faces the parking lot and a large patch of green space a little further out. The joggers are already outside, dressed in tight-fitting shorts and baggy shirts. I open the window and let the morning air in. It's refreshing. I let it run through my hair, which I realize I haven't seen yet.

A mirror on the wall above the sink glares back at me and I approach it. It's not as bad as I thought. Apart from bags under my eyes and my lips looking drier than the Sahara, I'm passable. My looks don't surprise me as much as I feared. Perhaps I remember myself more than I thought. My hair is dark, shoulder length, pretty straight, although right now it's greasier than all hell. I'm slim, which is good, mid-thirties at a guess, dark eyes, around five-six. If Wesley, my husband, is to be believed, a woman called Sierra Coleman is looking back at me from the smeared mirror. It's good to meet her.

The door opens, startling me.

"Hi. Mrs. Coleman, isn't it?"

"You can call me Sierra," I say, relishing the sound of my name on my tongue. It's the only thing that's remotely real to me.

"I'm Nurse Rodriguez," she says. She's my height, broad, smiling cheeks. "I've come by to check on you. I know it's early, but I saw you awake, so—"

"It's fine," I say. "I'm glad of the company."

"The doctor says you're suffering from acute memory loss."

I nod. The words sound horrible when they're spoken aloud. "He's got that right."

"I'm sorry to hear it. But the good news is, he thinks it's short term."

I smile, but it's a little forced. The doctor told me the same thing, but how can he be sure? Right now, my memory is locked in a box on an island located a thousand miles away. Sure, I could try to swim across the ocean, but chances are, I'll drown trying.

"You look a little pale. Do you want me to get you anything?" she asks. "A water, maybe?"

I'm still nauseous so I gratefully decline. I want to sleep, but I suspect I can't. Instead, I decide to probe for answers. Maybe this nurse knows something.

"Can you tell me how I was?" I ask, sounding like a child talking to her class teacher. "When I came in, I mean. Were you here?"

The nurse shakes her head and the disappointment suffocates me. I need to know what happened. I need to hear it from somebody other than the guy who says he's my husband and the woman who claims to be my lifelong friend.

"You were brought in by ambulance," she says, shocking me. "I wasn't here, but I've read the report. You were in a bad way, bleeding and unconscious."

I grasp at her words like pennies in a jar. "Was... was my husband with me?"

The nurse shakes her head. "No. He arrived around ten minutes later. The report says he drove here."

Her words are strange to me, a bizarre riddle. Why was I on my own? If Wesley truly is my loving husband, then shouldn't he have been with me?

"You look upset," she says.

"I'm confused, is all."

"That's understandable." She writes something in her notebook. "But don't worry. Your husband is a great guy."

My eyes snap to her. "Why do you say that?"

She grins from ear to ear. "As I said, I read the report. Your husband, he's a hero. He got to you real quick, saw you were trapped in the car, and helped the police pull you out. It was a close call, too. You could have both been killed."

I shake my head. "I don't know what you mean."

The nurse shudders. I shouldn't be surprised. What she says next makes me shudder, too. "As soon as you were pulled away from the car, the whole thing went up like a Roman candle."

CHAPTER 4

THE NURSE

THE DAY COMES and goes. It's like I'm in a dream state, not truly here, not truly anywhere. Everything is chaos in my head. I touch my face with fingers that are numb. My skin is like plastic, my body working in slow motion.

The doctor returns and tells me they plan to discharge me in the morning. I should be glad. I should be happy my condition has reached a point where the medical team considers me well enough to leave. The problem is, I have no idea where I'll go. I have no memory of owning a house, of living anywhere other than this hospital bed. I haven't set foot outside yet. I can't recall what the outdoors is like. Fear grips me, tugs at my stomach, pulls me around.

Wesley is more jubilant. "It's fantastic news, Sierra. I can take care of you, nurse you back to full health."

I wish I shared his optimism. I still have no idea who he is. I realize I'll have to relearn everything day by day. The nurse said my husband's a hero, and who am I to argue? He pulled me from a burning vehicle after all. He could have died. He risked his life for me. I should love him, but I don't. Not yet.

Mary Elisabeth doesn't show up today. Wesley says she had some urgent business to take care of. *Some best friend*, I think to myself, but then realize I'm being churlish. Other people have lives, too. I'm not the only show in town.

"I'll fix the house up for you," Wesley says, although I'm hardly paying any attention. "Make sure it's tidy and you have everything you need. Don't put any pressure on yourself. Everything's taken care of. You don't need to worry about it."

Taken care of? His words sound strange. If I hadn't crashed the car, I wouldn't need to be taken care of. I wonder what caused the accident. Had I been speeding? Drinking, maybe? Nobody has mentioned a crime being committed or of the police wanting to speak to me. I guess that means it really was an accident, but if no other cars were involved, why did I slide off the road in such a violent way? It's all a little odd, a little too clean.

When Wesley leaves, I wave him off with a smile, but I'm not happy. My overriding emotion is confusion. And anxiety. I can't shake either thing. It's all I've felt since I woke up in this room. I have a suspicion there is more going on here than meets the eye, although nobody has done anything to cause these crippling suspicions. Everyone has been nice to me—Wesley and Mary Elisabeth included.

I eat dinner—a chicken salad with extra sauce—and wash it down with ice-cold water. I can't get enough of the stuff. My body craves it continuously. I put my burgeoning thirst down to the stuffiness of the hospital room, but I have no idea if that's the truth of it. Maybe I have something wrong with me, some medical condition they haven't spotted yet.

I decide to go for a walk. I've barely traveled more than 20 feet outside of my room at this point, and I need to stretch my legs. I've been disconnected from the saline and the heart monitor, so I can walk freely without having to drag a half dozen contraptions behind me like I'm walking some sort of mechanized puppy around. I've heard the nurses talking about the staff cafeteria and the vending machines serving bars of chocolate, so I decide that's where I'm going. I grab my purse—Wesley handed it to me before he left—and I make my move.

It doesn't take me long to become exhausted. I hadn't appreciated how far the cafeteria was. I'm also pretty sure I'm lost. I thought it was a right followed by two lefts, but maybe I had it back to front. I'm in a corridor stretching on for miles without a soul in sight. I wonder whether I've inadvertently stumbled into a parallel universe where chocolate is outlawed and people are scarce.

Terror starts to grip me and I feel like I'm going to faint. I'm not sure what will be worse: the pain as I hit the floor, or the embarrassment when I wake up. This was a mistake. I should have stayed in my room and waited for Wesley to collect me in the morning. Perhaps my husband's right. Maybe I do need to take it slow.

I turn around, but I have no idea how to get back and barely any energy left to make the journey.

"Hey, what you doing all the way out here?" a friendly voice asks.

I turn around on shaky legs and come face to face with a man who I don't recognize. It's hardly surprising.

"Do I know you?" I ask.

"Nope. I don't think so," he replies, slipping an arm around me, causing my body to stiffen. "But I'm not going to stand here and watch you pass out on me."

"Should you be touching me like that?" His aftershave is nice. It smells of musk and spice.

"Probably not." He grins, amused. He holds out his other

hand and I take it. "Nurse Kaiden Marshall at your service. I was first on the scene when you arrived."

My heart leaps in my chest. A guardian angel, no less, and someone who might be able to give me answers.

He walks me to a seating area and sits me down. He perches next to me. He has smiling eyes, short, hazel hair, and a tiny scar on the left side of his chin. I find myself trusting him more than my own husband.

"Can you tell me what happened?" I ask. "I'm aware I was in an accident, and I narrowly escaped death."

"That's all true," he replies, nodding. "It probably doesn't feel like it right now, but you were very lucky."

"Yeah, I've been told that a lot." He has the face of someone who knows the truth and isn't afraid to speak it. I'm filled with hope. "But how was I? When I arrived I mean. How did I look?"

He shrugs. "You were pretty beaten up. You took one hell of a hit. I tried to talk to you, but you weren't in a fit state to hold a conversation."

His words stun me. How could he hold a conversation with a woman who was unconscious? "Are you trying to tell me I was awake when they brought me in?"

He nods. "Drifting in and out, but yeah. You were awake. Animated, too."

I'm so shocked, I can barely form a sentence. Why hasn't anyone mentioned this to me before? Why wasn't this in the report? "Did I... did I say anything to you? Anything at all?"

He pauses, and for a moment I think he's going to let me down. But then his head snaps up and he tells me something that makes my confused state go into overdrive.

"Mystic spring," he says. "You were saying those two words over and over again. You were trying to tell me something about Mystic Spring."

The Lies We Tell

CHAPTER 5

SOCIAL

MY HEAD IS in a spin. I have no idea what the words *mystic spring* mean, or if they have a relationship to each other. I run them over and over in my head, trying to dislodge something from the cluttered, dust-riddled attic of my brain. The nurse, Kaiden, seemed sincere enough. The concern in his eyes was obvious. He wanted me to remember. He wanted to help me. I am so sure of that it hurts. It's good to have someone on my side. Somebody I trust.

He helps me back to my room and eyes me from the doorway. There is something about him I can't place. I don't remember him, but I sense a compassion within him. I'm feeling closer to home than since I came round. I wonder if that's weird, that I have an affinity to a stranger rather than the man who says he's my husband.

"I'll be seeing you," he says as he starts to leave.

I don't want him to go, but I have no reason to ask him to stay.

"Thanks for your help," I offer, sounding feeble.

"It's no bother. I was glad to." He stops, half in and half out the door. "Did they give you back your things?"

I shake my head. I have things? I guess it makes sense. I must have come in with something. "I don't think so."

"I'll get someone to bring them to you," he says. I want to ask if he can be the one who gives them to me, but then he adds, "My shift started around five minutes ago, so I really should be going."

He smiles and my heart breaks a little. I have the sensation of inappropriateness again. I'm a married woman for heaven's sake.

The door closes and I slump into my pillow. I'm suddenly exhausted. I never made it to the cafeteria, but maybe it was for the best. I found out something about my arrival, something new, even if it made no sense at all. The words, *mystic spring*, could mean anything. I was barely conscious. I could have been reciting lyrics from a song, or a brand of soap I'd recently seen advertised on TV. I decide not to put too much thought into what Kaiden told me. In the absence of anything compelling, I could be wasting my energy.

I slip in and out of sleep. I dream about a shallow stream and cool, bubbling water; ghosts hovering over it like a morning mist.

When I come round, I see a bag inside my door. I smile. Kaiden managed to get it to me. I sit up, let the dream dissipate a little, and then collect the bag. It's not heavy. Only a few things. A fitness tracker watch, a necklace with a silver feather pendant, a pair of looped earrings, and a phone.

A phone! I hadn't thought about whether I had one of those.

I grab it, drop it in my excitement, but regather it. I stumble back to my bed, perch on the edge. I pray the battery is charged. I press a button on the side and thankfully the screen illuminates. My cover photo is a picture of a sunset in a place I don't remember. Palm trees line a golden beach. My phone only has fifteen percent battery life remaining, so I need to hurry. The display asks for a pin number but I have no idea what it could be. I hold it to my face, hoping the Samsung has facial recognition software.

For a moment, the screen stares back at me, daring me to do something rash, but then it blinks, and suddenly I'm in. I'm so elated, so energized. This is a link. A tether back to what I was before. I clutch it like a life rope. I want to kiss it.

I head straight to the photo gallery. It's blank. I shake my head. Who does that? Me, I guess. I try to access my emails, but I don't appear to have an email account, which startles me. I start to get suspicious. Has somebody wiped my phone? I have one last shot. My social media. I open Facebook and see a picture of me looking far more glamorous than I do in my hospital attire. My hair is brushed back, I have lipstick on, eyeliner. I'm wearing a white tee and figure-hugging jeans. I scroll through my posts. I find a picture of me standing with Wesley. We're in a garden, sipping cocktails. Another photo depicts a shirtless Wesley cleaning a pool. I was right about his physique. He clearly looks after himself. I find a photograph of me standing with a group of people I don't recall. I look out of place, like I don't belong with them.

I keep scrolling. I find an image of a house, of Wesley cutting a large red ribbon with an oversized bow outside. Is this our home? Did Wesley buy it for us? It's an impressive building with large windows, a sweeping balcony, modern, crisp architecture. It looks like something out of a brochure.

Once again, I wait for the memories to come, the images to come flooding back to me. Nothing happens.

I find yet more pictures, this time of Mary Elisabeth and I at some form of social gathering. We appear to be in a gallery surrounded by modern art and endless canapes. I'm drinking white wine, Mary Elisabeth, red. She's laughing, I look distracted. In another, she has her arm draped around a slightly older man with salt and pepper hair. I'm picking at the food and chatting with a group of women who are far more glamorous than me. I can't help but think there's something false about what I'm looking at, as if everybody has been asked to stand in a particular way and paint on the same fake smile. I'm probably being paranoid, deluded, whatever. I can't help the way I feel.

I don't find anything countering the story that Wesley told me. Everything matches perfectly. The home I share with him. Our marriage. My friendship with Mary Elisabeth. It's all a little too neat, too tidy, as if everything has been cleaned to perfection. This disinfected version of my life is like a movie I never starred in, a TV program I've never watched.

I throw the phone on the bed, frustrated. I can't work out whether I'm angry my perfect life has been interrupted by such a senseless, random event, or whether I'm pissed off that the life I almost lost is as staid and as boring as I was led to believe. Is this an existence I want to remember, one I can learn to cherish? I curse myself for being so self-centered, so entitled. What am I expecting to find? Kaiden is still on my mind, as is the little girl with blonde pigtails.

I curl my knees to my chest, ball my hands into fists, and will myself to sleep.

CHAPTER 6

MOM

I'M SHOWERED AND dressed. I sit on the edge of the bed in a pair of jeans and a black, strappy top, and wait for my husband to arrive. I haven't seen Kaiden today. I realize it's probably not his shift. Why would he come into the hospital on his day off to visit me, somebody he's literally only just met, leave?

I push aside my disappointment. It's not helpful. I have to get used to the fact I'm married. I have to learn to love Wesley again, assuming I ever did.

"Hey, Supernova," he says, using his annoying pet name for me again. "You're looking good."

"I don't have any makeup," I say, sounding like a sulking teenager.

"Heck, you don't need any. You're plenty beautiful without it."

I shrug, stand as he hugs me. His arms are so big, he could crush me at any second. I hope he never has the urge.

"It's so good to be getting you out of here, Sierra. I'm just so happy."

I look up at him. He looks like he's about to cry. I should be overjoyed, elated. Here's a man who says he loves me, who's moved to tears that I managed to avoid the grim reaper, and yet I'm ambivalent to him. I'm ashamed of myself, as if I've become a narcissistic socialite who expects others to love her without anything in return.

"I'm happy, too," I say. "Honestly."

He kisses my forehead, which I think is a little odd. He takes my hand and leads me through the door. I wave to the nurses, scouring the ward for a sight of Kaiden. It's a long shot and I get what I deserve, which is nothing.

"You expecting somebody?" Wesley says, catching the way I'm acting.

I shake my head. "Of course not. I don't know anybody else."

He smiles. "You will," he says. "You've got plenty of friends back home."

If only I knew where *back home* was.

We head to the parking lot. It's the first time I've stepped outside. It's a beautiful day. The kind of day that makes you remember you're alive, except I feel anything but. I still have the ridiculous sensation that I'm dreaming. Nothing appears real. I wonder whether I'm going to wake up at any moment, find myself in my real life, in my real home, with a husband I can actually remember. Deep down inside, perhaps that's what I want. To be anywhere but here.

"This is us," Wesley says, presenting me with a sky-blue, Ford F-Series. The words *Coleman Construction* are painted in bright red and white lettering down the side, the words slanted in italics, I guess to signify speed. I think it looks egotistical and loud, but maybe that's the way Wesley wants it. To be seen. To be noticed.

"Is it far?" I ask.

"The house?"

I nod, pulling myself into the passenger seat.

He smiles, showing me all his teeth. They're evenly spaced and well-looked after. I wonder once more why I can't accept this man as the person I'm supposed to be with. Maybe it will come with time, but doubt nips away at me like a hungry kitten. I wish I could be more sure.

"It's not far at all, Tiger," he says, chewing on a stick of gum. "Not far at all."

❉ ❉ ❉

We pull into a long driveway, the perimeter bordered by a half dozen Dogwoods. The gravel crunches beneath the wheels. It sounds like bones are being fed into a grinder. We pull up in front of the house. It's the one in the photographs. It's even more impressive in real life. The pool out front is big enough for a football team. I want to jump right in, let the water envelope me, for my body to sink to the bottom so I can hide from everybody.

"So?" Wesley says, helping me out of the truck. "What d'ya think?"

"It's beautiful," I say, sounding more convincing than I'd expected.

"Isn't she fantastic? We only bought her a year ago. She cost a small fortune, but she was worth every damn penny. Every darn one."

I walk toward the building, run my hand over the stucco plaster. I guess I'm trying to connect to the house in some physical, tactile way, if that's possible. The wall is cold, rigid. I have an overriding sensation of nothingness. The house could belong to anybody. It certainly doesn't feel like it belongs to me.

"Sierra, dear!" somebody calls out.

I'm jarred back to the moment. I turn to face a demure, older woman walking toward me from the garden. She's dressed in slacks, a floral top, and her silver hair is coiffured and immaculate.

I glance at Wesley, who is staring at the other woman as if she is a Hollywood star.

"I'm sorry," I say as she takes my hand in hers. Her fingernails are manicured and red-tipped. "But I don't remember you."

Her smile doesn't falter, not one bit. "I realize that, dear. Your husband told me all about it, but it's okay. All that matters is you're safe and well. You're back home with your family where you belong."

I want to believe her, but I still don't know whether I belong anywhere, least of all, here.

"I'm your mother, dear," she says, throwing me into a tailspin.

"My what?"

"Your mother. The person who conceived and gave birth to you."

"I don't understand." I'm completely side-swiped. This woman doesn't look anything like me. She's much shorter and her face is round. Mine is narrow.

"What's not to understand?" she replies.

"Evie has been living with us since your father died," Wesley says, placing his hands over this woman's and my own. "She's been sent from heaven to look after us. To look after *you*."

Sent from heaven? Who says that? "I'm so sorry," I say, realizing I'm being crass and more than a little rude. "I want to remember, I do, but for some reason, I just can't."

The woman, my mom, hugs me. I'm so shocked, my body becomes rigid. If she senses it, she doesn't let it show.

"You poor thing," she says. "You poor, poor thing."

"Listen," Wesley says. "I need to take a call in the house. I won't be long, but in the meantime, why don't you get reacquainted with your mom, and take a look around the place? Hopefully, it will help you remember." He cocks his thumb and forefinger and pretends to shoot. "I sure hope it does."

He stoops and kisses my mom on the cheek. He holds her a little longer than he should. Something about the way he's acting unsettles me, although I can't quite put my finger on it.

As he disappears inside, Evie takes my hand and leads me to the front door.

"Well then," she says, the scent of lavender and peach blossom wafting from her clothes, "let's give you the guided tour."

CHAPTER 7

LOVING HUSBAND

I'M ON THE couch, sipping a cup of coffee the woman who claims to be my mom made for me. The place is completely open-plan with high ceilings and a second floor overlooking the first. It's modern and contemporary, but stark and cold, without character. I wonder if the old me would ever have picked a place like this, or whether it was Wesley's choice. Is he the kind of husband who imposes his will on the women in his life? He doesn't give me those vibes, but let's face it, I don't know him. This new me only met him three days ago.

I'm so tired. The confusion is exhausting. The caffeine is doing nothing to diminish my fatigue. If only I could unpick this tangled web, somehow find its center. Maybe the truth is somewhere nearby, or maybe I'm already reclining within the truth, sitting in the house where everything I want to remember already exists.

"Hey," Wesley says, arriving in the living room like a whirlwind. "What do you need? Cookies? Ice cream? We've got it all."

"I'm good," I reply.

"Nonsense. You need to build your strength back up. You've been put through a horrible, traumatic experience. The worst. Your body needs sugar. It needs protein."

"A cookie then," I say to appease him, forcing a smile. "What you got?"

"Does double chocolate chip sound good?"

"Sounds great."

I force it down, even though I'm nauseous. The not knowing is like having the worst hangover. I come to the realization my stomach will never settle until everything has come back to me, however painful it might seem. I'll have to get used to it.

A little while later, Wesley heads out to get some things from town. "I won't be long," he says. "Do you want me to get you anything?"

I shake my head.

"I will anyway," he replies, laughing. "You try to stop me."

"I wouldn't dare," I reply, playing along, but wondering why I need to be so forced. Maybe this is all real. Maybe I'm being too harsh on the guy. He wants to look after me, after all. Am I being a bitch for resisting his kindness?

The door closes and I wonder what to do with myself. My phone glares at me from the coffee table, tempting me. I pick it up, unlock it. Maybe I missed something in my first go round. Maybe I can find something more.

I scan back through the images I've already seen, the "likes" from people I don't remember, the happy-face and laughing-face emojis. I have 217 friends on my account, but they may as well be aliens. I don't have any affinity with them. I feel like I'm standing at a football game, standing shoulder to shoulder with dozens of people, not knowing any of their names or anything about them.

I keep scrolling, hoping there's something. There has to be.

My eye is drawn to an image of me standing next to an older man, much older. He has deep lines in his face, thin white hair, a Dodgers baseball cap. His eyes are smiling, his lips drawn up at the corners. The photo must have been taken quite a few years ago because I look like I'm fresh out of college. My hair is glossy and long, and my skin is as smooth as silk. I look happy, and real, too. More real than I look in any of the other images. I wonder who this man is, the elderly guy with the hat.

I park it and start searching for photographs of my wedding day. If I truly am married, surely I would have posted something on my profile. Wesley said we got married almost three years ago, which isn't long at all. Those posts would still be available to access, displayed for all my 217 friends to admire. That's what newlyweds do, isn't it? Show off? Let the world bathe in how wonderful their nuptials were?

I scroll and scroll and scroll but don't find anything. No white dress, no tuxedo, no blushing bridesmaids or videos of Wesley and I dancing the night away to some cheesy pop band. It doesn't make sense, none of it. Why wouldn't I be proud of those moments? Why wouldn't I have them front and center on my profile? The happy bride, the beaming groom.

Come to think of it, I haven't found one single image of my mom, either. She's conspicuous by her absence, which I find odd.

I begin to wonder whether our marriage isn't a happy one, and whether my relationship with my mother is less than loving. Perhaps that's why I can't remember. Maybe my injured brain has pushed all the unhappiness, all the distress, right down to the farthest point of my psyche, burying it beneath a sea of darkness from which it will never return.

Suddenly, I get a bad case of the shivers, as if I've been cast adrift.

I scroll on, not wanting to consider that version of my reality. I want to be happy, I want to be loved, but I need to have some memory of the people who claim to be the main characters in my life. It isn't much to ask, is it?

I locate an old image. A really old one. I'm around nine or ten years of age. My hair is pulled back in bunches. I'm laughing so hard my face is screwed up into a tight little ball. Next to me is a young boy with tangerine hair, and next to him is a red-headed girl. She's laughing and pointing at the boy who has ice cream smeared across his cheeks. Behind us is a Winnebago, and seated in front of it is a younger version of the man in the earlier image. In this photograph, his hair is auburn, cut short into a buzz cut. He has an unlit Chesterfield between his lips.

My eyes drift to the girl with red hair. Could it be Mary Elisabeth? The hair color is a match, so too are the freckles on her cheeks. Maybe she's been telling the truth, just like Wesley and Evie. She said we've known each other since we were very young, and this is very young. Maybe this is all the proof I need to start believing.

I let the phone slip onto the sofa and I sit back, watching as the pool guy cleans the water.

Could this be my life? Is this who I am? If it is, it isn't too bad, is it? I've clearly got money and a lifestyle to go with it. If I learned to accept it, I would be comfortable. Real comfortable. I would be looked after, pampered, groomed like a prize thoroughbred. Why am I fighting it? Why can't I let this truth be my truth?

I pick at a nail, bite my lower lip. I understand why I'm so torn. It's because it's like a stage play to me, a bunch of actors reading their lines and standing where they're told to. Until I can get over that, this can never be my home, and this can never be my life.

CHAPTER 8

BIG DAY

I WAKE UP with a new resolve. I need to find out whether I'm being lied to. If this is my home, my family, then I have to locate evidence. It's not just that there are no images of me in this house; nothing links me to it, no lingering memory of me. I'm no more at home here than I was in my hospital bed. I'm as cut off from my life as I've been since I opened my eyes. A trail of crumbs must exist somewhere, a path back to the person I am. I have to believe that.

I shower, turning the water up so hot that every inch of me relishes the burn. I want to awaken something, to ignite a fire. I can't keep sleepwalking through the day.

I look at myself in the mirror; my whole self. The evidence of the crash is the only thing that makes sense to me. The bruising, the remains of the swelling. I push a finger against the tender spot in my ribs, digging the tip in until the pain is almost too much to bear, hoping the sharp pulse of agony will bring back images, sounds, smells. It doesn't work.

I get dressed, putting on clothes that could be mine, could be somebody else's. Black slacks and a light blue top. I have no way of knowing or identifying with either. I don't recall whether they're to my taste. What is my taste?

The smell of pancakes and fresh coffee wafts up from the kitchen. My stomach flips as I realize I'm ravenous. My appetite, at least, has returned.

There's the sound of laughter from outside and I go to the window. My mother is sitting at the garden table, finding something my husband has said to her amusing. Their closeness is strange to me, the way they are so comfortable around each other. I wonder if that's normal, but realize I have no way of knowing what normal is. I'm relearning everything. I can't take anything for granted anymore, because every event is another clue, another morsel on my path of breadcrumbs.

I head downstairs and relish the smell of food. If I could take my plate and head back to my bedroom, I would, but I'm aware a churlish action like that would be considered rude. Wesley has cooked for me, and that's an act of kindness I must repay with my presence. Anyway, I have questions for him.

"Good morning, Supernova," he says. "Did you sleep well?"

We didn't sleep in the same bed last night. Even he realized it would be weird, knowing that, in my head at least, we've only just met.

"Like a log," I lie. I hardly slept at all. "Something smells good."

"Pancakes and blueberries, just the way you like them."

"Sounds great."

My mom stands and hugs me. She is an alien in my arms.

She grips my hand and smiles at me. It's a smile that says she wants me to like her. I can't decide if that's a good or a bad thing.

"Sit. Eat," Wesley says. "The only way to mend your body is to give it the energy it needs."

I scoop four pancakes onto my plate, two large helpings of blueberries, and enough maple syrup to fill a small lake. I don't waste any time. I savor the sweetness, the soft pillow of pancake flesh, the crunching texture of the fruit. I close my eyes while I'm eating. I let out a little groan.

"There, see?" Wesley says, turning to my mom. "Didn't I tell you, Evie? A good night's sleep, and now her appetite has returned. Small steps, Sierra. Small victories."

I smile and dab a napkin on my syrupy lips. I find no victory here. No steps, small or otherwise.

"Tell me about us," I say, forcing my first question from my lips before I have a chance to change my mind. "Tell me about how we met, our first kiss, our intimate moments."

"Woah!" he declares, holding up his hands. "With your mother here?"

"Come now, Wes," my mom says, sipping her coffee. "It's nothing I haven't heard before."

"Right, but not the details."

"How we met then?" I counter. "Did you ask me out, or did I come on to you?"

He laughs, taking another bite of his pancake and looking down at the table. I sense uncertainty.

"I asked you, if you must know," he replies. "At the time you were working at a bakery in town, a place I used to go to every day to get coffee."

"And you just came up to me and asked me out for a drink?"

"No, not at first," he says. "I have to admit, I didn't think

The Lies We Tell 35

you liked me, so I waited it out, tried to build a relationship with you. You know? Use that old Coleman charm."

His body language is strange, unsettling. His eyes are jerky, flitting.

"And I eventually relented, right?"

"Sierra?" my mom exclaims. "What is this? An inquisition."

"I want to know," I reply. "I don't remember any of this. Not yet. Maybe hearing details about the most important moments of my life will speed up the healing process."

Wesley eyes me. I suspect he's trying to figure out where I'm going with this.

"You did," he says eventually. "Relent, I mean. I took you out to dinner. You had the fish, I had steak. We drank red wine and talked. It was a magical evening, for me anyway. I did the same the next week and the week after, again and again until, eventually, you fell in love with me. Just like I loved you, except for me, my heart was yours right from the get go, right from the first moment I laid eyes on you. You were so doe-eyed and innocent, but your face was so beautiful, it could light up the darkest of nights."

I blush then. I don't know how to react to compliments from a man I barely recognize.

"Why no pictures then?" I blurt out. I recognize it as a defense mechanism. I'm deflecting. "Our wedding day. I can't find anything. Not a hint it ever took place. Why is that? If it was one of the happiest days of our lives, why did we never memorialize it? Don't you think that's a little odd?"

My mother tosses her napkin. "Sierra! You're being rude."

Wesley looks wounded, which is a strange look on a man so big and strong. His face goes pale, as if all the color has leached from him. I wonder if this is the moment the lie unravels. I sense excitement burning in my gut. It sloshes around with the lingering remains of the sweet treats and coffee.

He stands and heads inside. I wonder whether he's retreating, running from the chaos, but in a few moments, he's back at the table with an album in his hands. He places it on the table in front of me. I look at it as if I have no idea what it is, but in truth, I'm pretty sure I do.

He opens it, and I'm right there in full technicolor, covered in white satin and chiffon. He's standing next to me in a navy tuxedo, he's smile as wide as the cake we're standing beside.

"They're all here," he says, turning page after page, revealing the hotel, the ceremony, the hoards in attendance. "Take your time. Believe me, there's a lot to look at."

CHAPTER 9

DADDY

WITH THAT LITTLE episode over, I'm emotionally drained. Perhaps we were married after all. He is my husband. I can't deny that one little fact now. I'm neither relieved nor deflated. This man who has been so nice to me is the man I decided to wed. That's a positive thing, something I should be happy about. The only problem is, I'm not and I have no idea why.

"That man loves you, you know?" my mom says. "He'd do anything for you. He was with you at the hospital every day while you were in a coma. He never left your side."

Is she giving me facts or trying to convince me of something? Either way, she's obviously the kind of woman who is unwavering in her conviction. I can admire her for that, at least.

"I wish I could remember more. Something to connect me to him. And to you, too."

She places a hand on my face, stroking my cheek as if it's

made from some exotic silk. Her palm is soft, the skin supple. She obviously takes care of herself.

"You will," she says, "I promise. You just need to give it time."

She's right, but it's the open-ended nature of it that terrifies me. How much time is enough time? How long will I need to wait until the first thirty-plus years of my life return? So much would have happened in those decades that shaped me, and without those memories, I'm a woman without direction, without a purpose. I need to anchor myself to something, a time in my past that will make sense of everything. I scour my brain for it, searching through a dark vault of endless nothingness.

"Let's go shopping," my mom declares out of nowhere. "You and me. Give you something to smile about."

"Oh," I stammer. "I don't know about that."

"Nonsense. Come on. It'll be fun."

She's up and organizing things before I have another chance to object. Before I realize it, I have my shoes on, a bag on my arm, and I'm being hurried into the car. As she drives us away, I'm left with the distinct impression I'm being railroaded.

Houses go by like tuna fish, swimming past us at speed as Evie navigates the winding streets of Lake Sherwood. It's an exclusive area; it's obvious by the cars in the driveways, the Olympic-sized pools, the tennis courts. Money lives here. Lots of it. I'm guessing I'm a wealthy woman, but I have no idea how much is in my bank account.

I go through my bag and glance at all the plastic. American Express, Platinum, two hundred dollars in cash. The money feels fake, as if it isn't mine. In some ways, it isn't. I have no idea who I am anymore, so how can this belong to me? I want to throw it out the window and give it to someone who truly needs it.

"You haven't asked about your father," my mom says. "Since you came home, you haven't mentioned him once."

I remember Wesley saying something about him, telling me my mom moved in after he died.

"Was he a good man?"

She smiles, tears glistening like diamonds in the corners of her eyes. "The best." Her hands grip the steering wheel. "You were a daddy's girl. Always by his side. Chasing him around the house as if you were attached to him."

I smile at that. It's a memory I don't have, but one I look forward to reconnecting with. "So, I had a happy childhood."

Her mom grins. "Our home was always a safe place, Sierra. You had the kind of childhood other people would die for."

I find her choice of words a little unsettling. "Was it painful? His death I mean?"

I endure a moment of silence as my mom composes herself. I can tell this particular memory is still raw on her, like an unwashed wound. "Cancer." She spits the words out like poison. "There wasn't much left of him to love by the time they put him in that box. Damn disease chewed him up piece by piece. He never deserved that. None of us did."

The thought chills me to the bone. A man I don't remember, but that the old me worshipped. I wonder whether I get to select the memories that come back, cherry-pick the moments I want to savor and discard those I never want to return. What would be the point of remembering my dad if the last meaningful interaction we had would cause me immeasurable pain?

Mom drives the car onto the parking lot of the mall. The place is over half full. I look at the other vehicles. Teslas, BMWs, Mercedes. Enough automobile aristocracy exists here to bankrupt the economy of a small country. Guilt consumes me. I was a part of this. I guess I still am.

"This is him," my mom says, fishing a tattered photograph from her bag. It's curled at the edges, as if it's been left out in the sun too long. The worn nature of it looks odd against her perfectly manicured hands and tanned skin. I wonder if she was always this way. Immaculate. Did she change when she moved in with Wesley and me? Did the transformation happen much earlier?

I take the photograph from her. The paper has lost its gloss. It's like old skin. I hold it up to the light. It's as old as it looks. I look at a picture of a man in flannel and corduroy. His hair is slick against his forehead, his arms like pistons. He's a man of the land. He's holding a shovel, gripping it like it means something to him.

In the background is a house. It's not like the buildings in Lake Sherwood, not a fraction of the cost. I'm right. My mom doesn't come from money. She acquired it at some point in her past. I wonder if it's been earned or taken. This man doesn't look like the one on my social media images. He's taller, thicker. I'm confused by the sight of him. Maybe the man I saw on my phone is an uncle, a family friend.

"What are you thinking?" my mom asks, watching as a truck pulls into the spot in front of us.

I shake my head, wanting to ask her so many questions, but not trusting myself to say the right things. "I'm not sure. Maybe I'm a little overwhelmed."

I start to cry. The suddenness of it surprises me, making me cry more. It's not that I'm sad my dad is dead. How can I be? The man in the photograph could be anybody, a magazine model, a movie actor. I realize my upsurge in emotional turmoil is being caused by the fact that not even this event, this tragic death, the loss of someone so dear to me, can ignite the smallest recollection in me. It's as though I'm without hope, as if I'm doomed to spend the rest of my days as no more than an empty vessel of lost moments and misplaced soundbites.

"Just give it time," my mom repeats. "Give it as much time as it takes."

I wipe the tears from my cheeks and hand her back the photograph. I wonder whether it's symbolic, whether I'm giving away yet another connection to my lost youth.

CHAPTER 10

BLACK ONYX

WE WALK FROM shop to shop, but I'm barely paying attention. I've got too much going on in my head to be concerned about Jimmy Choo heels, Burberry sweaters, and Ralph Lauren chinos. So far, the things I've learned have only served to heighten my unease. If everything in my life was so good, why can't I forge a link back to it? It should be the simplest thing to do, and yet it's almost impossible to achieve.

The mall is filled with designer clothing brands, jewelry that starts at a price point way above the average annual salary of an American family, and food that's low on calories and small in portion size. I don't like it. I don't like any of it. I want to leave almost as soon as we arrive.

"Oh," my mom says. "Cashmere. I promised myself I'd buy a sweater when I was next in town. Do you mind, dear?"

I wonder what she means by the question. Do I mind she's

buying a cashmere sweater, or do I mind she's dragging me to yet another shop?

"I'll wait outside," I offer. "You go ahead."

She glances up at me as her eyes narrow. I wonder if she can read my mind. "You'll be okay?"

"It's a mall," I say. "I think I'll survive."

She leaves me stranded in an ocean of people who clearly don't recognize me. That's something that's been bothering me since we started our little circuit of this mall of gregarious wealth. Nobody says hi. Nobody acknowledges me. Lake Sherwood isn't a big community. Less than two thousand. The fact I'm anonymous here is jarring, particularly since my mother has spoken to countless people since we showed up. They know her by name, ask after Wesley. It's like I'm a stranger in a strange land.

I stand by the railing, blowing hot air, foggy with claustrophobia, even though the mall is large and it's hardly shoulder to shoulder. My mouth is so dry. I click my tongue behind my teeth, tap my fingers against my thighs, do anything to distract my racing brain. I don't remember my family, and nobody here remembers me. If it wasn't for the photographs of my wedding, and my mom's emotional retelling of my father's death, I would be almost certain it isn't my life, and this isn't my town.

"Sierra!" somebody calls out, racing across from the other side of the concourse. "Sierra, it's me, Max."

I watch as the man approaches. Five-eleven, short, dark beard, heavy set. He's smiling at me. His smile sets my teeth on edge. I spot the large silver ring on the index finger of his right hand, the black onyx at its center. It's the kind of ring only a man who's yet to let go of the brashness of youth could ever wear.

"Sorry, do I know you?"

"Woah!" he exclaims, holding a hand to his heart as if I've shot him. "You really going to play it like that?"

"Play it like what?"

"You never struck me as the cold, calculating type."

I stare at his face, trying to find something in my memory banks that could tell me if he's a friend or an enemy.

"O-Malley's," he says, holding out his hands and grinning. "A little over two weeks ago. You were with friends having dinner. I came over, offered to buy you a drink. Your friends left but you stayed. Oh man, my head the next day. We must have drunk a whole bottle of Jack between us."

I shake my head, wondering what he's talking about.

"Oh, come on," he cries. "We danced."

I shrug.

"Okay, whatever. You want to keep it on the down low, that's fine by me. Casual is good. Casual is more than fine."

I decide not to say anything, to let him talk. If what he's saying is true, it means my marriage isn't a happy one. Happy wives don't stay out and get drunk with strange men, and they certainly don't dance with them.

"Anyway," he continued." How you been? You been good?"

His question snaps me back into focus. It's the first time anybody other than my husband has asked me that.

"Recovering," I reply, wondering if that's the truth. "Slowly, but I'm getting there."

He appears confused, like he can't decide where to take our conversation. I wonder if he's heard about the accident. If he hasn't, that's another red flag. In towns the size of Lake Sherwood, an accident involving the wife of a renowned construction company owner is big news.

I pick up the scent of lavender and peach blossom, and suddenly my mom is at my arm.

"Got it," she says. She's clutching a bag. She's bought more than one sweater. "Now, let's get out of here."

The Lies We Tell

I'm surprised we're leaving. She seemed to be settling in for the day. She tugs at my elbow, urging me forward like a little lost child. My feet move with her but not before Max grabs my hand and winks at me. Before I realize it, he's gone, leaving me with a sense our interaction never actually took place at all. Maybe he was a figment of my very active imagination, a mall ghost, a character I conjured up to reinforce my paranoia about my fake life and fake family.

Back at the car, I sit in the passenger seat while my mom loads the trunk with her expensive gains. I look at the hand Max grabbed. I can still feel his fingers in my palm. It's thrilling, the thought I had been keeping secrets from my husband, that I'd had an illicit rendezvous. I wonder if that makes me a bad person.

I turn my hand over and spy the business card Max slipped me. My mother hadn't spotted it, but I knew. The corners of the card dug into my flesh as I sought to conceal its existence. I need to. It's the only thing I have that disproves my imaginary friend theory. I read the words emblazoned on the black background in silver italics. *Max Cramer, Architect.* This means he's a real person, a real, living, breathing human. It also confirms his story I had a real hookup on a real night out with a man I'd never met before. I sense the tether being pulled tight, a rope that can lead me to the truth, even if the truth proves I'm the kind of person I don't want to be—or that my husband isn't the sort of person I wanted to spend the rest of my life with.

When my mom opens the car door, I slip the card into my pocket and close my eyes, feigning weariness. There's more to come from this story. Much more.

CHAPTER 11

HIDDEN VALLEY

WE ARRIVE HOME and my mom gives me a fashion show, wearing the cashmere sweater around the house like a second skin. I wonder if she realizes how entitled she's making herself look, how spoiled. I pretend to be impressed, smiling and making the sort of comments I think she wants to hear.

"Oh, it really suits you."

"If anything, it's slimming."

"The color is perfect for you."

"You look like a million dollars, Mom."

When she tells me she has to go to her hair appointment, I'm relieved. I can't walk around anymore with this smile on my face or these sugar-coated words spilling from my devious lips. The conceit is killing me.

As the door closes, I head to the bathroom, needing to wash off the remains of our tasteless outing. I'm still thinking of Max. Well, not *about* him, more about what the encounter represents.

It's a curveball of all curveballs, a significant shift in proceedings. I cherish it. I want to find out so much more.

I pause at the bathroom door, realizing I'm yet to look at each of the rooms in the house. Sure, I had a guided tour when I first arrived, but I was still in a state of shock at that point. I could barely breathe, let alone take anything in. All I can remember is doors and corridors, corridors and doors. Four large bedrooms occupy the second floor, but the only one I've noticed is the one I've slept in. Wesley sleeps in the next room with the adjoining door. I go to that room first. It's almost an exact replica of the master bedroom, but without the women's clothing. Wesley didn't make the bed either. The indentation where his body rested is still visible, his clothes tossed on the floor. I wonder if he was this messy when we shared a room. I wonder whether I nagged him for it, or whether I picked up after him like a doting wife.

Next up is my mother's room. It smells of her. It's clean, immaculate. She has an en suite bathroom which is also spotless. Her body sprays and creams are orderly, laid out in neat, straight lines. Her towels are crisp and folded perfectly. Her clothes hang in the closet, arranged by color and style. Her shoes are the same; daywear and evening wear are separated as if they are different races, or different species.

The last room is for guests. I wonder how many people have stayed in this private space. I imagine the kind of parties the Coleman's throw, and whether I'm a good hostess, witty and engaging. I can't picture myself in that scenario. It doesn't appear to be the kind of thing I would be good at, but I don't how I can spring to that conclusion.

I head downstairs and check out the kitchen. It's the kind of space that fills the pages of a homemaking magazine article. It's obscenely large with every kitchen appliance known to the human race. The central island is as big as a small truck. The oven is so clean, I wonder if I've ever cooked anything inside it.

I look through the glass doors leading to the backyard. The patio has an outside kitchen area; a stainless steel grill, wood smoker, skillets, and knives hanging from hooks beneath the sweeping overhang. I imagine Wesley standing outside, flipping steaks, sipping a cold beer and holding court with his business associates. Do I have a place in that life? Do I have associates of my own?

A door further down the long corridor stands out to me. I head to it, wondering if it's locked. It looks suspicious; gray wood with a black handle. I sense danger lurks within it. I'm almost disappointed when the door swings open with ease and I step into my husband's study. It's messy like his bedroom; filing cabinets where the drawers hang open like drooling mouths, a bookshelf containing anything but books, a half-eaten sandwich on a plate by the window, the bread curling. Paperwork litters the desk. The computer keyboard is barely visible.

On the wall is a framed photograph of Wesley with the people who work for him. They're standing in a parking lot, the offices of Coleman Construction in the background, the giant scoops of two digger trucks hanging overhead. Wesley stands front and center, holding up a banner declaring, "*Coleman's Construction: Ten Years of Shaping the Lake.*" I wonder if the ecologists would agree with him.

I run a finger across the dusty frame, search the walls for pictures of me. I realize that's a selfish thought, but aside from the album my husband shoved in front of me over breakfast, I find no trace I actually live here. Either Wesley is ashamed of me, or he's not a photograph kind of guy. I decide it's not the latter.

I get the sense I'm in a space where I don't belong, that if Wesley caught me in here he would be less than happy. The realization makes me all the more determined to snoop around, although my logic is flawed. If the office is off-limits, why wouldn't he lock the door? The alternative theory is it's a double bluff; that by leaving the door unlocked, it somehow demystifies the room, making it less interesting to me. I decide to counter his double bluff by rifling through the papers on his desk. It gives me a smug sense of satisfaction.

I find bills, invoices, account summaries that are meaningless to me. Money in, money out. I can't tell whether the business is making money or losing it. By the disorganized state of the office, I doubt whether Wesley understands that either. I hope he has a good accountant, because there's a lot of activity here. Next to the financial statements is a letter from the council offices, detailing what looks like an ongoing debate between Wesley and a guy named Frank Duvall. The language is mildly threatening, particularly from Wesley. I wonder what this guy has done to upset my husband so much.

I push those letters to one side and land on something that stands out to me. It's an information brochure detailing computer-generated pictures of a new development in the Hidden Valley, a large area of land northwest of the lake. The homes look plush, accompanied by a golf course, a shopping mall, and an exclusive hotel. I'm guessing a big slice of land is going to be chewed up to make way for this high-end development. Money will be made here, lots of it. My feelings are torn. I wonder how involved Coleman Construction is in the excavation and the construction work. I'm guessing Wesley wants in, otherwise, why have the brochure on his desk?

I flip the brochure over, the slick gloss of the document somewhat repulsive in my hands. I want to wash my fingers, rid them of the stink of money. I almost don't notice the name of the development at the top of the brochure.

I gasp out loud. I'd almost forgotten about what the nurse, Kaiden Marshall, had told me that night in the hospital. The two words I'd spoken over and over again when I was first admitted. They're right here, printed in bright blue font. I'm so shocked, I can barely catch my breath. I read the words again. My heart pounds in my chest as I trace a line beneath the headline with my index finger.

"*Welcome to Mystic Spring.*"

CHAPTER 12

THE DEAL

THOSE WORDS ARE the bridge back to my life before, I'm sure of it, and now they're also a link to the man I married. It can't be a coincidence. It's not possible. If Mystic Spring was emblazoned on my concussed brain, then they meant something to me. They were important. Now I realize they're important to Wesley too. I study the brochure once more, checking whether I was seeing things. I wasn't. It's as clear as day. A development is being planned, and Coleman Construction is in the running for it.

I hear the sound of the front door opening, keys being tossed on the side, followed by the meaty stomp of somebody pacing down the hall. My heart leaps in my throat. I almost stumble into a chair. The footsteps are getting closer. I'm sure I'm going to be caught, a deer in the road, a truck bearing down on me. They're so close now, no more than a few feet away.

I glance at the window, but I'll never make it out in time. I can't open it and pull myself over the windowsill before whoever's outside catches me in the act. I'm trembling now, terrified, but I wonder why.

There's the sound of a phone ringing, and then the footsteps falter. It's my husband's voice.

"Hello?" he says. He's right outside the door, so close I could almost touch him. "Okay. Yeah, just give me a second."

He's retreating, heading back toward the rear of the house. I sense this is my moment, and after allowing enough time for the way to become clear, I pull the door open. I'm slow, deliberate, not wanting to give myself away. Although this is my house, and as far as I'm aware, nobody has committed a crime here, I have a burning in the pit of my stomach, warning me of impending danger.

I sneak into the living room, glance through the windows facing the front of the house. My husband's truck is outside, basking like a giant alligator in the afternoon sun. There's the sound of the rear door opening and closing. I turn to the kitchen. There's the distant strains of Wesley's voice. He sounds animated.

My instant reaction is to leave, or at least go somewhere in the house where my presence isn't a threat. I don't want to poke the bear. Then I realize this is an opportunity that's too good to miss. The call Wesley took could be about the development. I need to hear what's being said.

I decide taking the direct route could arouse suspicion, so I head out the front door and make my way to the rear of the house. I pass the pool on the way, raising a hand to the pool guy who nods back at me. He seems oblivious to my presence. My mother's still at her hair appointment which means only the three of us are at home; me, my husband, and the hired help.

I slip around the edge of the building and work my way between a wooden outhouse and the eastern edge of the property.

Wesley's voice fades in and out. I picture him pacing the garden, his ear pressed to the phone. I step between two rose bushes and snag my pants on some gnarly thorns. I ease myself out of my ensnarement, but my pants don't make it out unscathed. I look down at a tiny hole and a hanging thread where the sharp barb caught me.

Wesley's around the next corner. I can hear the sound of his voice, but not well enough to make out every word. Closer. I have to get closer. My pulse is thrumming in my neck. I have sweat on my forehead and upper lip. It's like I'm breaking and entering, which is crazy. This is my house.

I drop to my knees and peer around the corner. He's there. He looks agitated, desperate. He turns in my direction and I duck away, realizing I'm taking one hell of a chance spying on him like this. I'm not behaving like a wife, particularly not one who's recently come out of a coma. I've never met this version of myself. I've never met any version of who I am.

"Well, tell him I need it signed," Wesley says. "Tell him it needs to be done this week."

Whatever it is, there's urgency in his voice, the necessity. I wonder once more whether the financial viability of my husband's business is more fragile than he lets on.

"I don't give a damn whether he needs more people on his side. Tell him to give me names and phone numbers and I'll pay them all off. Every last one of them."

His tone is becoming bitter now, nasty. I haven't heard him like this before. It heightens my anxiety considerably. I chance another peek. The veins in his thick neck are protruding, the pulse in his forehead twitching.

"Whatever it takes," he reiterates. "Tell them I'll pay whatever it takes. I need that contract, and I can't afford to wait for it. And remind that sonofabitch he owes me. He owes me big time."

He ends the call and tosses his phone onto the table. He clenches and unclenches his fists like a bare-knuckle fighter about to go into battle. It appears this fight is on hiatus, and the very thought of it is killing him. His mouth is drawn down in a hateful snarl, his jaw tightly clamped. I realize this man is capable of anything if the circumstances dictate it. I wonder how hard it is for him to play a different role in front of me.

He slumps into a chair and lights a cigarette, inhaling deeply before blowing smoke. I back away, knowing I've got everything I came for, but also knowing I'm still in the dark. I never actually heard him mention the Mystic Spring development. I could be putting two and two together and coming up with a number that suits the narrative I'm developing in my head, but I can't deny the existence of the brochure on his desk, or that my husband appears to be in a desperate situation.

How long has this been going on for, and what does it have to do with me? Was my accident even an accident at all? Is Wesley capable of more than just bribery and corruption? Does he have violence in him?

I can't put the pieces together, not in any logical order. What does any of this have to do with anything? Is it linked at all? I'll find out. It's only a matter of time. Eventually, the truth will be revealed, and I plan to be first in line to watch the big show.

CHAPTER 13

QUESTIONS

I'M IN THE bedroom, running everything backwards and forwards through my mind, when my mother arrives home. She brings me a coffee. Her hair looks the same as when she left. I wonder if that's the point, to stave off the regenerative process. I realize I have no idea how old she is, but I don't have the cojones to ask. She doesn't look like she's the kind of woman to be receptive to a question like that. I suspect she's older than she looks, which is actually a complement to her.

Not long afterward, the doorbell rings and my mother answers it. A female voice responds. It's Mary Elisabeth and she's asking for me. I head to the railing overlooking the downstairs area and call down to her.

"I'll be there in a minute or two," I say.

She's carrying a tray of brownies and a smile a mile wide.

I take my coffee and meet her in the living room. We sit on the couch, sip our warm drinks, and eat chocolate cake. At least, I do. There's no evidence Mary Elisabeth has actually eaten anything. I wonder if she ever cooks anything for herself to eat. She's so painfully thin.

"I wanted to make sure you were settling in okay," she says with a grin, her teeth so white they're literally blinding me.

"Well, I'm comfortable, if that's what you mean. I'm still a little beaten up and bruised, but physically I'm okay."

"What about your memory?" she asks, cocking her head as though I'm a patient to be studied.

"It's no different. Still nothing. I mean, I understand what things are, I'm not completely in the dark, but when it comes to my life, the things that really matter, it's all a blank sheet of paper."

She sighs, touching my hand. "It will come," she says. "Don't rush it. There's no need."

If only she knew. The weight of so much on my shoulders, the burning, incessant need to figure out what's happening to me.

"I feel like I'm out in the cold, you know?" I'm being honest with her now. "Like you're all around me, but you're not really. I feel alone, cut off from you. If I can't remember who you are, how can I ever be at home in this town, in this house? I can't even remember my own mom, and she's living right here."

"You poor bunny," Mary Elisabeth replies, handing me another brownie. "I just wish I could help you in some way."

I should tell her that fattening me up isn't the answer, that giving me body confidence issues on top of my own paralyzing insecurities won't help in the slightest, but I take the brownie anyway. They're good. Maybe too good.

"I've been going through my social media," I say, speaking through a mouthful of chocolate crumbs. "Searching for something that might help me."

She eyes me over the rim of her coffee cup. "And?"

"There isn't much. Some pictures of Wesley and I, some with you in them."

I wonder whether I should tell her about my trip to the mall with my mom, figuring if she truly is my best friend, she would be all over my alleged hookup with Max Cramer. Maybe she's another link in the chain, another way back to whatever it is I'm missing.

I decide to give it a try. What do I have to lose?

"I met a guy in town," I say, realizing how sordid it sounds.

Mary Elisabeth's expression is passive. "A guy? What sort of guy?"

I shrug. "He claimed to know me."

"Well, you've lived here for over a year, Sierra. People are bound to know you."

"He didn't know me like that. Not like a friend would know me." I sense I'm standing on thin ice. It's cracking and splintering beneath my feet. I have no idea how loyal my friend is to my husband. This is dangerous ground, truly treacherous. I decide to be less direct. "Was I always faithful, Mary Elisabeth? To Wesley, I mean?"

She sets her cup down, glances toward the kitchen. I can't decide whether she's worried about my husband hearing her answer, or whether she's considering how to respond.

"Are you asking me if you ever had an affair?" She looks serious now, grave.

"I guess that's exactly what I'm asking. Yes."

She takes time to answer. Too much time. My mind goes into overdrive. Have I revealed too much? Should I have kept these questions to myself until I had more evidence to go on?

"What's that?" she asks, pointing at my left thigh.

I follow the line of her finger which points to the loose thread hanging from the small tear in my chinos. I'd forgotten all about it. The remains of a thorn still hangs from the ripped material. Color rises in my cheeks. I've been busted.

"Darn it," I say without thinking. "I must have caught them

on a bush when I was outside in the garden. Home for two days and I'm already ruining my clothes."

Mary Elisabeth doesn't laugh. She only stares at the hole. I realize she's never going to answer my original question. Maybe she's avoiding it. Part of me is relieved. The exchange wasn't going as I'd planned anyway.

"You ought to be more careful," she says, her gaze unflinching. "Wesley spends a lot of money on you. Those pants are Gucci, pure wool."

I'm stunned by her response. What does that have to do with her, and why would she be interested in how much my husband spends on me, anyway?

"Yeah, I'm such a klutz." I finish the last of my brownie and stifle a yawn. I want our little exchange to be over. "Anyway, I'm a little tired. Maybe we can continue this chat another time?"

She snaps back into focus, as if somebody has changed the channel on the TV. "Nonsense. I'm here to help you, not let you sleep yourself into a pit of despair."

"I don't think that's what I'm suggesting."

"Of course not," she says, standing. "But you want to remember who you are, and I want my best friend back." She grabs her keys and her bag and heads for the door. "Now why don't you go and change those pants and meet me in the car in, say, five minutes?"

I'm on the back foot now, wondering what I've managed to get myself into. "But, where are we going?"

She smiles. "The last place you visited before your memory went for a little walk around the block."

"But that would mean—"

"That's right," she replies. "We're going out to the crash site."

The Lies We Tell 59

CHAPTER 14

PIGTAILS

I HAVE NO memory of the crash at all. I have no idea what caused it, where I was headed, what state of mind I was in. The police haven't contacted me, so I assume I wasn't on drugs or acting in some sort of diminished capacity. I don't remember collecting my keys, getting in the car, starting the engine, gunning the accelerator, taking the corner. It's all a blank. Zero. Nada. I'm only aware of the exact spot it occurred because Kaiden told me.

I was driving on the Yerba Buena Road through the Santa Monica Mountains, very close to the unique rock formation that's visited by thousands of tourists and nature lovers every year. God's Seat. I have no idea what I was doing in the area surrounding the landmark, but that's where the police found me, and where my husband dragged me from the wrecked vehicle before it literally exploded.

It's also where Mary Elisabeth has decided to take me, and for once, I agree. I wonder why I didn't think of it myself. It's a brilliant plan. If anything is going to kickstart me back to normality, surely it's the place where I very nearly drew my last breath.

Mary Elizabeth's car is a Lexus LC500 with all the extras. I wonder how she afforded it, what she does for a living. It's the kind of car women of power and means have. She looks tiny in it, diminutive, but she drives it like it's an extension of her. She's confident, bold, assured. I wonder if I was like her before the crash. If I had a fraction of her presence. If I had a career.

"Let's go get that memory of yours back," she says in a singsong voice, as if finding my past is as simple as a shopping trip to Sears.

"I hope so."

"Me too. I want the old Sierra back. The one who used to hold the best parties, make me laugh until my sides hurt, and who would cuss like a sailor with Tourette's."

We make small talk for a while as she drives. Her demeanor opens me up a little. She's trying to help me, that much is clear, and now I'm away from Wesley, the sense of impending doom has lifted a little.

"I've been having these dreams," I say, unclear about where I'm going with this.

"Dreams? That's pretty normal, isn't it?"

"It is, but this one dream, well, it's a vision, really."

"Like a ghost?"

I shake my head. "Not exactly. I first saw her when I was unconscious. At least, I think I did. When I came round, she was all I could think about."

Mary Elisabeth's eyes flit to me and then back to the road. "You say she. You're dreaming of some woman?"

"A little girl. About eleven years old."

"Do you know her?"

"That's the point," I say. "I have no idea. I'm guessing whoever she is, my memories of her are buried along with the rest of my past, way, way down deep in my subconscious."

Mary Elisabeth grips the steering wheel, navigating around

The Lies We Tell

the tight turns. A truck comes past us at speed and something inside me skips a little.

"What did she look like? This girl in your dreams?"

I close my eyes and she's standing before me. Alone in the darkness, a single spotlight illuminating her young face. It's like she's in the car with me. I can almost feel her breath on my skin.

"Blonde hair," I say without opening my eyes. "Pigtails. Freckles on her cheeks. Sad eyes, as if something had upset her."

"And you didn't recognize her?"

She's already asked me that question but I decide to suppress my frustration. I shake my head. Mary Elisabeth is silent once more. I look up at her but she appears distracted. She turns the radio on and the car is immediately filled with the sound of a young female singing about lost love and broken hearts. If I have a heart to break, it's currently keeping itself in the shadows. Love is the last thing on my mind.

I glare out the window, look down at the valley. I wonder if Mystic Spring is below us somewhere, nestled within the rolling landscape. hidden beneath the wild sage and dense scrub. I'm still so confused. My thoughts are so disparate. I can't decide whether I'm being intensely paranoid, or whether everyone around me is duping me.

"You had blonde hair when you were younger," Mary Elisabeth says, turning the radio down. "You know that, right?"

My eyes snap to her. "What?"

"When we were kids, your hair was so blonde, people used to say it was practically kissed by the sun."

I think of the photograph I found online. She's right. My hair was a lot lighter back then. Maybe not as blonde as the girl in my dreams, but pretty damn close.

"I'm not certain," she continues, "but I think your mom

said she used to tie it back in pigtails, too. You know, to keep it off your face."

I chew my lip. I watch as she navigates the road. She could be telling me the truth or this could be another way to distract me. A moment ago I was beginning to trust her, but now I'm not so sure. This all sounds too convenient.

"You think I'm dreaming of my younger self?"

She pats the steering wheel to the faint strains of an old rock classic. "Well, I'm no psychiatrist, Sea, but I would suggest a traumatic incident like a near-fatal car crash could cause your subconscious to regress to a much earlier time. Like, say, when you were eleven years old."

She's making sense, although I don't like the answer. My brain has been battered into submission and maybe that's triggered a restart mechanism, sending me back to a safer place, a safer time. Maybe the blonde girl inside of me is trying to protect me, to stop me from slipping into a state of paranoid delusion. If that's the case, maybe I should start listening to her rather than suspecting everyone I come into contact with of trying to pull the wool over my eyes.

"It's a theory," she says. "No more than an idea, but I think you should consider it at least."

I nod, but inside I'm still fighting with myself. I guess this modus operandi will continue until everything comes flooding back, if it ever does.

"Anyway," Mary Elisabeth says, swinging the car onto a dirt track at the side of the road. I look at the curve of the highway and the smears of black rubber and scorched asphalt. "We're here." She turns and grips my hand. Her fingers are like icicles against my palm. "Let's see if you can't remember something important."

CHAPTER 15
REDSHOOT

"WOAH, WHAT A view," Mary Elisabeth says, standing with her tiny hands on pencil-thin hips. "I hardly ever come out here, but I gotta say, you picked a beautiful spot to trash your car."

I try to ignore her barbed comment. She doesn't mean anything by it. I step out onto the highway. The mid-afternoon sun beats down on me, the heat is soothing on my skin. I realize I've felt cold ever since I left the hospital.

I approach the tire marks. They're erratic, jerky. I obviously lost control as I rounded the corner. These marks are followed by a long stretch of unmarked asphalt, and then further along, signs of the road being churned up by a heavy object hitting it at top speed. A scorched area is beyond, blisters on the road and blackened scrub. I realize my car left the road as it flipped, and then slammed down hard.

My bruises scream out at me as if the accident is happening

all over again. I can't get enough oxygen into my lungs. It's like I'm suffocating. I drop to my knees, close my eyes.

"Sea, Sea!"

Mary Elisabeth's voice is in my ear, but I'm not paying her any attention. How can I? I'm not in the present anymore. My hand goes to the asphalt, touching the tire marks. I can hear noises now, loud scraping sounds as if gears are grinding. Glass strikes my face, my hands fighting to control a wheel that's turning away from me violently. The sounds of my own frantic breathing resonate all around me, my screeching voice as I cry out. I'm terrified, fearful for my life. I try to wrestle the wheel back in my direction, but it's a big mistake. The car jerks hard to the left and then gravity takes charge of the situation and I'm flying. I have no idea which way is up or down, or why the outside world is spinning around the car like a Ferris Wheel. I'm buffeted by strong wind on my face and glass in my eyes, and then something slams into the road, something massive, and it crumples in on me, jarring my neck to the side. So much noise, a loud metallic cacophony of sound that hurts my ears. The wheel is against my chest, crushing me, and something is digging into my ribs and arms. Everything goes black.

I wake to the smell of gas. It's stinging my eyes and nose. Something sticky is on my face. Everything is blurry. It's a patchwork of colors and lights, but nothing looks real. My body is wracked by a lot of pain but I can't place where it's coming from. It hurts all over. My head is the worst. It's like a hot boulder nestled on my shoulders. I'm so desperately tired.

Everything goes black again, but this time, when I come round I'm surrounded by a sea of red and blue, swirling and dancing in front of me. A loud noise hurts my ears, too, a wailing sound like a warning siren. I want to sleep. I want to disappear.

There are people shouting at me. Somebody touches my

body, tries to pull me toward them. I resist this intruder. I don't want to leave. I want to close my eyes. The stench of gas now is overpowering. The air is stifling hot. It's coming from somewhere close to me. Another hand reaches round me. Somebody close by says, "This might hurt a little," and then I'm falling head first, crumpling into a little ball as my body folds in around me. Everything hurts now. Really hurts. It's like somebody is kicking me repeatedly in the head. If I could disappear, I would. I want the pain to stop.

I peep through my half-closed eyelids a little. It hurts even more. I'm confronted by two faces, one I don't recognize and one I do. They are on the floor, their arms outstretched toward me. I'm not sure whether they are trying to push me away or pull me to them. My question is answered pretty quickly. I slide through what would have once been a window. Glass scrapes at my belly and my side, but a cool breeze is suddenly on my face and neck and the familiar man's lips are on my cheek. I try to turn away from him, but everything is swimming and spinning. A loud boom resounds from a place behind me, followed by a ferocious heat and by lots of shouting and running. The pain becomes so unbearable, the darkness creeps up on me. In an instant, the blackness has returned and the pain is pushed somewhere where it can't get to me anymore. Not for a little while anyway.

I open my eyes and I'm back in the sunshine, looking at scorch marks on the highway while the sun gradually burns the back of my neck. I realize I've just had the first bona fide memory recall since coming round. It's a tiny victory, but one which I savor. The crash definitely happened, and Wesley had told the truth when he said he'd helped the police pull me from the wreck. I guess I should be grateful to him for what he did, but why did I turn my head away when he kissed me on the cheek?

It's that little innocuous moment that rings like a church bell in my head. Perhaps I'm too readily focusing on the negatives.

"Sea, are you okay?" Mary Elisabeth crouches beside me, hugs me.

"Just had a moment," I say.

"A moment?"

"You were right to bring me here. I saw the crash. I even saw myself being rescued."

One of her eyes twitches. It's a subtle movement, but in my heightened state of self-awareness, I'm missing nothing. "Is that so?"

I nod.

"Well," she cries, standing. "That's fantastic news! I told you, didn't I? I said if you didn't put any pressure on yourself that everything would start coming back to you."

"Woah there," I say, following her. "Let's not get ahead of ourselves here. I only remembered a snippet."

"But a snippet's a snippet, right? It's something."

She's right. Perhaps that's why we're friends. She's the positive to my negative, the light to my shade. Her phone rings and she holds up a finger. "I have to take this. Is that okay?"

I nod. I'm getting used to the people in my life taking urgent calls.

I stand on the side of the road, wondering whether my little moment of recollection is a precursor to the floodgates opening. If it is, I'll find out soon enough who the real heroes and villains are. That's when I will have decisions to make. I only hope I'm strong enough to make them.

The sun catches something in the scorched scrub and my eyes flit to it. It's around ten feet away from the side of the highway. I push through the dry bracken which claws at my legs and ankles, and I stoop down. I reach for the metallic object that's half in and half out of the undergrowth. I collect it into my palm, hold it close so I can study it. It's a single key with a hard plastic fob. One word is written on it in black ink. *Redshoot.*

"Sorry about that," Mary Elisabeth says from the other side of her car.

I slip the key into my pocket and stand abruptly. My best friend doesn't need to be burdened with this. Nobody does. A lock exists out there somewhere matching this key, and I intend to find it.

CHAPTER 16

DEPARTURE

WE PULL UP outside the house. My husband's truck is still out front, as is my mom's car. It's late afternoon now and the sun is starting to slip to the west. It's been an eventful day but I'm still no closer to truly understanding who I am. Sure, I've made steps in the right direction, but they're barely baby ones, tiny little stumbles.

"Let's celebrate," Mary Elisabeth says.

"What are we celebrating?"

"Your memory coming back, silly." She pulls me toward the house. "I make a mean margarita. Of course, if you had all your memories back, you would know that, but what the heck."

As we step over the threshold, Wesley is coming at us. His face is a ball of anger, his skin the color of raw meat. I've never seen him this way before. He looks so different.

"Where the hell have you been?" It takes a moment before I realize the question is directed at me.

"Mary Elisabeth and I headed up to the crash site to see if it could help me remember things."

"The crash site?" He's practically spitting now. His eyes flit from me to Mary Elisabeth and back again.

"Right. The place where I crashed the car." I realize I'm being churlish, but his demeanor is pissing me off.

"And you didn't think to tell me?"

I'm offended by the inquisition. "Is that the kind of relationship we have, Wesley? Do I have to get your permission to go out?"

He turns to Mary Elisabeth. "And this was your idea?"

She retracts from him like a beaten dog. "Well, I—"

"No, it was mine," I lie. "I'm fed up with not knowing who I am."

"But you do know who you are. You're my wife!"

"So you keep telling me, but I don't remember you," I reply. "I don't remember my own mother."

"But you will!"

"When?"

He does the thing with his fists again. For a moment I think he's going to hit one of us or both, but then he walks away, breathing through his nose like a bull.

"Mary Elisabeth, I'd like you to leave," he says, barely attempting to control his tone.

She looks at me, her lips drawn together in a thin line. "I'd better go."

"You don't have to."

She slides toward the door. "Yes. I think I do. I'll see you tomorrow."

As the door closes, the tension in the room becomes almost unbearable. I want to run from it, but I'm acutely aware I have to confront this situation head on. Is this what I was living with? A controlling relationship? Was I accepting of the way things were? If that's who I was, perhaps I don't want to remember.

"What the hell was that?" I yell at him, but he's circling me like a tiger. I'm suddenly afraid. I realize I don't know who this man is or what he's capable of. He's under pressure at work, that much is clear, and my near-death experience would have been an additional burden for him. Is that what this is, or is something more sinister going on here?

"She had no right!" he yells. "You had no right!"

"What? To go outside? To spend time with a friend?"

"To leave me here, wondering where the hell you are, or if you're even okay. Don't you realize, the crash almost killed you, Sierra? We almost lost you?"

"And you think I would just run off and never come home? Where would I go?"

"I never said that."

"But you implied it."

His fists are still clenched, the muscles in his forearms bulging. "Mary Elisabeth knows how hard this has been for your mother and I. She should have known to give me a heads up."

I'm literally spitting feathers now. How dare this man try to manipulate me in this way, to make me feel guilty for having the audacity to leave the house.

"So you can go out at the drop of a hat, but I can't. Is that what you're saying? That two sets of rules exist for the people who live here? One set for you and my mother, and a whole different set for me?"

"Just while you're recovering," he offers. "Just while you're getting yourself back together."

I throw my arms out. "Are you aware of how long that could take, Wesley? Do you even have any understanding about what this process is I'm going through? I could be like this for months, years," my voice cracks, "forever."

"You don't know that."

I front up to him, stand toe-to-toe as I tip my head back and look into his eyes. I realize it's a bold play, a dangerous one, but I'm so outraged. This man doesn't get to tell me how to live my life or how to behave. He isn't in my head, walking in my shoes, discovering piece by tiny piece what kind of a person I was before my whole body was thrown into a grinding machine and spat out in little chewed-up bits.

"I know enough," I hiss. "And I won't be imprisoned in this house or babysat by you and my mom while I wait for the fog to clear. If my old memories aren't coming back to me any time soon, then I plan to make some new ones."

He's still breathing heavily, his cheeks puffed out, his teeth clamped together. I have no idea which way the chips are going to fall here, but I have no intention of giving ground to him. If he wins now, he wins forever, and I can't have that. If he is the love of my life, he needs to re-earn his badge. For now, he's just another guy whose ego is bruised.

We stand chest to chest in silence, waiting for the other to make the first move. I almost crack first, but then I watch as his eyes twitch and the muscles in his neck relax a little. I sense his anger is dissipating. It's either that or he realizes this approach isn't going to get him anywhere. I wonder whether I've earned his respect, or if he realized I had this in me. I'm guessing he didn't, because I didn't realize it myself.

His shoulders drop and his hands open, and then they're on me, resting on my shoulders. He looks down at me and smiles. If he wanted to, he could throw me through the window, stomp me into the gravel.

"You're right," he says eventually. "Of course, you are."

My eyes narrow as I wait to find out if he's playing me.

"I overreacted," he continues. "And I'm sorry."

"You'll need to apologize to Mary Elisabeth, too."

He seems to react, but he catches himself. "Of course."

I let him hug me. His chest is like steel and concrete against my cheek.

"I have an idea," he says as he strokes my hair. "A way to make it up to you."

I don't want him to make it up to me. I'm now more anxious than ever. He could pulverize me in his strong arms and I would have no way of escaping. I can't pull away from him now. If I do, he'll sense weakness. We're locked in this embrace for as long as he wants us to be.

"Dinner," he says, releasing me and reaching for his phone. "Get yourself ready. We're heading into town."

CHAPTER 17

DINNER DATE

I RELUCTANTLY ACCEPT. Perhaps he is truly sorry, and perhaps I have been unfair, but I'm still nervous of him, and I can't forget the brochure on his desk or the way he spoke to Mary Elisabeth. A romantic dinner at an Italian restaurant in town is hardly fair restitution.

I get dressed, putting on a black thigh-length dress he picked out for me. I apply lipstick, a touch of gloss, some perfume. I don't want to overdo it and give Wesley any ideas, but I'm enjoying the way I look. It's the first time I've felt like anything other than cannon fodder.

"Look at you," he says as I descend the staircase. "Man, you look the bomb."

The flattery doesn't go unnoticed, but it's no more than that. I want to look attractive, to be something better than the person staring back at me in the morning.

We drive into Thousand Oaks. It's not a long drive, fifteen

minutes, but he keeps glancing at me. I try not to notice, try to look away. I watch as the traffic speeds past us in the opposite direction, but I sense his gaze on my legs, my hips, my body. I suddenly wish I'd worn something else, something less revealing. I'm practically naked beside him.

I think about the way Mary Elisabeth looked when he practically threw her out of the house. She looked taken aback, hurt. I'm guessing this hasn't happened to her before. I wonder if she's okay. She's been a good friend to me so far. She is the only one who's helped me to remember, even though the memory was painful. I can still recall the scratch of the glass on my stomach and the crunch of the steering wheel against my chest.

"You're going to love this place," Wesley says. "You do love it. Well, the old you did."

I force a smile, wondering where he's going with this.

"Every time you came here, you would rave about the seafood linguini. Me, I could take it or leave it, but you? Man, you loved that dish."

He's making small talk, which is fine. Small talk I can handle. What I can't take is the side of Wesley that showed itself in the house. The Mr. Hyde version of him is terrifying.

"You know, we came here on our first date," he adds, not waiting for me to speak. "Once I'd convinced you to take a chance on me, that is. Man, I was so nervous. Didn't want to mess up. You looked so beautiful that night, just like you do tonight. I was stumbling over my words all evening, spilling my drink, making an ass out of myself. I thought I'd blown it, that you would never agree to come out with me again, but I must have done something right, because you did. You kept coming back."

I try to picture myself falling in love with this man, of being so impressed by him I'd be literally bursting to meet up with him again. I can't. It's not real. If something exists between us, some chemistry, it's either gone, or it's buried way, way down.

"Maybe it was the linguini," I say, joking, but realizing as the words spill out of my mouth I sound like a bitch.

"Yeah, maybe," he laughs, taking it on the chin. "You sure like that pasta."

We sit in silence for the rest of the journey. I wonder if I've hurt him, and I'm suddenly filled with guilt. He was trying to express his feelings for me and I burst his love bubble. Maybe I'm the problem, not him. Maybe I've always been the problem.

I shut my eyes to the headlights racing past us. Everything is so bright, so loud, so overwhelming.

I picture Max's face, the smile on his lips, the business card he slipped into my palm like a five-dollar bill. He told me we'd hooked up. Why would he lie about that? He has nothing to gain from convincing me we'd been out for drinks. Mary Elisabeth didn't appear to be aware of it, which I think is strange. Girlfriends tell each other everything. It's the unwritten code. It either means I didn't have time to catch up with her after the date and before the accident, or I kept it from her. I'm not sure why I would do that. If my marriage was having difficulties then surely she would be the first person I would speak to.

I think about Mystic Spring and Wesley's call. A link has to exist between that and my accident, I'm sure of it. Wesley was so animated on the call, so desperate. I wish I'd spent more time looking into his accounts, because it could have backed up my theory. Max is an architect. Is he involved in some way? Maybe this is some kind of complex, intricate web I'm ensnared within. Can I actually trust anybody?

And then I recall the key. *Redshoot.* The only thing left at the crash site. It came from the car; I'm absolutely certain of it. It was right next to the scorched scrub, in a spot where it could have easily been tossed from the wreckage. I have no idea what Redshoot is, or where the matching lock is located, but it's linked to all of this. It has to be.

"You're deep in thought," Wesley says, touching my leg. "You wanna share?"

I glare at his hand. I fight the urge to push it away.

"Just trying to remember things," I say. "Trying to recall anything about our first date."

His fingers tense against my thigh. Did I say something to unsettle him? I wonder if he'll squeeze my leg until it hurts, dig his fingers in, maybe break the skin.

"It'll come," he says, moving his hand away. "Of course, it will."

We turn off the freeway and head through town. It's a bustling, vibrant place. I wonder how many nights I've come here with friends, how many adventures my younger self would have had. Dozens of restaurants and bars line the streets, an open-plan shopping mall stands on a hill. Country music plays in the street. People crowd around donut stands, pizza joints, burger bars. A motorbike gang sweeps past us, all leather jackets and bright bandannas. A group of frat boys stand on the corner, watching as the college girls walk past. I envy them, their youth, their freedom.

We pull into a parking lot. Up ahead is a red neon sign that reads, *Vincenzo's*.

"This is the place," Wesley says, turning to me. "I am sorry, you know? For what happened earlier."

"Yeah, me too," I reply, opening the door, stepping outside, and leaving him in my wake. I'm not in the mood for his apology. If Thousand Oaks signifies freedom, I want some of it.

CHAPTER 18

CHANCE ENCOUNTER

WESLEY ORDERS FOR us. I'm okay with that. By now, he knows my mind better than I do. Much better. We start with antipasti, a glass of Malbec for me, a beer for him. It's the first alcoholic drink I've had since leaving the hospital and it goes straight to my head. I can't wait for the main course to arrive. I need it to soak up some of the booze. The restaurant is busy. Every table is full. Wesley tells me a packed restaurant is the sign of good food, and he's right. The seafood pasta is delicious. King prawns, clams, a couple of crab claws. I wonder how much all of this is going to cost.

"You like?" he asks me, chowing down on a calzone.

"I do," I say, dabbing my lips with a napkin, trying not to spill pasta sauce down my dress.

"I told you."

I have another sip of wine, not sure if it's a good idea. I'm on my second glass and getting increasingly inebriated. I don't want to say anything I shouldn't. I try to be sensible, place the glass back on the table, and inadvertently almost knock it over.

"Woah there," Wesley says. "Almost lost the whole thing."

"I need the bathroom," I say, standing, taking care not to crash into the table.

"Okay. You know where it is?"

I don't, but I'm pretty sure I can find it.

I head toward the coat room, thinking it has to be somewhere nearby. I'm wrong. I find myself in a separate eating area with another half dozen tables. All eyes are on me, the slightly drunk woman in the inappropriate dress.

"Sorry," I say, backing away. "Took a wrong turn."

I realize I'm blushing and so I quicken my pace. My first night out and I'm already making an ass of myself.

"Sierra, are you okay?"

I turn, expecting my husband to be looking down at me through those semi-patronizing eyes, but it's not him at all. It's my friendly nurse. Kaiden. His smile makes my heart hurt. My head, too.

"Oh, hi," I stammer, more drunk than ever. "Just... looking for the bathroom."

"Right. It's over there, beside the bar."

I follow where he's gesturing, and within a second or two, I spot the sign. I've no idea how I missed it before. It's not exactly discreet.

"Sorry, I'm still... getting used to things."

He steps toward me and I catch the scent of his aftershave again. It's mysteriously enticing to me. Maybe it's the effect of the red wine, but my heart is pounding in my chest.

"You don't have to apologize," he continues. "You had a bad accident, Sierra. It's going to take some time for things to return to normal."

"I'm starting to believe normality is a long way off."

His eyes don't move from mine. I sense the compassion, the genuine concern for my predicament. I wonder why that notion seems so alien to me.

"You shouldn't put pressure on yourself."

"Funny," I reply. "You're not the first person to say that to me."

"Your husband?"

I nod, avert my eyes. Since my fight with Wesley earlier, whenever I'm near him, I feel intense pressure.

Kaiden glances in the direction of a table for two against the far wall. A pretty woman sits there. She looks up from her phone and raises a hand in our direction. Kaiden waves back. I realize I'm stepping into something.

"That's Ruth," he says. "We work together."

"I'm sorry," I say. "I'm interrupting."

"No, not at all. She'll be fine. We've known each other for, like, forever."

Right at that moment, I want to be Ruth. I want nothing more of this life I once had. I want the life Kaiden's forever-friend has instead. The one where she gets to go to dinner with this handsome nurse with no added complications, no memory loss, and no unsolvable riddles hanging over her head.

"Who are you here with?" he asks, and for a moment I can't remember. I'm not even sure where I am.

"My husband," I say, remembering Wesley is waiting for me back at the table. I've been too long, I realize. If our earlier exchange is anything to go by, he'll be slowly boiling in his own anger.

"Is he taking good care of you?"

"Sure," I reply. "Real good."

"That's great."

It gets awkward between us then, as if something isn't being said that ought to be. I fidget with my hands, step from side to side, still needing to pee.

"You probably should get to where you're going," he says, smiling.

"Yeah, I probably should."

"It was great seeing you, Sierra."

"You too, Kaiden."

I turn toward the bar, but I sense movement behind me.

"Wait," he says, turning as he grabs a pen and a slip of paper from a waiter. He writes something down. "Here."

I take it, peering down at the hurried scrawl, wondering what the heck is going on.

"In case you need to talk," he says, his fingers grazing mine. "About anything. Anything at all."

I stifle a smile. He's the second person today who's given me his number, except this number is one I actually want.

"Thanks."

Our eyes connect and I sense something between us. I'm aware I'm married, but for some reason, I don't care. Why doesn't my husband look at me like this? Why don't I feel this way when I'm with him? Maybe it's the natural reaction of a crash survivor, becoming emotionally attached to the nurse who first took care of me. Maybe it's a condition with a name, like Munchausen or Stockholm Syndrome.

"You take care of yourself, Sierra."

He heads back to his table and there's a sharp pang of disappointment in my abdomen. I stagger toward the bathroom, head to the stall, lock the door, and sit down. The room is swimming a little, but I try to focus on the note Kaiden has given me. It has his number with a little handwritten note.

Don't be a stranger. xx

Two kisses. *Two kisses?* What does he mean by adding those? Does he want me to call him? Does he want me to go behind my husband's back and meet up with him?

I recall Wesley's face when we came back from God's Seat, and the way he went for Mary Elisabeth. I can't risk that with Kaiden. I can't put him through it. I fold the note in half and tuck it into my bra. It's a tacky move but it's the only place I can hide it in this goddam dress. Wesley can't find out my nurse gave me his number. That would only end badly for all of us.

I realize if I'm going to solve this riddle, I'm going to have to do it on my own, without any help from Kaiden Marshall or anybody else.

CHAPTER 19

STANDOFF

I SMOOTH MY dress down, pour myself a glass of water from the jug at the bar, and head back to the table. Wesley watches me approach. His eyes follow my every move. I realize he's not blinking, that he's barely breathing. My anxiety peaks again.

I grab my chair and sit down, glugging my water.

"Where you been?"

"I told you. To the bathroom."

"You've been twenty minutes."

"I really needed to go."

I don't like the tone of his voice. He's not quite as riled up as he was earlier, but he's heading in the same direction. I notice he's ordered himself another beer, a tall one. An empty whiskey glass sits beside it, moisture still on the rim.

"I saw you talking to that guy."

Okay, I think to myself. *Here it comes.* "Oh, yeah?"

"Yeah, Sierra. The guy by the coat room. You two seemed pretty friendly."

His face is changing color again. I take another large gulp of water. I need to sober up quickly. I can't risk another blow out. Not here. Not in public.

"He's Kaiden, the nurse who admitted me into the hospital."

"And he just decided to come up to you in a restaurant while you were having a romantic meal with your husband?"

I scoff. My immediate, sarcastic reaction clearly annoys him. "This is hardly romantic."

"So what is it then?"

"It's just dinner, Wesley. Just some pasta."

His neck muscles bulge again. "Just some pasta. Just some pasta." He throws his napkin onto the table and stands. "Well, let's see about that."

He stomps across the restaurant, past the coat room, and into the second dining area. I race after him, almost tripping over my own chair in the process. He's at Kaiden's table before I have a chance to stop him. His fists are opening and closing, opening and closing.

"You the nurse?" he bellows, standing so close to the table his feet are practically touching the legs. Everybody looks up at him. The surrounding diners give us nervous glances, followed by a smattering of whispers.

Kaiden stands. "I am. Name's Kaiden Marshall."

He holds out a hand. Wesley looks down at it as if it's the vilest thing he's ever seen.

"And do you know who I am?"

"I'm sorry, sir. I do not."

"Well you oughta, seeing how you're so close to my wife."

The two men glare at each other with simmering discontent.

I have a lingering, persistent sensation something is going on that I'm not seeing.

The woman sitting across from Kaiden sets down her glass. "Kaiden, what's going on here?"

"I have absolutely no idea," he says, his jaw clenched. "Perhaps Mr. Coleman can enlighten us."

"Oh," Wesley says. "So you do know who I am."

Kaiden looks at me, but I avert my gaze. I'm ashamed of what's happening. If it wasn't for me, this confrontation wouldn't be happening. The slip of paper containing Kaiden's telephone number and his affectionate message, "*Don't be a stranger. xx*," burns hot against my skin.

"Well, as Sierra is standing behind you, and given that she and I spoke earlier, I'm going to make the assumption you're her husband."

"So, you're a wise guy," Wesley retorts. "Well listen to this, wise guy. My wife has had a major, life-threatening accident, which means she's vulnerable, particularly to health care professionals on minimum wage like you who apparently prey on vulnerable women."

"What the hell is that supposed to mean?"

"Whatever you want it to."

Kaiden steps away from the table, closing the distance between himself and my husband. He's shorter and less well-built, so there's only going to be one winner in this fight. Nevertheless, he stands chest to chest with him, his eyes never flinching. The panic rises in my gullet. I can't let this happen.

"You want to make a move... *Kaiden*," Wesley spits.

The nurse's lips curl at the corners. He looks like an old dog who's got one last bite left in him. "You tell me... *Wesley.*"

A waiter comes racing into the room, putting himself

between the pair. "Sirs. We do not want any trouble here. This isn't that kind of establishment."

The pair of them don't blink, don't speak. You could cut the atmosphere with a butter knife. I'm torn between pulling them apart or running out of the restaurant. If I'm the cause of all of this, maybe I shouldn't be here.

"Wesley," I say, my voice like tiny bells. "Please don't."

He chews his lip, exhales. "Stay away from my wife," he growls.

I eye Kaiden over his shoulder. He looks relieved. I don't think he wanted this any more than I did. If only I hadn't gone to the crash site with Mary Elisabeth, and if only I hadn't angered Wesley by not telling him where I was going. We would have never been at this restaurant at the same time as Kaiden, which would have meant all of this would have been avoided. It's like my accident has set off a chain of events that are leading inexorably to some sort of catastrophe. The only problem is, I don't have any idea how it can be avoided.

"Anyway," Kaiden says, visibly shaken. "It was nice meeting you, Mr. Coleman."

"I wish I felt the same way," Wesley says, taking my hand in his. "But I don't."

We walk out, leaving Kaiden to make things right with his date. The guilt eats away at me. If he was trying to make a good impression, I did a pretty awesome job of making sure he failed. As Wesley pulls me toward the door, I wonder why everything managed to get so heated so quickly. The look in Kaiden's eyes, the spite in Wesley's. It was almost as though the two men knew each other, which I guess is possible. It's a small town, after all. But if that were true, why had they claimed to be meeting for the first time?

"Wait here," Wesley says as we stand on the sidewalk. "I'll get the car."

As he walks off, I retrieve Kaiden's note from its hiding place and study it. I realize I'm being paranoid. I have to trust somebody. Not everyone is against me. I decide my nurse in shining armor is the least likely to be a threat, making him the only person I can wholly rely on. I extract my phone from my bag and enter his number, filing it under a fake name, *Kara*. Something tells me I'll be calling it at some point in the very near future.

CHAPTER 20

HOOK UP

I STAND OUTSIDE in my ridiculous dress, watching as the young partygoers walk by, laughing and hollering, feeling far older than my years. What makes it worse is I can't remember being that young; not because it was so long ago, but because I can't remember anything at all. At least if I had memories I could dwell on the nostalgia of it all. I don't even have that.

Wesley has been a while. I don't recall us parking the car so far away. I start to wonder whether he's left me alone as punishment for my daring to talk to another man. I wonder how things have turned so quickly. Up until this afternoon, he has been the epitome of a loving husband, catering to my every whim, even if I couldn't bring myself to fully trust his intentions. Now he's turned into a jealous, possessive control freak.

I try to plan my next move, but it's like I'm all out of them. Unless I can find a connection with Mystic Spring or locate the lock for my key, the riddle will remain unsolved.

I wrap my arms around myself, trying to push away the cold night air. I'm still a little heady on red wine and pasta.

I spot a couple approaching and step back to let them pass. The guy presses the fob on his key chain, and a set of lights blink into action from a Ford Taurus across the parking lot. The woman is laughing. I recognize the man, and he recognizes me.

"Well, if it isn't Sierra. Twice in a day, right?"

It's Max, my architect friend from the shopping mall.

"Hey, what are the chances?"

Max's date—a tall peacock with short hair and a piercing through her right nostril—looks me up and down. A smirk spreads across her lips. I'm guessing she thinks my dress looks a little stupid on me. I'm beginning to think that myself.

"I was going to call you," I say.

"Okay," Max replies, but it's obvious the exchange is awkward for him. Here he is, out on a date with a hot young thing, and here I am, middle-aged and desperate, acting like we're old friends.

"I wanted to talk to you about what you mentioned this morning. The thing about the drinks."

"Right," he says, glancing at his date. "Can this wait?"

"I just wanted to let you know I wasn't being intentionally rude earlier. It's just that I've been in an accident, a bad car accident, and, the thing is, I've lost my memory." I sound like a crazy person.

"Right." He looks relieved, as if his ego has received a double-strength boost. "So I'm not as forgettable as I thought."

"No, not at all," I laugh. "I'm sure if I hadn't had the accident, I would have remembered every sordid detail."

I regret the words as soon as they leave my mouth. The peacock with the piercing doesn't appear to be too fond of them either.

"Max," she hisses. "I'm getting cold. Can we—"

"Oh, sure," he says, gesturing toward the Taurus. "The car's right over there. I'll just be a minute."

His dismissal doesn't go down too well and she disappears with an exhale and a wave of one long-fingered, manicured hand.

"Sorry about that," I say, offering an apologetic smile.

"No problem. It's a first date and I'm not sure it's going anywhere, anyway."

"Still. I seem to be making a habit of getting in the way."

He shoots me a sympathetic look which takes me by surprise. Is this what I'm becoming? A sad case? Somebody who needs sympathy?

"You wanted to ask me something?"

He's getting me to hurry up, which means he's not lost hope on his date yet. I guess that's a good thing.

"About that night," I say. "If there's anything you can tell me, anything I said or anything peculiar about the way I was behaving, it would be really helpful."

His eyes narrow as he considers my question. "Not particularly. It was just a fun night. We had a blast, believe me. I was kinda hoping it would go on a little longer, but you seemed in a hurry to be somewhere."

"Any idea where?"

He shrugs. "Beats me. You were pretty coy about your personal life."

The peacock hits the car horn and I almost jump into Max's arms.

"I think she wants me to hurry up," he says, grinning.

"Yeah, you'd better go."

I was hoping for more, hoping for some big revelation. With all other roads leading to the same dead end, this was sort of my last big chance.

"I guess there was something, though," he adds. "Although it's probably nothing."

"Go on," I urge him. "Anything you have is better than what I've got, I can tell you."

He purses his lips as he tries to remember the details. "You said something about a big project you were working on with some friends. Something you were really excited about."

A sharp jab of excitement digs me in the ribs. "Any idea what it was?"

"Not exactly. You said something about the wildlife in Ventura County and the need to preserve what we have. You seemed like the kind of person who cared about things like that."

"About the environment?"

"Right."

Maybe that was who I was. Maybe that was my passion. The thought ignites something inside of me. Maybe I'm not the self-serving, wealthy socialite I was starting to believe I might be.

Another sharp blast from the car horn jerks Max into action.

"Look, this has been fun, Sierra, but I need to go."

"I understand," I reply. "I hope the rest of the night plays out how you want it to."

He smiles. "Maybe it will, maybe it won't." He turns to go and then turns back. "Call me. Let me know how you get on with the whole memory loss thing."

I smile back. "You'd better believe it."

As he disappears, I stand on the sidewalk, wondering what this new revelation means. If I was working on a project, surely there has to be some record of it, and if there is, I'll find it, even if I have to go behind my husband's back to do it.

❊ ❊ ❊

Wesley sits in the car, watching as she chats to the guy with the beard and the insanely tall bitch on his arm. Two men in one night. Who the hell does she think she is? And there he was, trying to make her feel at home by spending an outrageous amount of money on a dinner he could barely afford, and instead of being grateful, she goes off and whores herself to every guy who pays her the slightest bit of attention. Well, she won't get away with it, and neither will the architect. Nobody makes a fool out of Wesley Coleman and gets away with it. *Nobody.*

CHAPTER 21

DREAMS

WESLEY DRIVES US home and barely says a word. I figure he's still upset about Kaiden, which is frankly ridiculous. We only spoke for a few minutes. He couldn't have picked up on how the nurse made me feel. I'd tried to keep those emotions in check, tried to bury them in a place they couldn't be found. He had made me feel those things, though. He'd made me feel so much.

We head inside and Wesley stomps off to his office. There's the loud crack of the door slamming. I suppose there's safety in my husband being in another room, even if it is only temporary.

My mom's watching TV, some old cop show. She glances at me as I pass.

"Nice night?" she asks.

I decide to lie. "Yeah. It was great."

"Wes looks upset."

"I think he has some urgent business to attend to."

I surprise myself at how easily I come up with these stories. It's like I'm an old pro.

I wish my mom a good night, and then I head upstairs. Although I have no affinity toward this house, I cherish the thought of being behind the closed door of my bedroom. I'm exhausted. It's been a long day with a lot of questions being uncovered. I just wish there were more answers.

I head to the dresser and open the drawer. The Redshoot key looks up at me, daring me to do something with it. It sits on top of Max Cramer's card. I slip Kaiden's note out of my bra and place it beside the two items. I read it again. *"Don't be a stranger. xx."* The only clue I haven't managed to scoop into my possession is the Mystic Spring brochure. I figured that removing it from Wesley's office would have been a step too far. It doesn't matter. I've already seen it. It exists not more than fifty feet from where I'm standing.

I slip out of the dress. I silently swear I'll never wear it again and pull on a nightdress that's far more suitable. I stretch my arms and yawn. I could sleep for a week, which is ironic, considering I've just been in a coma for four days.

I peer at myself in the mirror. I wonder who's looking back to me. The face isn't familiar to me, although I'm starting to learn more about this woman's inner resolve. I'm beginning to like that about her, her strength. Whatever happens, I vow to hold onto it.

I pull the covers back and fall onto the mattress. The blanket of sleep drapes itself over me in an instant, and before I have the chance to resist, it consumes me.

❄ ❄ ❄

I'm rolling again. The world is spinning around me like some sort of weird, stop-motion cartoon. My ears are assaulted by that noise again, the horrible scraping, shattering, screeching sound.

I realize I'm back in the car after it flips over, and gravity is trying to suck me down once more. It's like I'm reliving the horror over and over, as if this is purgatory and some otherworldly entity is forcing me to repent. I would willfully do it if I could remember what I needed to ask forgiveness for.

The car comes to a halt and the police officer is beside me again. Wesley's with him. The only difference is, this time I pay attention to the look on Wesley's face. It's the same look he gave to Mary Elisabeth when we arrived back from the crash site, and to Kaiden when he confronted him in the restaurant. It's hateful, spiteful. Resentful. I try to push myself away from him, to escape through the other door, but he grabs my arm and tugs me so hard it hurts. I scream at him to let me go, but he laughs at me, the sound a cruel, sniggering rasp.

When I emerge from the vehicle, they've all disappeared. The police officer, Wesley, the ambulance. I'm in darkness. It's terrifying. I'm so cold, as if all the oxygen has been sucked out of the night. I wonder if this is it, if I actually died after all. Perhaps it would be for the best. I've been causing nothing but trouble ever since I left the hospital.

A little girl speaks to me from someplace outside of my consciousness. I whirl around, but everything is covered in a blanket of mist as thick as cotton. I step through it, not knowing where I'm placing my feet or where I'm headed. I could be walking into more trouble, or worse still, stepping off a cliff. I'm not cold anymore. I'm hot. Sweat glistens on my cheeks and forehead. I look down but I can't my own body is invisible to me. I could be floating in space, drifting in the darkness.

I'm confronted by her face. She emerges from the swirling cloud. She could be mistaken for an angel if it wasn't for her clothing. She's in an orange dress and white sneakers. Her hair is as yellow as buttercups in a meadow. Her pigtails rest on her shoulders. Her long fringe hangs just above her deep blue eyes. They glisten with tears. It's the girl I've been dreaming about ever since the accident, and now she's standing right in front of me, her arms held out, beckoning me.

"I don't know what you want," I say.

Her finger curls up, pulls me toward her. It's like we're attached by an invisible thread because I float through the mist, moving closer and closer.

I look up. Something is behind her, a darkness in the mist, its heart as black as coal. Fear squirms in my chest like a coiled snake. I want to grab the girl's hands and get out of this darkness, but I have no control of my legs. I'm right in front of her now, almost close enough to grab her. I reach out, but I'm an inch too short. The darkness slips over her shoulders and caresses her gullet. She lets out a soundless scream. I'm screaming with her, telling her to run, to get the hell away, but the darkness won't let her go. It's consuming her, sucking her into a black pit, thick tar covering her torso as she disappears beneath its bubbling surface. The last thing to vanish is her hair. Bright yellow strands remain visible until the tar slips across them, sucking them downward.

I drop to my knees, my hands held out, stretching, reaching. Tears soak my cheeks and chin. The blackness makes a spitting, bubbling sound as I search for her. The tar bubbles like boiling water. Something rises to the surface. Something metallic. It floats to the top, rests in the black ooze. I realize it's a key with a blue, plastic fob. Written in thick black letters is the word *Redshoot*.

CHAPTER 22

RAMMED

I OPEN MY eyes. The saltiness of fresh tears is in my mouth. I've been crying. The little girl's face is still painted across my mind. I'm shaken by what I witnessed. Although I'm aware that what I saw was merely a figment of my exhausted brain, it's still as real as the sheets covering me from the waist down, or the pillow I've buried my head into.

A shuffling sound emanates from the doorway and my head snaps toward it. Somebody is in my room. I rub my eyes with sweat-soaked fingers and wait for everything to come into view. It's my mother. Evie. She looks as immaculate as ever, a floral top, pleated slacks, her lipstick carefully applied.

"You're awake," she says.

"Barely."

"You have a visitor."

I push myself up into a sitting position, pull the sheets across myself. I glance at the clock. It's eight in the morning. "At this hour?"

"It's a police officer. He has some questions for you."

She doesn't say any more than that before disappearing. I leap out of bed, brush my teeth, and make myself look as presentable as I can. I'm nervous even though I've done nothing wrong. This has to be routine. A few standard questions, nothing more. I'm sure of that, sort of.

I head out into the hallway, glance at the door to Wesley's room. It's ajar, giving me a good view of what's inside. He's nowhere to be seen, just his usual mess of screwed-up clothes and assorted litter. I'm pleased. I'm not sure I can face him again this morning. Not the Wesley I met yesterday.

Downstairs, my mother is reading the day's news and drinking coffee. She eyes me as I pass, lifts a hand. She's strangely quiet today, which I find odd. She doesn't ask me how I am.

"He's out back," she offers, creasing her nose. "Smoking."

I pass through the kitchen. He's standing on the patio. He's tall with short, red hair. He's wearing light gray slacks, a blue flannel shirt, and a white undershirt. That means he's not uniform, which heightens my anxiety. He has a couple day's stubble on his cheeks and chin. He drags on a cigarette and blows smoke.

"Hi," I say, stepping outside, catching him off guard. His head jerks up.

"Mrs. Coleman?"

"The very same."

I hold out a hand. He pitches his cigarette and takes it, pumps it twice.

"Detective Brady Wilson," he says. "Ventura County Major Crimes Bureau."

Those five words instantly sharpen my focus. It's the first time anybody has mentioned the word crime in relation to my accident. That's assuming that's what this is about.

"How… how can I help you?" I say, sounding nervous. He picks up on it. I can tell by the way his eyes shift.

"Firstly," he says, gesturing to a chair. We both sit. "How are you feeling?"

"My body's healing well," I say. "My mind, not so much."

He nods. "The doctors tell me it could take a while for your memory to come back, but that it should. Come back, I mean."

I smile, noticing the awkwardness about him. "Thanks. I appreciate the vote of confidence."

He folds his arms, looks up at the house. "Nice place."

"Yeah, I guess it is."

"I assume you don't remember much about your home, either."

"Not a thing." I laugh and he laughs with me. "Could I get you a coffee?"

"No. Thanks anyway. I already had my fill at the station. It's not exactly coffee shop standard, but it's free, so…"

I wonder what the detective's building up to. Part of me hopes he's going to get it over with quickly. Rip off the band aid. The other part of me wants to sit out here and talk. It's nice, chatting to someone who's real and who doesn't expect me to remember who they are.

"I wanted to ask you about the crash," he says, his expression shifting to business mode. I notice he uses the word crash rather than accident.

"Of course." I wonder why this is the first time I've been asked, but my thoughts immediately go to my husband. Perhaps he kept the police away from me.

"Your mom says you went to the crash site yesterday."

"I did."

"God's Seat."

"That's right."

"Did it help you remember?"

I think about the screeching noise, the twisted metal, and broken glass. "A little."

"Anything useful?"

I shake my head. "I remember the car being out of control then flipping. When I came round, I recall the police officer and my husband pulling me from the wreck before it went up in flames. That's about it."

"It must have been traumatic."

"From what I can remember, yes, it was."

He nods again, peers into the distance. I wonder if this is a detective tactic; ask a question and pause, ask another question and pause again. Do it a few times before slipping in the killer blow. I'm not falling for it. I'm aware it's coming, even if I don't know from which direction the uppercut will land.

"We had our guys check out the wreck," he says eventually. "Man, you were lucky to walk out of that."

I want to say that, actually, I didn't walk away, I was pulled away, but I don't want to sound too pedantic. Anyway, I need to hear what he has to say. I suspect this is going somewhere important.

"They tell me they found something on the rear fender that's unusual."

Now I'm interested. Super interested.

"What do you mean by unusual?"

He pulls a packet of cigarettes from his pocket, looks at it, and then thinks better of it. "Do you have any enemies, Mrs. Coleman?"

The question is like vinegar. It stings. "I... I don't know. I hope not."

"Has anybody made you feel unwelcome since you came out of hospital? Anybody threatened you?"

"You mean, aside from my husband?"

He laughs at my jibe. He thinks I'm joking. "Seriously, has anything out of the ordinary happened?"

I shake my head, not wanting to throw Wesley under the bus for what was basically a petty argument.

"Can I ask where you're going with this?" I ask. "I'm starting to get the impression something's going on here. Something you're not telling me."

He leans forward. The morning sun highlights the sharp line of his jaw, the slight scarring on his forehead. "The local PD initially thought this was a run-of-the-mill accident, Mrs. Coleman. That's what they thought. Those roads can be treacherous, and in a car like that, driving that late at night. It happens."

I'm literally bursting at the seams now. He's dragging this out far longer than he needs to.

"Except, the guys who look at this kind of thing, they know what they're looking for. Thank God for them, right?"

I want to drag him across the table and literally squeeze the information from him. "What did they find?" I ask as calmly as I can, but inside I'm screaming at him.

"Mrs. Coleman," he says, his voice a little lower, a little quieter. "We have reason to believe somebody rammed your car off the road."

CHAPTER 23

SR22

THE SHOCK OF his words registers with me like hot pellets in my brain. Somebody rammed my car? Why would somebody do that?

"What does that even mean?" I ask, sounding shaken.

"We're not sure yet."

"What do you mean, you're not sure?"

"We're not jumping to conclusions. It's possible the perpetrator collided with you by accident and then drove away."

"You mean, like a hit and run?"

He nods. "It's a possibility."

"But not a certainty."

He scratches at his stubble. "Not yet."

"And the alternative theory is?"

My question gives him pause. I wonder whether this is another technique from the detective school of interrogation.

"The alternative theory is a little darker," he says eventually.

"Hence me asking you whether there's anybody you can think of who might wish you harm."

I grip the table, my knuckles white. "You're suggesting it's possible somebody deliberately tried to kill me."

He nods again, this time much more seriously. "I'd be lying if I said it wasn't one of the scenarios we're considering."

Murder? Somebody may have tried to murder me. I can't believe what I'm hearing. If that's really true, then can I trust anybody? Isn't everybody a suspect until ruled out through all the available evidence?

"I have no idea how to process that," I say.

"I realize this is a shock, but as I said, we shouldn't jump to any conclusions. The investigation still has a long way to go."

I'm literally shaking now. I look back at the house, wondering where my husband is. "What if I don't have long?"

He looks at me, retrieves a notebook from his pocket. "Is there something you want to tell me, Mrs. Coleman?"

I think about it. Of course, there is. There's lots I want to tell him. The development at Mystic Spring, my husband trying to illegally buy the contract, the key I found near the crash site, the way Wesley's behavior shifted after my trip to God's Seat. None of it is useful to him, none of it is evidence. I can't spill the contents of my paranoid mind all over our discussion. I'd look even more crazy than I feel.

"No," I say. "Nothing that helps your investigation."

He stares at me, his eyes unblinking. He's watching the way I act, studying my body language.

"There's something else," he says, bending down to extract something from his backpack. I hadn't noticed he had one with him when I came down from the bedroom.

"Sure," I say. "Whatever you need."

He grabs a clear plastic evidence bag and places it on the

table between us. It takes me a moment to realize what's inside. It's black and sleek, with an indented handle.

"Is that—"

"It's a gun, Mrs. Coleman. A handgun. A Ruger SR22."

I'm stunned by the proximity of it. I don't ever remember being this close to a weapon before, although my memory only stretches back a few days.

"Why... why have you brought a gun to my house?"

"I didn't bring it anywhere," he said. "We found it."

"Where?"

He's still watching me intently, his eyes not leaving my own. "It was in the glove compartment of your car."

Now I'm really shocked. A gun in my car. Why would I have had a gun in my car? Unless—

"Is it mine?"

"I was hoping you might answer that question for me."

I have no idea. I have absolutely no idea.

"I don't think so," I say, looking at the bag containing the gun, unable to take my eyes off it. "Aren't you able to find that out from the serial number of something?" I'm not sure that's even a thing they can do, but it seems like a logical approach.

"We tried that," he said. "But this gun is unregistered. If it was yours, you had it illegally."

I slump back in my seat. It's like I've been hit by a truck. Again. Firstly, this detective tells me somebody may have tried to kill me, then he tells me I'm the potential owner of an illegally obtained lethal weapon. I have no idea what to think, what to do. I suddenly realize I have absolutely no idea who I am or what I am capable of. Not for the first time since I left the hospital, I wonder if I'm the bad guy here, if I'm the one I should be suspecting, not every other living person who has the audacity to talk to me.

"Was it loaded?" I ask, not really knowing why that's important to me.

"It was. Full clip. More bullets in the glove compartment. If this is yours, you were preparing to defend yourself, or—"

"Planning to hurt somebody," I say, completing a sentence I already knew the answer to.

We sit in silence for a moment. I understand what Detective Wilson is doing. He's waiting for me to blurt something out, reveal something I don't want to reveal. He has me all wrong. I don't have anything else to say. I'm the literal equivalent of an open book. I'm not hiding anything here. I'd be crazy to.

"What happens now?" I ask.

"We keep looking," he says. "See what we can find."

"Do you have any other leads?"

"It's not appropriate for me to comment on an ongoing investigation."

"But it's okay for you to give me a bunch of information that has me thinking somebody close to me is trying to murder me, right?" I sound spiteful, which isn't what I intended.

"I'm just doing my job, Mrs. Coleman."

"I know. I'm sorry. It's just that I'm pretty vulnerable right now."

He nods to show he understands, but it's obvious he has nothing else to give me. Not yet. Maybe I should be grateful somebody is looking out for me. It's better than what I had.

"If we find anything, you'll be the first to hear about it," he says, standing. "In the meantime, don't leave town."

It's the kind of thing the police say to suspects, which I guess is what I am. I had the gun, after all.

"Do I get protection?" I ask. "Somebody in a car outside, at least?"

He smiles. "This isn't a TV show, Mrs. Coleman. That sort

The Lies We Tell

of thing isn't easy to obtain, and until we know your life is in danger, I'm afraid the chances of me getting it approved are slim to very slim."

I nod. I knew the answer before the question left my lips. "I'll just sleep with one eye open then."

As I watch him leave, I realize the game has gotten real. This isn't a puzzle anymore, a collection of pieces I need to organize in some logical order. This is a dangerous game of cat and mouse, and something tells me the cat isn't too far from home.

CHAPTER 24

FACEBOOK

I ROAM THE house, pacing like a crazy person. My mind is a scrambled mess of anxiety and paranoia. I had a gun. A goddamn illegal handgun. If it was mine, it meant I was afraid of somebody or something, and why shouldn't I be? Somebody drove me off the road. Even if it wasn't a murder attempt, the end result would have been the same. If it wasn't for my husband and a heroic police officer, I would be dead, burned to a crisp. I have to find some answers and fast, because if somebody wanted me dead, they're probably planning to come back to finish the job. Without knowing who my potential attacker is, I'm completely exposed, a red snapper floundering on a mudbank, gasping for much-needed oxygen.

I make myself a coffee, drink it too fast, and burn my tongue. I curse out loud.

"Sierra," my mother says. "Maybe you should slow down a little. You're going to hurt yourself."

If only she knew the truth. The real truth.

"Yeah," I say. "Sorry, you're right."

"Is everything okay?" She's suddenly interested in me. I find myself wondering why.

"I'm fine."

"Is it something to do with the police detective?"

"No. Maybe. I don't know."

"What did he say?" Straight away, I'm suspicious of her questions, which is crazy. She's my mom. Why would I doubt her?

"He's looking into a potential cause of the accident."

"I thought it was obvious. You skidded off the road. You were probably driving too fast. I'm always telling you about it. You've never been a careful driver. You've never been careful about anything."

Her accusations only serve to intensify my paranoia. I push past her and head upstairs. I can't be around her negativity. I have enough negative thoughts of my own.

She calls after me but I'm not listening. I have to be alone. I have a hundred different suspicions crashing against each other in my skull. It's like happy hour at the pinball arcade. I need to find a way to calm myself, otherwise I won't be able to think about this logically.

I fall onto my bed, peer up at the ceiling. I want to close my eyes, but that's a slippery slope to oblivion. I have to be conscious. I've got too much thinking to do.

The smoke alarm blinks at me. A single red light flashes repeatedly. I have a thought. Cameras. Surveillance. What if somebody's watching me? The idea consumes me. It would make sense. If my husband is involved in this in some way, then wouldn't it be logical for him to spy on me?

I leap up, grab the plastic cover of the alarm and twist it. It comes away in my hand with a loud crack. A nine volt battery is attached to two thin wires, one red, one black. Everything is normal. I have a closer look. A tiny hole is pressed into the plastic but I suspect it's too small for a camera, not that I understand anything about miniature surveillance equipment.

I head to the lamp, the telephone, the hairdryer. Anything with a plug. I go downstairs, grab a knife from a kitchen drawer, run back to my room. Nothing is spared. I pull it about, probe the shit out of it. I won't be spied upon in my own home. I have to be sure.

I don't find anything. Of course, I don't. My husband had nothing to do with this. He pulled me out of the vehicle, after all. Why would he have done that if he wanted me dead? Unless, of course, he was playing the double bluff. I laugh out loud. I realize I'm being ridiculous. Wesley might be a lot of things but he's not a murderer.

I sit on the edge of the bed, exhausted. My paranoid episode has drained me of all energy. I lie back, stare at the ceiling once more. Something jabs against my thigh. I reach into my pocket and pull out my phone. An idea comes to life in a spot just behind my eyes. I open up my social media accounts and head to Facebook. The only other person who has willfully been making contact with me is the one person I would never have thought about. What if it is him? What if he followed my mother and I to the shopping mall and acted all innocently to throw me off the scent? What if he then followed us to the restaurant, brought a date along for the ride, and then accidentally bumped into me? I mean, I saw him twice in the same day. That's more than a coincidence. That's deliberate. What if this whole story about my secret hookup with him is his way of getting me to suspect my own husband? Maybe I've been played.

I type his name into the search bar. Max Cramer. A few people with that name spring up so I keep scrolling. A zookeeper, a financier, a guy who looks like he carries rugs for a living. I eventually find his face. It's a posed shot. The lighting's just right. I'm guessing he paid for it.

I click on his profile picture and his page opens up. It's not private. I scroll through his other photos. He likes himself. That much is obvious. He's something of a narcissist. I look at a picture of him by Niagara Falls, another of him with a group of beautiful women. It looks like he was in Vegas when that one was taken. That figures. His posts are self-congratulating, too, a series of soundbites about how wonderful his life is. I realize I'm starting to dislike the guy, even though I've only just met him... again.

I start to think about our meeting the night prior. He said I was working on a big project I was really excited about. Now I'm not sure if that's true, but I have to find out. Is Max being genuine with me? Is this environmental project real? Is there something about him I should be afraid of? He said he was an architect, and according to his Facebook profile he was telling the truth. His offices are in Casa Conejo, a stone's throw from Lake Sherwood.

I sit up, toss my phone on the side. I need to get across town. I need to figure out what the hell is going on. One way or another, Max Cramer is going to tell me everything he knows about my past life.

CHAPTER 25

WALKING THE DOG

I HEAD DOWNSTAIRS and spy my mom's Buick parked in the driveway. I glance at the hook on the wall, her keys dangling next to my own. I grab my boots.

"I need to go out," I say to her. "For a little while. Is it okay if I—"

"If you what, Sierra? Come on, spit it out."

"Borrow your car?"

"My car?"

"Yes. I need it for an hour or two. No more."

She looks shocked. I realize I have to seal the deal. I go to her and grab her hand.

"I promise I won't be any longer."

She looks up at me, torn between letting me have my own way and disappointing me.

"He won't be happy. He really won't."

"He won't know."

I take her silence as a tacit acceptance and I grab the keys on the way out.

Her car smells of her. It's just as tidy, too. It's an SUV, four-wheel drive. I wonder whether Wesley bought it for her. It doesn't matter. It's got four wheels and an engine, and that's all I need. I punch the address I found linked to Max's Facebook profile into the GPS, and I gun the accelerator.

It's not a long drive, but long enough for my brain to start playing with me. This is going to go down one of two ways. Either Max is going to prove to me that what he told me was the truth, or I'm going to find out he was behind the wheel of the vehicle that ran me off the road. If it's the former, I'll walk away with at least some more information, something to aid my investigation. If it's the latter, I might not walk away at all. I think it's a risk worth taking.

I have to find something to give to Detective Wilson. I can't keep living my life with a cloud of suspicion over everybody I meet. I have to get used to the idea my memory might not return for years. I can't wait that long to start rebuilding what I had, or to begin to build something new.

I'm in Casa Conejo before I realize it. I've been so consumed by my own thoughts, I barely noticed the journey. Max's business is on the other side of town, so I travel another five blocks before pulling into a parking spot. I walk the rest of the way. It's a beautiful day and I need the air. This could be the moment everything starts making sense to me. The pinch point.

A police car goes by on the street, its siren blaring. An old lady walks past and smiles. She has the look of somebody who's at peace with herself. I'm envious. A kid on a skateboard swerves past me, music blaring from a portable speaker tucked into the pocket of his baggy pants.

The park is up ahead. From what I can remember, it's two

blocks over from Cramer Designs. I walk toward it but realize the far end has a police cordon around it. The squad car with its siren blaring packs nearby and the two officers inside emerge to join a collection of other officers, investigators, and journalists surrounding a white crime scene tent. I have no idea what's happened but it looks serious.

I pass it, keeping my distance. A large gathering has started to form around the park. I have to weave in and out of people to get past. They all look concerned, anxious. They're all talking about it.

"Damn shame."

"Yeah, such a nice guy."

"I can't believe something like this could happen in this neighborhood."

I try not to get distracted. This has nothing to do with me. I've got more important things to worry about; namely, getting my life back.

"Sorry," I say, trying to get through a densely packed group of people.

"This way, please," an officer says, trying to direct the crowd to a spot a little further away.

I'm getting crushed now, sandwiched between an overweight guy and a group of teenagers. I don't like it. It's like I'm back at the hospital, trapped on the bed with all those tubes protruding from me, the damn machine beeping like crazy.

"Just a little further back," the officer continues. "Back toward the sidewalk."

I try to move with the crowd, but the teenagers are stubbornly refusing to give way, and the fat guy is backing into me. He steps on my foot, crushing my toe, and I try to pull it away. Instead, I end up tripping over my own ankle, sprawling toward the ground with the big guy stepping back. I realize I'm going to

The Lies We Tell   113

be trapped on the floor with the crowd treading on me, pressing me into the asphalt, suffocating me, crushing my bones.

As my hand hits the ground, somebody grabs me and hauls me to my feet, dragging me out of the crowd. I'm in the open now, fresh air on my face. I look up at the police officer's face. I realize he must have stepped out of the melee to help me.

"You were nearly in trouble there," he says.

I stand up, hands on my hips, breathing hard. I look back toward the crowd I've been pulled free of. They're frantic, excited. They look like rats around roadkill. What are these people expecting to find here?

"Thanks for getting me out," I say. "I'm not trying to interfere in what you're doing. I just have someplace I need to be."

He grabs a pen and notebook. "Where you headed?"

I gesture to our left. "Two blocks up. Cramer Designs."

"Max Cramer's place?"

I smile. "How did you know?"

He approaches, his expression shifting. "I need to take your details, Mrs—"

"Coleman. Sierra. May I ask why you need them?"

"Let's just say they may be important to what's happened here." I'm so shocked that I give it to him. I give him everything; my home address, my phone number, my next of kin.

"Why do you need all of this?" I ask. "What's going on?"

He gestures toward the park. "The man you were meeting? Max Cramer? He won't be at his office, not now, not ever." He heads back to his post. "Keep your phone on you, okay? We may need to talk to you."

I shake my head in shock. What does he mean when he says Max Cramer won't be in his office?

The air is filled with the babble of talk and I turn as the

crowd nears. I step aside and as one of the reporters talking into a handheld camera starts to speak.

"The thirty-three-year-old was walking his dog in this park last night in his hometown, Casa Conejo, when somebody stabbed him eight times in the chest. The victim died instantly from his wounds. Max Cramer leaves behind a sister and an elderly mother."

My knees go weak. Max, dead. How can that be true? What the hell is going on here?

My vision becomes a dark tunnel as everything goes numb. My legs turn to jelly, my arms become Styrofoam. I don't realize I'm falling until my body hits the ground.

CHAPTER 26

MYSTIC SPRING

WHEN I COME round, I'm back home, lying on the couch. My mom is with me. She's holding a glass of water to my lips. I have no idea how I got here, or what happened after I learned Max was dead.

"That nice detective brought you home," she says. "Apparently the local PD called him, and as your assigned officer. He thought it was only right he should be the one to hand deliver you to us. Fortunately, he brought my car back, too."

I sip yet more water. I can't believe Max is gone. I can't believe I fainted. I can't believe all this is happening to me. Can it be another coincidence in a long line of them? I don't think so. It's all too convenient. The very night Max tells me about a major project I'm working on, he ends up with a knife in his chest.

"What were you doing out there?" my mother asks. "What was so urgent that you had to take my car out to Casa Conejo?"

"I was meeting with someone," I say. "A friend of mine."

"Sierra, don't lie to me. You can't remember who your friends are. How can you expect me to believe you were meeting one of them?"

I don't try to answer her. What's the point? I'm in no fit state to win an argument. Max was my only connection to who I was before, and now he's gone. Somebody is deliberately shutting all the doors on me. I'm closed in, imprisoned. My next steps elude me like a forgotten dream. My memory is showing no sign of returning, and every time I think I have a route to figuring this whole crazy thing out, I hit a roadblock.

Aside from a key without a lock, the only thing I have left is Mystic Spring. That's the one clue I haven't chased down yet. I thumb through my phone and find the location in the Hidden Valley. It's so close, just south of Thousand Oaks and north of God's Seat. I've been circling around it without realizing it. All this time, it's been hiding in plain sight. I've been such a fool.

"Mom," I say, trying to sound as pathetically needy as possible. "Can I borrow your car again?"

❄ ❄ ❄

I drive into the valley and follow the dirt track. Farmland stretches for miles on either side of me. A ranch is nestled beneath the hills, a dozen horses running free on the wide expanse of land. The road is rough beneath the wheels, orange dust kicking up as I wind through the scrub. It's a hot day, too hot. I have the air conditioning cranked way up, but even so, the hot sweat is pooling at the nape of my neck.

A sign on my right reads "*Mystic Spring*," and I swing onto another track, this one a little narrower, a little more uneven. I hope the car's suspension doesn't give out. I've already lost my mom's car once today. Twice would be careless. The gnarled branches of Californian Oaks stretch across the trail, attacking the roof of the vehicle. I try to avoid them, but the way ahead is overgrown and wild. I decide to park up and walk.

I step out into the open. I'm dressed in tight-fitting jeans and a black vest. I have no hat. With the sun beating down on me, my neck is like a steak on a hot grill. A narrow stream winds lazily beside the track and I follow it, figuring if I'm looking for a place called Mystic Spring, following the water wouldn't be the worst idea in the world.

I walk for twenty minutes or more, keeping to the shade as best I can. It's a large plot of land with plenty of potential. Lilacs, buckwheat, brittlebush, even sage, cover the soil. The land is fertile, if a little dry. The stream is helping, I realize. Keeping the land irrigated.

A noise comes from my left and I look up. A deer steps out onto the trail. It bows its head to me, chews at the grass. I don't move, not wanting to scare it. It looks so peaceful, so serene. I watch it eat some more. It stops, looks up and down the path and then back at me. It bows its head again, and then it's gone, disappearing among the oaks. I afford myself a smile. With everything else going to hell around me, I can appreciate something as calm as a deer grabbing some lunch.

Two male voices come to me on the slight breeze, and I head toward them. Somebody else is here. I walk parallel to the stream as it widens. The bubbling water threatens to drown out the distinct sound of conversation, throwing me off the scent, but the sounds are clear enough to let me know I'm going the right way. I'm much closer now, no more than seventy feet away. I push on, keep myself hidden in the shadows, hoping my decidedly amateur attempt at surveillance doesn't bite me in the ass. One thing is for certain, I wasn't a private investigator in my old life.

I can barely take two steps without stepping on a twig or a pile of dried leaves.

The voices sound more urgent now. It sounds like two men. One of them is agitated, his voice raised, the other more passive, as if he's trying to defuse some sort of escalating situation. I hurry. I have a suspicion what I'm about to witness is important. Things are starting to click into place, although the picture being created is still a confused, jumbled mess.

I step across the stream, get my feet and ankles wet, climb the bank on the opposite side. I scramble up the incline, taking care not to disturb any rocks or stones; anything that might give me away. I realize my growing anxiety is ridiculous. I can't see any sign of danger, no immediate threat, but something about the situation is making me nervous.

The voices are louder, much louder. Somebody says, "What the hell do you mean you can't guarantee it? I'm paying you for certainties, pal, not your best efforts."

I can picture who it is, even before I peek over the top of the bank. Two trucks are parked in the middle of a wide expanse of land. Two men are talking, standing face to face, one of them a little smaller, a pot belly hanging from a thin frame, the other bigger, bullish, all riled up. I tense up and slip on a pile of stones. The bigger guy's head snaps in my direction. I duck out of the way just in time.

I lay on my back, hoping my cover isn't blown. There's no doubt I would struggle to explain this away. He'd never believe my story if I did.

The smaller man I don't recognize, but the bigger man is much more familiar to me. He should be. I'm with him every day. We're married, after all.

CHAPTER 27

KNOCKOUT

THIS IS IT. This is what I've been searching for. I knew this place was important, but I had no idea why. This could be the glue binding it all together. Not only have I seen the brochure for the Mystic Spring development in my husband's office, sitting among the heaps of trash littering his chaotic desk, but now I have him slap bang in the middle of the location, talking to the man I assume I heard him trying to buy off.

I reach for my phone, pull it from my pocket. If only I could record what they were saying, I would have something. Sure, it doesn't link anybody to my supposed accident, or the murder of Max Cramer, but it could give me leverage.

I move along the bank, keeping the stream to my right and then to my left and up ahead. I realize it's not going to bring me close enough, but further along, there is a copse of bushes that just might. I'll have to break my cover to get close, but if I time it right, I'm confident I'll be able to do it.

I'm starting to sweat again. It's a hot day with no shade in this part of the valley. I start to wish I'd brought a hat, or some sunscreen at least. The last thing I need is a trip to the hospital for sunstroke.

The two men are shouting at each other now. Whatever they're arguing about, it's heating up fast. I quicken my pace, heading for the bend in the stream. Once I get to my destination, I climb the bank again. I'm much closer now. The trucks are less than twenty feet away now. I'm slightly behind and to my husband's left. I realize I'll have to wait for the other guy to be distracted before I make my move to the cluster of foliage. He's currently got a clear line of sight to my position.

I watch as my husband points at the land around them and raises his hand. He says, "You stand to get a lot of political leverage out of this development, don't you," but the other man retorts, "And you stand to make a lot of money. In fact, if my memory serves me correctly, this project will make you one of the wealthiest property developers in Ventura County."

These are all things I'm aware of. None of this is new information. What I need to find out is who this second guy is, and I need evidence my husband is planning to buy the contract.

I crouch down at the edge of the bank, biding my time, growing increasingly frustrated at how long this is all taking. I have to get closer.

My moment comes a few seconds later in the worst possible way. I didn't predict it. Hell, the other guy certainly didn't. It becomes clear something's about to happen when my husband's neck turns the distinct shade of crimson I've seen before. Then, before I have time to wonder what it means, he throws a fist, swinging his arm around in a wide arc. It connects with the smaller man's jaw, sending him staggering.

I gasp and place a hand over my mouth, trying to stifle the

sound. It's the first time I've seen Wesley be violent, although he's been on the precipice a couple of times. He throws another punch, and this one dances off the other guy's temple, knocking him to the ground.

I'm frozen to the spot, unable to think or move. I was waiting for a distraction, and this is a humdinger of one. My husband steps forward. I'm behind him so I can't see his face, but I can picture it; a twisted ball of pent-up fury, his eyes buried under heavy lids, the snarl at the corner of his mouth.

Something spurs me into action and I dash across the ten feet or so to the clutch of bushes and crouch behind them. I pull them apart and peer through the dry branches. The other guy is on his side, barely conscious. My husband looms over him like a bear, his fists clenching and unclenching, blood pouring from the knuckles of his right hand.

I try to activate the video recorder of my phone, but my hands are slick from sweat and it slips from my grasp. It goes tumbling into the thorny scrub. I curse under my breath, but then the stricken man shouts, "No, please!", and when I look up, Wesley aims a boot at his ribs and swings his leg. There's the unmistakable sound of air escaping and a cry of pain, and then Wesley swings his leg again, his boot connecting viciously with the other guy's cranium, knocking him out cold.

I realize I may have just witnessed a murder, and what's more, my husband is the killer. I want to go over and help the man, but I'm so terrified. What if he attacks me? What if I'm his next victim?

Wesley leans over the unconscious guy and smirks. He actually smiles.

"You had that coming," he says. "I told you what I would do if you didn't play nice."

I'm sick to my stomach. I've been living in the same house

as this guy, breathing the same air. He even has my mother living with him.

What he does next makes my stomach flip. He makes a strange gargling sound in the back of his throat, opens his mouth, and unloads onto the other guy's face. I turn away with the back of my hand to my lips.

"I'll be seeing ya', Frank."

The truck door opens and then the engine roars into life, followed by the crunch of gravel as Wesley swings the vehicle around and heads back up the hill. I look down and spy my phone lying in the dirt at my feet. I realize it was within reach all along. I grab it and tuck it into my pocket, cursing myself for my own ineptitude. If I'd been calmer, smarter, I could have recorded everything.

I peer back toward the prone body on the trail. I pause, waiting for the truck to disappear out of view, not knowing what to do. If the guy's dead, I'm now at the scene of a murder with nothing but my own word as proof of what happened. I realize that's a dangerous game. My husband is an important guy around these parts, and I'm merely a woman who doesn't remember her own history.

I stay seated, trying to control my ragged breathing, silently considering my next move, wondering how it has all come down to this; but then the man beside the beaten-up truck starts spasming uncontrollably, and before I realize what's happening, I'm up and running toward him.

CHAPTER 28

RESCUE

I SKID TO a halt beside the man's jerking torso and place my hand beneath his head. Frothy saliva bubbles in a grimace of a mouth, his eyelids fluttering like the pages of a book. His teeth are clenched tight, and I realize he could choke on his own tongue. I push his lips apart, get my fingertips between his teeth, and pull his jaw open, trying to clear his airway. I roll him onto his side, but his arms are thrashing and his legs kicking. One of them catches me in the thigh, causing me to cry out.

I wrestle with him, doing everything to keep him calm. As far as I'm aware, I've had zero medical training, so whatever I'm doing is coming from some faded recollection of something I've seen on TV or in a movie. I keep his head off the floor, cradling his cheek in my hands, and I wait for the spasming to stop.

Gradually, the thrashing starts to slow a little, and before long, he's still once more.

I let out a long breath. I hadn't realized I'd been holding it all this time. I slump onto the ground, hold myself up with my hands on sharp gravel. I'm exhausted. My pants are covered in dirt, my forearm scraped by thorns.

I check the man's pulse. It's still racing, but he's breathing at least. A few moments ago, I thought he was dead. One thing's for certain, he needs medical attention. I can't leave him out here with the sun beating down on him.

I head to his truck. It's not as new as Wesley's. The front fender is damaged, the rear wheel arch rusted beyond repair. I open the passenger door, and flip the glove box. I find a bunch of documents, a packet of cigarettes, some gum. I push it all to one side and find what I'm looking for. His wallet. I pull it out and open it, fingering some bills before finding his driver's license. The guy's name is Frank Duvall. I have no idea who that is. I look a little harder and find a couple of official-looking documents. They're on Thousand Oaks letterhead. One of them is to the mayor of the town, advising him of the idea to force through a development in the Hidden Valley, putting Coleman Construction forward as the proposed construction company. It's signed by none other than Frank Duvall, Senior Councilman.

I pocket the letter and head back to the unconscious man. I have to do something other than go through his personal possessions, but I have no idea who I can call. I realize I can't call Mary Elisabeth. She's already terrified of Wesley after their confrontation, and this will send her over the edge. I need somebody who can get Frank Duvall the medical attention he needs.

I scroll through my phone, passing over a dozen people I no longer recall. One name leaps out at me, and I mentally slap my forehead. *Kara*. Of course. Why didn't I think of it sooner? Of all the people I've encountered since waking up at the hospital, this is the one person who could get me the help I need. I hit dial and wait for the call to connect. I have no idea what the signal is like in the Hidden Valley.

Luckily, within a few moments, I hear the resounding whir of a ringtone. I wait impatiently for the other person to pick up, my feet tapping out a samba beat in the dirt.

As I'm about to give up, my thoughts are interrupted by a voice on the other end of the line.

"Hello, this is Kaiden Marshall."

"Oh thank God," I say. "I'm so glad you answered."

"Sierra?" he replies. "Is that you?"

"Yes. Look, I'm sorry for disturbing you. I'm guessing you're busy with work or whatever, but I've kind of got a situation here."

"Wait," he says. I hear him opening and then closing a door. "Okay, I'm all ears. What's going on? You sound worried."

He's not wrong. I'm terrified. I fill him in on what's happened, my voice breaking. I tell him about Detective Wilson suspecting my crash wasn't an accident, of the untraceable gun in my car, of Max's murder, and my subsequent trip to the Hidden Valley. When I tell him about Wesley knocking the councilman to the ground and then kicking him until he was unconscious, his tone shifts. Suddenly, he's in medical practitioner mode.

"Okay, tell me where you are."

His decisiveness catches me off guard. I realize I'm exposed out here. Too much is already going on all around me. I can't afford to be dragged into this without any evidence to back me up.

"I can't be here when you arrive," I say.

"Wait. Why not?"

"The detective already has me owning an untraceable firearm, and now he has me visiting the scene of Max Cramer's murder. If he then finds out I was here when somebody almost killed a Thousand Oaks senior official, he might begin to think I'm involved in some way."

Kaiden lets out a long breath. "So you want me to send an ambulance to the Hidden Valley, but not disclose who called it in?"

"Right. That's exactly what I'm asking."

Kaiden pauses on the other end of the line. "You know I think you're being ridiculous, right?"

"Walk a mile in my shoes, Kaiden, and then come back and tell me if you still think that."

My words have the desired effect, because he reluctantly relents. "I tell you what, I'll do as you ask. I'll collect this guy, make sure he gets the medical attention he needs, and I'll keep you out of it."

I look down at Frank Duvall. He's starting to stir. "Why do I get the feeling there's a catch?"

"No catch," Kaiden replies. "Just a request."

"Go on."

"Lunch."

I glare at the phone. Is this guy kidding me? "Are you asking what I think you're asking? You know I'm a married woman, right?"

"Hey, I'm not inviting you out on a date. Just some lunch and some conversation."

"Kaiden, a guy has almost died out here. I don't think this is the right time to be making some sort of proposition."

He laughs. "As I said, no proposition, no date. Just meet me. Tomorrow at Charlotte's Café. It's over on Fifth."

Frank Duvall is moving now. I duck behind the truck, scared he'll open his eyes and realize the wife of the man who attacked him is standing right beside him. If that happens, my chances of staying out of this evaporate pretty quickly.

"Okay," I say, heading back the way I came. "But hurry. I think Frank's about to wake up with one hell of a headache."

CHAPTER 29

PIECE BY PIECE

I DRIVE HOME with my head all over the place. Everything is happening too fast. My accident, Mystic Spring, Max's murder, and now this. I'm trying to figure out how it's all connected, if it's connected at all. One thing is for certain, the man I'm married to isn't the man he was purporting to be.

I turn into the driveway and park by Wesley's truck. My anxiety levels hit a new high. This man is capable of horrific violence. I have no idea whether he saw me at the site, or if he realizes I've not been home this whole time.

I slip inside, opening and closing the back door as quietly as possible. When he eventually walks into the kitchen to find me making coffee, he glares at me as if I'm an intruder.

"You want one?" I ask, trying to control the obvious tremor in my voice. "I'm making a pot."

"No, I'm fine," he replies, waving a hand dismissively. "But

I'd be grateful if you could keep the noise down. I've got a lot of work to do. This house doesn't pay for itself."

I want to snap back at him, to tell him I have no intention of being a kept woman, particularly not by him, but then he moves his hands and the wrapping across his knuckles is revealed. Blood is starting to seep through. I don't mention it. I can't. I doubt I could control what comes out of my mouth.

When he leaves the room, the tension slowly dissipates. I pour myself a cup, sit at the table, and stare out the window. I think about Kaiden and Frank Duvall, wondering whether he got to him in time, and whether the councilman is okay. I would never forgive myself if he died because of something I did or didn't do.

Then I think about Kaiden's offer of lunch and what it all means. Could I really allow my friend to put himself in danger like that? If Wesley found out about our proposed rendezvous, he would react in the worst way possible. He's already shown himself to have an uncontrollable temper. If he was willing to kick a man unconscious over a construction contract, what would he do to a guy if he was caught secretly meeting with his wife?

My memory is still a faded patchwork of inconsequential things. I'm no closer to remembering who I am than to knowing who rammed my car off the road.

I decide to start organizing my thoughts, laying the events of the past few days out like a confused jumble of jigsaw pieces. It's all a series of threads that appear to be unconnected. Life is rarely like that. Everything has a place in the chaotic, random order of things. You just need to find the right sequence.

Firstly, we have my supposed accident. It's become clear it was either a murder attempt or a hit-and-run. Either way, my husband helped pull me from the wreckage, potentially ruling him out as a suspect. On top of that, we have the gun in the glove box. Why did I have it if I didn't think I was in danger?

Secondly, I have to consider Max Cramer, now deceased. According to Max, the two of us hooked up prior to the crash. We then bumped into each other, not once, but twice in the same day. That night, Max was stabbed to death while walking his dog in the park. It couldn't be a coincidence, could it?

Thirdly, Mystic Spring is still a riddle I have to solve. I'd mentioned it to Kaiden at the hospital in my state of delirium, and then I saw the brochure on my husband's desk mentioning the location. I'd now been a witness to Wesley kicking a councilman unconscious over the proposed construction contract. That made him a bad person, but it didn't necessarily make him a murderer.

Lastly, I have the key from the crash site. *Redshoot.* The lock is out there somewhere, keeping something important from me. If that isn't true, why was the key on the side of the road? Maybe I'm reaching, jumping to the conclusion that it was thrown from my car during the crash. In reality, it could have been dropped by anyone at any time.

I run these jigsaw pieces over and over through my mind, consuming cup of coffee after cup of coffee as I try to make sense of it all. Is the key matched to a lock in the house, possibly to a cabinet in my husband's study? Are Max and Wesley connected in some way? Max was an architect and Wesley works in construction. Did they work together? Was Max bidding for the same job? Why was I carrying a gun when the crash occurred? Who was I afraid of?

An idea begins to form in my mind. What if I had found out about Wesley's plans to bribe a council official and confronted him about it? At the same time, what if Wesley found out about my drunken night with Max, sending him into a fit of jealous rage? He's certainly capable. Was his behavior reckless enough for me to fear for my life? If that was so, was that why I had the handgun? That night, was I driving through the mountains because I was trying to escape my murderous husband? Did I tell him I would go to the police about his illegal involvement in the Mystic Spring development if he didn't leave Max alone? Was that what all this was about? Did he try to kill me, and then, realizing I wasn't dead, tried to save face by helping the police to pull me from the burning vehicle? It was a possibility, if not entirely credible. For a start, it didn't give me any answers regarding the mysterious Redshoot key, but maybe that's a red herring, no pun intended.

My head's beginning to hurt. I can't tell whether it's the caffeine or the confusing jumble of thoughts in my head.

I decide it's probably both. I close my eyes, but the girl with the blonde hair glares back at me. She's the other part of the mystery I haven't yet been able to lock into place. Who is she, and why does she look so sad? I'm so confused, I lay with my head on the table and try to blot everything out.

I don't expect the hands on my back, or the fingers pressing into my shoulders.

"Does that feel good?" Wesley asks, rotating his thumbs until they hit a hard knot of muscle at the base of my neck. "You're a little tense. I've been neglecting you, and I'm sorry."

I'm so afraid, I can barely think straight. I want to slip out from beneath him, to open the back door and run until the house is out of sight and the sound of his snide, sneaky voice is a distant memory.

"Remember," he says, gesturing toward the upstairs hallway to a door that stands half open. "If you get lonely tonight, I'm right next door. I have plenty of space in my bed."

CHAPTER 30

KARAOKE

THE MASSAGE GOES on forever. I try to slip into a state of unconsciousness, praying for the relative comfort of my coma to return. At least no one can hurt me when I'm in that state, and if they can, I wouldn't be consumed by the kind of mind-numbing fear that's suffocating me right now. I would scream, but nobody but my mother would come running; and Wesley wouldn't hesitate to hurt her, too.

When he finishes, he runs his hand through my hair. I wait for his fingers to tighten, for him to tug my head backward, to scream into my exposed face, but he lets them slide through, his hard callouses rubbing against my scalp until he's gone.

I wait for a moment, my head still on the table, my hands tucked beneath my face, until I'm sure he's left the room. Even then, I still imagine him rushing me, his fists raised, eyes like blazing coals.

I breathe out, wrap my arms across my body. I need to check on my mother. I have no idea whether she's safe.

At first, I can't move. It's like I'm glued to the chair, my feet nailed to the floor. I realize I have no idea where Wesley went, but then I realize his truck is no longer in the driveway. I'm safe, at least for now. I have no idea how long it will last. He can't find out about my visit to Mystic Spring or that I saw him beat the living shit out of Frank Duvall. If he's playing nice, I need to ensure things stay that way; at least until I'm able to prove my theory.

I head upstairs and check in on my mom, dreading what I might find. Fortunately, she's in her room, reading some cheap romance novel, one of the paperbacks with the raunchy covers.

"Everything okay, dear?" she asks.

I nod my head, unable to speak without revealing my emotions. No, I'm not okay. Nothing is okay. I want to curl up in a ball and wait for everything to go back to whatever I had before the car careened out of control. I hope it was a better existence, because this is no fun.

For some reason, I decide my bedroom is a safe space. I have the adjoining door to my husband's bedroom to think about, but luckily it has a lock. I turn it and sit at the dresser. I spy myself in the mirror. My mouth falls open in horror. There are dirt stains on my top, the smear of red dust. It's not obvious, but it's definitely visible. What if Wesley had seen that? It's not the same color as the soil of Lake Sherwood. In fact, it's identical to the dust bowl of the Hidden Valley.

I'm now more afraid than ever. I need to crack this mystery before I end up dead. As crazy as it might have sounded twenty-four hours ago, it's now more real than ever. If I don't get to the end of this ugly, blackened rainbow sometime soon, I have the feeling things will spin dangerously out of control. I can't let that happen. I have to get ahead of it.

I open my phone. My past has to have more to it than what I've been able to ascertain so far. From what I've gathered since coming round, people live their lives on social media to the detriment of their actual, real world existences; but as far as I can tell, I'm the exception. My posts are infrequent and without character. I could be a machine posting stock photos and cutting and pasting words from elsewhere.

I decide to head back to the photographs of the party I apparently attended with Mary Elisabeth. Something about them was off. I didn't look real in those pictures, as if I had been transported in from some other place. Mary Elisabeth, on the other hand, looked like the life and soul of the party.

The first image is of me standing on the balcony with the colorful lights of downtown Thousand Oaks at my back. Mary Elisabeth is standing next to me, holding what looks like a margarita. In the next image, I'm talking with somebody I don't recognize, but I'm peering off into the distance, as if I want to be somewhere else. I study these photographs as if they are rare artifacts, trying to understand what is making me so indifferent to them. None of them spark a memory, none of them make me *feel*.

I hit the video media button and find three files. One of them is of me jogging in the hills. I'm on my own. I have no idea who's taken the video, but I appear to be friendly with them. More than friendly. The film goes on for a little over a minute. A man laughs. It doesn't sound like Wesley. The voice is slightly higher in pitch, a little cleaner. I scroll back through the file and let it play again. I don't find anything else that's useful.

In the second file, I'm sitting in a garden, drinking tea and watching the sunset. I don't recognize the garden or the furniture. It appears I'm unaware I'm being filmed. This video is a little longer, but once more, I don't find anything else. Unless I can find the garden, I've got no way of knowing what all of this means.

I'm hopeful for the third file, praying it holds something revealing. I click and hold my breath. After a moment, the video springs to life. The picture erupts in a blur of colors and activity. It appears to be taken in some kind of bar. The lighting is dimmed and the sound quality is poor. Dozens of people litter the floor, some standing at the bar, some on the dance floor. Mary Elisabeth runs past the camera and grabs somebody's hand. I realize this somebody is me. I'm dressed in a figure-hugging dress and heels. We head up to a small stage where some guy with large glasses and spiky hair hands us each a microphone. Mary Elisabeth and I break out into fits of giggles as the music roars into life. Shania Twain's *Man! I Feel Like A Woman!* We do our best Shania impressions, trying to command the stage and sing in tune; no mean feat. We're barely passable. At one point, I almost stumble off the stage, but Mary Elisabeth catches me and whirls me around. We seem to be having the time of our lives. People are hollering and cheering. One guy high-fives me.

I realize I'm smiling, enjoying a memory that isn't mine, but one I at least participated in. If only I could recall it.

My enjoyment is cut short when I spy the guy standing in the background. He's a little away from everybody else, sipping a beer and watching the awkward performance. I realize he's staring at me. His eyes barely leave me. I'm suddenly self-conscious, embarrassed. I want to shut the video off, forget I ever saw it. Then I look a little closer. The guy is familiar. I spoke to him this afternoon. He was the first person on the scene at the hospital, and the one person who I've felt most comfortable with ever since I woke up from that damn coma.

The guy watching me like I'm a prize he simply has to have is Kaiden Marshall.

CHAPTER 31

DENIAL

THE NEXT DAY I wake with a renewed vigor. I'm more determined than ever to connect the dots in this confusing, ever-changing puzzle. First stop, lunch with Kaiden.

Last night I lay in bed, fearful of Wesley coming home and heading to my room, perhaps slipping into my bed while I was asleep. All the doors in the house have locks, so I latched the door shut and put a chair under the handle to make sure I was safe. I wasn't about to take any chances. I'd already decided at this point I was going to Charlotte's Café the next day, and I was going to confront my nurse. He kept things from me, and I had no idea why.

Wesley told me a courtesy car was on its way, and sure enough, when I go down to breakfast, a shiny new Chevrolet is sitting on the driveway. That's good. My need to constantly borrow my mom's immaculately clean SUV is getting a little tiresome. I live in fear of leaving a mess, or worse still, damaging it.

I eat my cereal and read the newspaper while Wesley gets ready for work—he's late leaving.

He shoots me a cursory glance as he passes by, barely says good morning. I wonder if he's ashamed of manhandling me the way he did the night before, but then I realize it was a massage, not an assault. He's very careful about the way he does what he does. I realize he's much smarter than I've been giving him credit for.

When he leaves, I wash the dishes and get myself showered and dressed. Although my lunchtime meeting with Kaiden isn't a date, I want to look presentable. Despite him keeping things from me, important things, he's been a good friend. A friend I like being around.

I throw on a long skirt and cream blouse, complementing it with a silver necklace and silver bangles. I check myself in the mirror, deem myself passable, and grab the car keys. The Camaro is bright white with a sleek exterior. It also has that new car smell. I slip inside and take a breath. I have some hard truths to get out of Kaiden, but I plan to tackle them tactfully. I don't want to push him away. I need him. He's my anchor to some sort of sanity.

I drive into town and park a block up from the café. It's a small place facing the square. It has two large windows and a set of double doors. The tables and chairs outside are half full, but I decide to head into the building. I can't risk being seen by my husband, so I take a booth at the back and order coffee from a pretty, young waitress.

The distinct scents of cinnamon, chocolate, and caffeine assault my senses; the three staples of a good coffee shop. I check my makeup in a handheld mirror, not certain why I'm so self-aware. I check my watch. I'm a little early, but that's okay. I have time to prepare.

I still have the toxic sensation of Wesley's hands on the base of my neck, his thumbs rotating against the hard muscles beneath my shoulders. I picture him aiming a heavy boot at Frank Duvall's midriff, the councilman's body spasming and jerking. The two memories make me nauseous for very different reasons. I'm not sure how long I can stay in that house with my husband, but one thing's for sure; I can't leave my mother on her own for much longer. It's too dangerous.

Somebody blocks out the light from the windows and I look up to see Kaiden standing there, looking down at me and grinning.

"You look like you're deep in thought."

"Something like that," I say, gesturing for him to sit. "You're on time."

"And you're early. You ordered yet?"

"Only coffee."

"Good, because the New York Delhi sandwich here is out of this world."

I peer over the rim of my cup. "Kaiden, we're in California. How good can it be?"

He winks. "Trust me, you won't be disappointed."

I take him at his word and order his recommendation. He's not wrong. It's probably the best sandwich I've ever tasted, which is a low bar as I have little to no memory.

"Thanks for meeting me here," he says, wiping mayo from his mouth.

"Hey, no problem. I wanted to find out how Frank's doing."

If he's disappointed at my ulterior motive, he doesn't show it. "He's doing great. He's awake and he's eating."

I nod and smile. I'm happy and nervous in equal measure. "Can he remember what happened?"

He shakes his head. "Not yet. I guess he's got a little bit of what you have."

I wince at the irony. I secretly wonder whether Frank Duvall truly can't remember, or whether he just doesn't want to. "I'm glad he's okay."

"Yeah, me too." He takes another bite of his sandwich. "Do you think it's safe for you to be around that guy? Wesley, I mean?"

I nod. "For now."

"He could have killed him. If you don't go to the police, they could arrest you for being his accomplice."

The thought has crossed my mind, but my pursuit of the truth is far too important to allow it to be hampered by legalities. "I don't have any evidence he did what he did," I say. "I'd lose."

He glares at the table. "I'm worried about you."

I have to agree. I'm worried about me, too.

"I have a question for you," I say, remembering why I agreed to this meeting in the first place.

"Sure, go ahead."

I take a sip of my coffee. "Had we... had we met before my accident?"

He thinks about it for a second, and for a little while, I think he's going to say yes. He eventually responds almost nonchalantly, "No, the first time I saw you was at the hospital a few days ago. Why do you ask?"

I shrug, casual, but the disappointment is eating away at me. "Just wondering, I guess. You look familiar."

"Hey," he says, holding out his hands. "What can I say? I have a familiar-looking face."

I laugh but it's shrill and awkward. I tear off a strip of pastrami, pickle, and rye bread. I go in for the kill. "One other thing. My friend, Mary Elisabeth—"

"The woman at the hospital? Slim, red hair?"

"Right," I chew my mouthful, swallow like I'm eating my last meal. "Anyway, she keeps trying to get me to go with her to

The Lies We Tell   139

some bar in Thousand Oaks called The Blind Pony. I'm not sure if I want to without some idea of what it's like. Have you heard of it?"

He pauses again, wrinkles his nose as if he's picked up a bad smell. "I don't really drink. That stuff doesn't agree with me." He cocks his head. "Sorry, I guess I'm not the kind of guy you thought I was."

No, you aren't, I think to myself, wondering if anybody in this damn town is trustworthy.

My phone goes off in my pocket, breaking the silence. I reach for it and realize it's Mary Elisabeth.

"Hello?" I say, thankful for the distraction.

"Sierra?" she sounds harried. "Where are you?"

"I'm in town... with a friend. What's up? You sound upset?"

"I need to meet with you." The panic is evident in her voice. "Can you come here? As soon as you can? Say you will."

"Of course," I say, but before I can ask why, the line goes dead. I know where she lives. She's a block over from the house I share with Wesley. I can get there in thirty minutes, tops.

Kaiden leans across the table and grabs my hand. It's an innocuous act, but one that sends my pulse racing. "Everything okay?"

No, it's not, I think. *Nothing's okay.*

I try to blot everything out. I stand and grab my bag.

"I have to go."

CHAPTER 32

CONNECTION

I'M HEADING FOR the door, my emotions a heady concoction of anger, disappointment, and fear. I reach for the handle. I have the door half open when Kaiden calls me back.

"Sierra, can you stay, for a little while at least."

I turn back to him. He's standing now, too. He holds his hand out, as if he expects me to take it. I can't do that. Mary Elisabeth needs me, and right now, I can hardly bring myself to speak to him. He's lying to me, pretending to be somebody he's not. He told me he'd never met me before, had never heard of The Blind Pony, but I have video evidence of him standing at the bar, watching me sing as if I'm some kind of world-famous country star.

"That was my friend on the phone. She needs me to go over there, urgently."

He cocks his head again, in a way I'm starting to find more and more attractive. "It won't take long, I promise."

I pause, wanting to leave, but finding it increasingly more difficult to do so.

"Two minutes," I say, relenting. "That's all I have."

I sit down, watch him as he prepares himself. I wonder if he's going to confess everything, tell me why he's been deceiving me. I want him to. I want him to be the kind of person I think he is. I'm not sure if I can cope with the disappointment of yet another person in my life letting me down.

"I... I'm not sure how to say this."

It's my turn to grab his hand now. "If you've got something to tell me, Kaiden, just do it. I promise, I won't judge you."

He studies my hands, laces his fingers between mine. He looks up, and the hope is like a burning light in his eyes. I wonder if this is it, if this is the moment he becomes the person I've always hoped he was. "I know we haven't known each long, and this is going to sound as crazy as it sounds in my head, but ever since I met you, Sierra, I can't get you off my mind. You're there when I go to bed at night, you haunt my dreams, and when I wake up, you're still with me, consuming my thoughts. I... I think I'm falling for you."

His words completely sideswipe me. This isn't what I was expecting at all. He's falling for me? Why? How? We barely know each other. "Kaiden, I'm married."

He grips my hands a little harder and runs his finger across my palm. I don't stop him. "You can't trust Wesley. He's no good for you. He... he's dangerous."

I'm so shocked, I can barely look at him. Although he's been lying to me, what he says about my husband is true. He is dangerous. There's no denying it. Frank Duvall is evidence of that.

"I can't listen to this," I say, attempting to stand. "Not now. I have too much going on in my life. I'm still trying to remember who I am. This is another thing I'm going to have to deal with, and I just can't."

He doesn't let go. "I know you feel it too, Sierra. I can see it in you. This isn't only coming from me. I've known it ever since we first met, ever since we bumped into each other in the hospital corridor. Tell me I'm wrong."

I slip my hands from his, run my fingers through my hair. I look around the coffee shop, wondering if anybody is listening to this. I'm so confused. I do care for Kaiden. Really. He's been on my mind for days, but I'd thought it was because he was a good friend, somebody I could trust. Now he's confessed his feelings for me, it's making me second-guess myself. Have I been falling for him too? Is that what's been happening? Is that the kind of person I am?

Then I remember his deception, the way he lied to my face without blinking. I can't trust him, just as I can't trust my husband. They're both the same, two men who want something they can't have but are willing to do whatever it takes to get it.

"This is crazy," I say, heading for the door once more.

The waitress looks up, half smiling, wondering if she's witnessing a Hollywood romance movie in real life.

Sorry, sister, I want to say to her. *Real life doesn't play out that way.*

"Sierra, wait!"

Kaiden comes after me, but I'm already on the street, looking for an escape route. My life is becoming more insane by the minute. It's all too much. It's like the walls are closing in all around me.

"Think about it," he says as I walk away. "Think about what I said."

I am thinking about it. It's driving me to the point of distraction. First, I find out I'd hooked up with Max in a bar behind my husband's back, and now I've somehow given Kaiden a whole bunch of signals I wasn't aware of. Is Wesley right to not trust me? Can I even trust myself? I do like Kaiden. I have to be honest with myself about that. He's right. Ever since that first meeting, I've been thinking about him. Sure, I've been thinking about a lot of things, not least who I am, but Kaiden has been the glue that's been holding me together.

One thing's for certain, even though I'm married, I don't feel any love for my husband. I'm terrified of him. If Kaiden hadn't lied to me, maybe I'd ask him to help me, to unpick this ball of twine that's wrapped around me. I'm a mash of tangled emotions, just so confused. Nothing is real anymore. I'm walking around in a fantasy realm, bouncing from one crazy adventure to another, never really finding my true north.

I don't notice the Toyota as I step off the sidewalk or hear the loud blast of the car horn until the vehicle hits me and I go spinning onto the asphalt.

CHAPTER 33

DOUBLE CROSS

I'M SO STUNNED, the driver's voice is a scrambled series of consonants and vowels. I'm cast in his shadow as he looms over me.

"Are you crazy, lady? You didn't even look. You just stepped out in front of me."

I stand, but the bruise is already starting to form on my hip. I was lucky. He wasn't going fast. If he had been, I'd be dead right now. Dead a second time. Maybe I'm like a cat. If that's true, I still have seven lives to go.

"I'm sorry," I say, looking up at the guy. He's right to be angry.

"You could be roadkill, right now. You are aware of that, right?"

I nod. He's right on so many levels.

His anger slips as he sees how upset I am. I'm such an idiot. I deserve everything that's being thrown at me. I don't deserve to have come out of the coma. Everybody's lives would have been so much easier if I just slipped away.

"Are you okay?" he asks, looking me up and down.

"I'm fine," I reply, but I'm really not. Not in my head, anyway. My head is a mangled mess.

"Do you want me to take you to the hospital?"

That's the last place I want to go. "No. Really. I'm more embarrassed than anything. Sorry for almost ruining your day."

He smiles. "You didn't, and maybe I should have been paying more attention. You sure you're okay?"

I nod. "Honestly. Thank you for caring."

As he gets into his car, I hurry along the street. I can't be here anymore. I can't be out in public. I'm obviously a danger to people.

I find my car parked between two larger vehicles. I climb in, happy to be out of the public eye and away from Kaiden. He's given me too much to think about. My hip hurts, but worse than that, my head is spinning, and not because of the accident. I speed away, knowing the place I'm headed toward is no more comforting than the place I'm departing.

On the drive home, I try to unpack what I've learned. Kaiden told me he started falling for me when we first met, citing us bumping into each other as the exact moment he started his feelings began to develop. The problem is, I can't forget it was Kaiden who was at the bar with Mary Elisabeth and me way before my accident. Does that mean we've met before, and if it does, has he always had these feelings for me? Did I have feelings for him before I ended up in a hospital bed, hard-wired to heart monitors and saline drips? If that were true, why didn't he disclose it? Why keep it from me?

I'm back at Lake Sherwood before I realize it and cruising past my house on my way to Mary Elisabeth's. I spy the car parked next to my husband's truck and recognize it. It's been at our house before. The sight of it startles me. I decide to park in the street and investigate.

Mary Elisabeth said she needed me, so I can't be long, but I need to find out what this is. The car belongs to Detective Brady Wilson, which can only mean one thing; Frank Duvall must have recalled what happened out at Mystic Spring and called it in. If that's true, my husband is in hot water. Boiling hot. If Duvall decided to report the assault, I'm guessing he's also reported the bribery attempt. That kind of thing means jail time. Wesley can't worm his way out of that. Although it's not what I was looking for, perhaps it's a partial solution to my problems. With Wesley out of my hair, my life will be a whole lot less complicated.

I approach the house with caution, not wanting to be seen. The detective's car isn't clean. It's littered with takeout cartons and drink containers. It's the kind of decor reserved for the kinds of people who spend far too much time on the job. It doesn't surprise me. The detective is all business. If my husband believes he can convince this guy the whole thing has been some big misunderstanding, he's mistaken.

I inch ever closer to the house. The place looks peaceful, serene. My mother's car is missing from the driveway. I guess she's gone into town. That's good. She wouldn't want to witness this. She's close to Wesley. I decide I'll break the news to her gently when he's out of the house and we're on our own. It will be easier for her to accept. So much has happened that she's oblivious too. I'm glad. She doesn't deserve to be wrapped up in this.

I'm by the entryway now. The whole front of the house is glass so I have an unobstructed view inside. Neither Wesley nor the detective are there. I wonder if they're out back, but then I spy movement from the rear of the house. Somebody's approaching. I duck behind a Yucca plant and watch as the two men walk into the living room. They're both drinking coffee. Wesley says something amusing and the detective laughs. He says something amusing in return, and my husband reciprocates.

This isn't a tense exchange. Nobody is being arrested here. These two guys are familiar to each other. They're laughing and joking like they're old friends. I have no idea what's going on, but it isn't what I expected. Maybe I'm missing something. Maybe Frank Duvall didn't report Wesley to the police, but if that's the case, why is Detective Wilson here? Is he looking for me? Is he in on the whole thing with my husband? Does he plan to cash in on the Mystic Spring development too? If so, does that mean he was involved in the attempt on my life?

Something else catches my eye. I notice it as Wesley raises his cup to his lips. On the middle finger of his right hand is a silver ring with a black onyx at its center, the same ring I last saw Max Cramer wearing, the very same guy who is now in the morgue with a knife-shaped hole in his chest.

I stagger backward, almost tripping over a pot plant. These people are murderers, cold-blooded killers, and they're out to get me. Whatever I did in my past life, whoever I was, these people are closing in. I'm being punished for sins I don't recall. I have to escape. I have to run.

As I turn and hurry down the driveway, I come to a conclusion about what to do next. I need a gun, and I need one fast.

CHAPTER 34

FIREARM

I DRIVE BACK toward Thousand Oaks. I spotted the store the day prior. It was set back from the road, hidden between two larger buildings, but the logo out front was unmistakable. It's the kind of store that will have exactly what I need. I rifle through my bag and find my purse. I only hope the plastic in my name has enough credit. I don't want Wesley to find out what I'm planning to do. I need protection. I don't trust my husband anymore, and now I can't trust the police.

I park in the lot and head toward the door. It rings as it opens, announcing my arrival. I don't like it. I wanted to slip in unannounced. I haven't got a clue what I'm doing or what I'm looking for.

A guy approaches, wearing a green life preserver and a Jack Daniels baseball cap.

"Can I help you, ma'am?"

"Yes," I say, turning to him. "I... I'm looking to buy a handgun."

When he realizes who I am, his expression changes. "Sierra? Sierra, is that you?"

I nod. Have I met this guy before? I hold out a hand and he takes it. "Yes. I'm Sierra."

"Man, I didn't think you'd come back here in a hurry."

Now I'm starting to get anxious. "I'm sorry. I was in a car accident and my memory's a little fuzzy. Do I know you?"

"Car accident, you say," the guy replies, heading toward the counter. "That figures."

"I'm sorry."

"Don't be. I'm sure it wasn't your fault."

I'm undecided whether this guy is being deliberately vague or whether he's trying to make a point. "You said, *that figures*. What did you mean by that?"

His eyes narrow. I wonder whether I've done something to offend him. The door to the store opens and an elderly couple walks in. I want to leave, to get away from prying eyes, but not before I have what I came here to obtain.

The store owner gestures to a clerk. "Gabe, would you mind dealing with these fine people? The lady and I have a few things to talk about out back."

"Sure thing, boss," a young man with braided hair says, sliding his fingers across his pencil-thin mustache as the elderly man asks him about a hunting rifle.

I'm ushered toward a door to the right of the counter, and I follow the store owner into a dimly lit room stacked high with files and empty boxes.

The guy turns to me and holds out a hand. "First things first, as you don't remember me, I'll reintroduce myself. Name's Bob McAllister, and this tidy little establishment belongs to me. It's been in town since the start of the Korean War, give or take. My daddy started McAllister's Firearms when a license was a thing you handwrote at the counter before you took the customer's money, but I've been looking after the place ever since the old guy started forgetting where to take a crap in the mornings."

I take his hand and shake it. I'm unclear where this conversation is headed, but I like Bob. He seems like he's the kind of guy who is honest with people. I decide to be cautious, however. I've been wrong about people before. So wrong.

"So you want a gun?" he asks.

"That's right. Something light and easy to use."

He runs a hand across his whiskers. "Can I ask what you did with the last one I sold you?"

I shake my head. "The last one?"

"Right. The Ruger you brought from me a few weeks back. "

A Ruger? Just like the gun the detective said I had in my glove box. "You mean an SR22?"

"The very same. You said the same thing to me back then, light and easy to use. You had the same look in your eyes too, like you were scared of your own shadow."

So the gun had been mine, and if I'd bought it a few weeks ago, that meant whatever I was scared of, it had ramped up to breaking point right at the time of my crash.

"I need you to tell me everything I told you back then," I say. "Everything. Don't leave out any detail."

"Woah, lady," Bob replies. "I don't want to get involved in anything here. If you had a crash not long after buying the gun from me, and this crash was bad enough for you to forget who you are, it means the people you were afraid of caught up with you, and if they can catch up with you, that means they can catch up with me."

I'm starting to shake now. Bob's logical rationalization of what happened to me is serving to heighten my fears.

"The police told me the gun was untraceable," I say. "So you sold me an illegal firearm?"

Bob pushes his hand against the door to make sure it's closed. When he turns back to me, his finger is pressed against his lips. "Keep your voice down. That isn't a service I offer to everybody."

"Well, that's what I want again. Same gun, same deal. Whatever it costs."

"Maybe I don't want to do that again."

"Then maybe I'll go to the police and tell them it was you who sold me the Ruger."

Bob's mouth twitches at the corner. "You wouldn't do that. And even if you did, you have no proof."

"Try me," I say, trying to sound as steely as possible but feeling like I could throw up at any second.

I must sound convincing because Bob's expression softens. "Look, I don't know what you're mixed up in here—I don't wanna know—but the last time you were here, you told me you suspected someone was trying to kill you, and unless that person or persons was somehow killed in the crash you survived, that means he or she is still out there, which I guess is why you want more of the same. I don't blame you. If I was in your shoes, I'd want protection too. However, let me make this as clear as I can. If I agree to get you the Ruger, I want my name to be put in the same place your other memories are kept, the ones you can't remember, and I don't want it to ever make its way out of your mouth. You get me?"

I nod slowly, not knowing whether Bob confirming what I suspected makes me happy or scares the living shit out of me. "I get you."

"Good," he says, reaching for the door. "Then come back after closing and I'll get you what you need. And, Sierra?"

"Yes?"

He slips a rolled cigarette between his lips and reaches for his matches. "This time, make sure you pull the trigger before they do."

CHAPTER 35

COUNCILMAN

I STEP OUTSIDE and take a deep breath. Bob's honesty has shaken me. I'm now aware in the weeks leading up to the crash I was fearful for my life, and the gun the detective found in my glove box was mine. Sure, I suspected both of those things, but hearing them spoken out loud as candidly as that made me even more nervous about my situation. If I thought I needed a gun before, I'm now absolutely certain I do. I'm not sure whether I'll be able to use it when it comes down to it, but there's no doubt in my mind I'll feel a whole lot safer with one in my hands than without one. Right now, I'm like a chicken in a coop with a fox hunkered down on the other side of the fence. A fox who looks like the man who sleeps in the next room.

I turn toward my car and that's when a guy I hadn't spotted gets up in my face.

"Sierra?" he asks, his face bruised and swollen. "It's you, right?"

I don't answer. I'm too shocked by the sudden arrival of Frank Duvall to speak.

"Yeah, it is you," he says. "I knew it was."

My mouth opens and closes again. I wonder if the councilman saw me standing beside him at Mystic Spring. I wonder if he thinks I was involved in my husband beating him to a pulp. I wonder if he thinks I've been benefiting from the shady deals he's been doing with my husband.

"You're Frank Duvall," I say. "You're a councilman for this town."

"That's right. I am a councilman. An important guy around these parts, too. Used to be, anyways."

He appears nervous around me, as if he thinks I'll lash out at him. It couldn't be further from the truth. He looks so broken, so wounded. I want to help him, but I have no idea how.

"Your husband's a bad man," he says. "A real bad guy."

I want to tell him I agree with him, that I'm doing everything I can to stop him, and if he testifies to my husband beating him, that I'll confirm his story. But I don't. I just stand on the sidewalk, looking at his split lip, his fractured nose, the eyeball where the blood vessels have burst. I open my mouth to speak, but only air comes out. It's like I've lost my tongue.

"You need to get away from him before he does something like this to you. He will, you know? It's only a matter of time."

"I thought you didn't recall what happened," I say, somehow finding the will to speak up.

"That's what I told the police, but that ain't the truth. That ain't the half of it. Your husband doesn't take no for an answer. He won't listen. He just won't listen. No matter how many times I tell him I can't make it work, he keeps going on and on like a broken record."

His voice cracks as he fights to compose himself. His eyes flit to the street and back to me again, his actions jerky and fitful. I realize he has one eye on me and the other on the people passing by. He's nervous about who might be listening. He doesn't want another beating. I think he's right to be afraid. I saw the look in my husband's eyes. I figure next time, calling Kaiden to take him to the hospital will be a waste of time. It'll be way too late for that.

"You took money from him," I say, accusing him. "Doesn't that make you as bad as he is?"

He laughs, but it's shrill and uneasy. "You think that makes me like him? Sure, I'm not a good guy, I've done things I'm not proud of, but Coleman? Wes Coleman?" He blows air through his swollen lips. "He's something else. A next-level sleaze."

A car backfires two streets over. I think Frank Duvall is going to drop dead of a heart attack right in front of me. He leaps into the air, the color instantly draining from his face. He watches as a car approaches slowly, curb crawling, the single occupant obscured by the shadows.

"Look," he says, his voice more urgent than ever. "There's some things you need to know. Some things they're keeping from you."

My heart skips a beat. What can this guy tell me about my past?

"Like what?" I ask. "Frank, if you know something about my life before the crash, you have to help me."

His eyes flicker at the mention of my crash. He can tell me something about that too. I'm sure of it.

Somebody yells from somewhere behind us, and then a group of kids come running, one of them on rollerblades, the others shouting obscenities at him.

I step aside to let them pass, and now I've lost Frank. He's on the other side of them, somewhere between the group and the road. I wonder about the car, about the man in the shadows sitting behind the wheel. I try to push through the crowd but there's too many of them. I'm knocked backward, almost sent sprawling onto the sidewalk.

"Hey!" I yell. "Watch where you're going!"

"Screw you, lady!" one of them yells back, flipping me the finger.

I decide to go around them, find out what's happened to the councilman, but then he emerges from among them with a piece of paper held out in one trembling hand.

"Take this," he says. "Use it. Do what you can, but don't get me involved. I have to stay out of it. I can't be linked to this."

I take the note, try to ask him questions, but he's moving back among the throng, retreating to the road. I push through, barging my way past them, using my arms as battering rams.

I emerge at the edge of the sidewalk, breathless and anxious. Frank has gone. He's disappeared. A car door slams, and Frank's face is behind the glass, the collar of his jacket pulled up to his cheeks. He has sunglasses on. He looks in my direction, but it's as though he doesn't recognize me. The car pulls out into traffic and keeps moving, and within a few seconds, it's gone.

I don't know whether the councilman is in trouble, or if he just wanted to disappear. I remember the note in my hands, the sharp crease of the crumpled paper against my palm. I unfold it carefully and take a look. It's a telephone number and five words:

805 654 2319 call before it's too late

CHAPTER 36

BLOOD

OUR FRAUGHT DISCUSSION has sent me into a spin. The councilman was all over the place, at times belligerent, at other times like a rat caught in a trap. The note intrigues me. It's another breadcrumb in a long trail through the black forest.

I decide to call it, but then I remember the phone call I took in Charlotte's Café after Kaiden told me had feelings for me. *Mary Elisabeth.* She wanted to see me urgently. My discovery that Detective Wilson is allied with my husband, coupled with what Bob McAllister told me about the unlicensed Ruger, has served to distract me. I need to get to her, and fast. By now, I could be way too late.

I jump back into my car, tucking Frank Duvall's mysterious note in my back pocket, and head to Lake Sherwood. I've been a shitty friend, the worst. Mary Elisabeth needed me, and I've allowed myself to be sidetracked for my own personal gain. My selfishness appalls me. Am I really this shallow?

I floor the accelerator, wondering whether my friend's in a whole load of trouble. What if she was hurt? What if Wesley got to her, or what if somebody involved in Max's murder found out she was helping me? It didn't sound like she was in danger, but what if I'm wrong?

I can't think of that now. I have to get to the house and deal with the consequences.

I pass my own home without looking. I don't want to know if my husband's home or if he's still fraternizing with the detective. It can't be my priority now.

I park outside Mary Elisabeth's house and walk swiftly up the path. If she's home, she's going to be really annoyed at my lateness. If she's not, I'll think again. Make it up to her somehow. Buy her a gift. Isn't that what people do in the suburbs? Spend money to make up for their personal inadequacies. I almost forget how worried about her I am. That is until I realize the door is open.

I pause outside, wondering if something has happened here. I ring the doorbell but nobody comes. I tap on the window but get the same nonexistent response. The house is an empty vessel, a ghost ship stranded on uncharted waters. I get that nervous sensation again, like somebody's standing behind me, looking over my shoulder, watching my every move. I glance behind me but thankfully I'm alone. I'm still unsure of myself. What if someone is standing at the tree line, peering out at me?

I push these thoughts away as ridiculous, irrational notions. I'm a grown woman, not a kid from kindergarten. Those kinds of illogical fears should have evaporated years ago.

I realize I've never been in Mary Elisabeth's house before, not as this version of myself. I wonder if being here will spark a memory, light a fire that until now has been completely dormant. I'm not surprised to find it doesn't.

I step over the threshold and take in my surroundings. I don't recognize anything. Not the hessian rug with the Moroccan pattern that decorates the hallway, or the standing lamp with the intricate, art deco design. I don't remember the crisp, white walls, or the ebony furniture that stands in stark contrast to the sweeping cream-colored sofa. I don't recognize the oak bar at the rear of the house, or the wine rack that occupies a whole wall in the reception room. I don't even remember the seven-foot giraffe carved from mahogany that stands in the kitchen, overlooking a huge marble island in the center of the room. This is the house of a woman who knows her place in the world and isn't afraid to declare it. I'm envious of her, of the space she occupies. Maybe that was me before. I can only hope.

The fact is, nobody's here. I find that odd. Even in a place as high-end as this, people don't leave their front doors open. And with everything that's happened to me in the past few days, I'm not about to leave anything to chance. I have to make sure she's okay. I've abandoned her once. I won't do it again.

I spy a door across the hallway and wonder if Mary Elisabeth is inside. I approach it with caution. I have no idea what's behind it.

I glance outside. The driveway is empty. The street is deserted. There are no sounds, no happy chirp of birdsong or the insidious hiss of traffic. It's as though everybody has vacated the area. I immediately think of zombies and slasher movies.

I place my hand on the doorknob, take a moment to compose myself, let my fingers slip around the smooth metal, and turn it. The door opens, revealing a home office. It's not like my husband's, which is a wreck on the highway in comparison. This office is clean, orderly. An Apple computer with a large, curved monitor stands atop the desk. Photographs of Mary Elisabeth at awards dinners and benefit functions stand beside it. A bookcase stuffed with reference texts and assorted classic literature lines the rear wall. Everything appears to be in its specific place, located in the exact position it needs to be. Everything, that is, except the paperwork that's scattered all over the floor. It looks odd, jarring against the rest of the house which is so crisp and refined. I realize something has happened here. Something bad.

A locked cabinet occupies the corner of the room. It has been turned inward, as if somebody has taken a long hard look at it. I notice a smear of something across one of the drawers, and my stomach flips. I look a little closer, and that's when the pattern becomes clear: a thumb, four fingers, a smeared palm.

A hand has been pressed against that drawer in the not too distant past. A hand that was covered in blood.

CHAPTER 37

ASSAULT

NOW I'M STARTING to panic. Mary Elisabeth had called me, wanting to speak to me urgently, and if I hadn't been so self-obsessed, so completely consumed by my own life, I might have gotten here before whatever this is happened.

Somebody has been attacked—that much is obvious. The question is, who? Did somebody break in, looking for whatever is in that cabinet, and was then confronted by Mary Elisabeth? Did she try to stop them but was then attacked by the intruder? Is it her handprint on the drawer? Oh God, is Mary Elisabeth dead?

I begin to run potential suspects through my head. Frank Duvall is a possibility. He looked like he was halfway to crazy, but even in his paranoid state, why would he go after our neighbor? If he had violence in him, surely he would take out his anger on the one guy who almost put him in the ground. Mary Elisabeth mentioned her ex-husband on the ride over to God's

Seat, but he's in another state now, and from what I can remember from what she told me, they're back on speaking terms after years of avoiding each other.

That only leaves one other person, and it's the one guy I've suspected all along. The only guy who I've seen raise a fist in anger. Wesley.

Maybe Mary Elisabeth was writing something for the magazine she told me she works for, an exposé on bribery and corruption of county officials. It's a far-fetched notion, but it's more than plausible. I can imagine Wesley coming over, confronting Mary Elisabeth about it, and demanding to see the evidence she's planning to reveal. She would never have given it to him willingly, even though it's clear she's wary of him. She would have stood her ground, defended her beliefs. That would have led to only one possible outcome—the kind of outcome that leaves a bloodied handprint on a filing cabinet.

My eyes are drawn to it. The fingerprints pressed in dark, coagulating red, the smear of the palm, the crimson spatters beneath. I imagine the pain Mary Elisabeth was in as she tried to escape, the fear that was crippling her. I picture Wesley standing behind her with a knife or some sort of blunt weapon. I imagine his mouth twitching, his fist opening and closing. I picture the muscles in his neck, the pressure behind his eyes. I imagine him talking to her, screaming at her, threatening her.

I scour the rest of the office for a sign, anything to tell me what happened next. If he rendered Mary Elisabeth unconscious—or worse, oh God, don't let it be worse—then he would have had to carry or drag her out of the house. I can't find any more blood, or any sign anybody has been forcefully removed from the room. The hallway's clear too. Whatever it was, it happened in here and in here alone.

I pause. What if my husband is still in the house? What if

he saw me arriving and hid? What if he's in the basement with Mary Elisabeth's body now, the bloodied dagger dangling from his fingers? What if he's standing beside her, readying himself for his next move as my best friend's body starts to decompose at his feet? I can't believe it. I won't. The door was open. If Wesley was still here he would have closed it. He might be violent, but he's not stupid. Far from it. He would never willingly give me the advantage like this.

My finger slips against something in my pocket, and then I remember the Redshoot key. I took it with me to the coffee shop, planning to show it to Kaiden if he somehow convinced me he was once more a person I could trust. That was before he lied to me, before I saw Detective Wilson drinking coffee with my violent husband, before Frank Duvall handed me the note, and before I knew I'd let my best friend down in the worst possible way. The lock on the cabinet is to the left of the handprint. It looks like it's the same brand as the key.

My pulse quickens. Could I be this lucky? Could this really be it? Could I have stumbled onto something that could bring the whole world crashing down around my husband?

I hold the key in my hands, my anticipation like amphetamines in my veins. I step over the scattered paperwork, slide around the desk while taking care not to touch anything. I'm already in Detective Wilson's crosshairs, and contaminating the scene would only serve to solidify his suspicions. Mary Elisabeth peers up at me from a photograph beside her computer. It's a shot of the two of us. We're standing beside a large, rolling waterfall, holding each other like sisters, as if we could never bear to be apart. We're laughing at something out of shot, a joke only the two of us and the photographer will ever find funny. It would be an endearing image if not for the blood spatters creating a fractured line from the bottom left of the frame to the top right. I'm nauseous. I want to throw up.

I turn back to the task at hand. I hold out the key and use my other hand to steady my shaking arm. I curse myself, angry at my weakness. The key catches the edge of the lock but slips away.

Frustrated at myself, I try again. This time the key makes good contact. I start to push it home, but sense a presence behind me. I'm interrupted by the sound like a magazine being folded, but I realize, too late, that what I'm hearing is the crunch of feet on crumpled paper.

I start to turn, but my reactions are too slow. The blunt object strikes me behind the ear, and the jolt of pain resonates through my skull and across my shoulders, and then I'm falling, falling, falling. Darkness comes like a black tide, and within seconds, I'm entirely consumed.

CHAPTER 38

WHISPERS

I'M IN A house I don't recognize. It's a little overcast outside; I pull my sweater around myself to dampen the chill. I think it's going to rain, although the weather forecast is for sunshine and heat.

A stack of paperwork is on my desk, filed in an orderly manner. I have to get through it soon. I have a magazine article to write, and a project to start pulling together, but right now I have more important things to think about. Things have gone haywire and I have to make them right. I've found out things, things I can't get straight in my head. People who are close to me have done things I can't forgive.

A car pulls up by the house. My mood flips on its head in a heartbeat. I head to the window, but for some reason, outside is now nothing more than a blur to me. I need to get out. I can't be here anymore. If I stay, I'm in danger.

Somebody approaches the front door so I run down the hall,

grabbing my keys and jacket. The back door is open, and luckily I had the foresight to park the car a block over. I can make it without being seen, as long as I'm quiet.

The back porch is ahead of me, the swing set in the garden beyond, the dark billowing clouds gathering overhead. I run faster, pumping my arms and my piston legs, but then the shadow passes by the side window and I lose my concentration. My left foot gets into a fight with my right ankle, and then I'm tumbling down the porch steps like I've had too many glasses of wine, and my car keys spill into the long grass where they disappear out of sight. I regather myself, get up onto my knees and frantically search for them.

Somebody is approaching, and when I turn around, I'm now envisioning the cars racing past on the street through the window of my car, and I look down at my hands on the wheel.

I'm going fast, way too fast, but I have to. I'm being followed. I'm in a world of trouble, the kind of trouble that can put you in a box. I won't let them get to me. No way. I have too many responsibilities, too many people I care for. Something has been taken from me, something important, and I need to get it back. I want to go to the place where I'm sure it is, but danger is waiting for me. I don't care. I'll risk my life to retrieve it.

The road ahead is narrow and winding. I have to really concentrate to make the turns. At this speed, if I make one wrong move, I'm gone. I can't slow down. If I do, they'll catch up with me, and then I'm in a whole world of trouble. I've been standing up to them for far too long. Their patience is wearing thin.

Headlights loom behind me, and the inside of my car is suddenly a sea of light. I shield my eyes, almost missing the next turn, and push my foot even further to the floor. I have to get away. Something strikes the rear fender and the back of the car slides out from beneath me. I wrestle with the wheel, alternating my foot on the accelerator and brake to bring the car back under control. For one moment, I think I've lost her, and I'm going to go careening over the edge, tumbling down the bank in a ball of tangled metal and flames, but then the tires find a purchase, and suddenly I'm back on the blacktop. It doesn't matter. They're still with me, right behind me, so close I can almost see the whites of the driver's eyes.

If I can only get back to Thousand Oaks in one piece, I'll be okay. They'll never come for me in town. Too many people, too many friendly faces. I'm less than a 20-minute drive away, but it may as well be an hour, a day.

The headlights behind me grow closer still, and I'm bathed in white light now, as if I'm driving my car to the pearly gates. I brace myself for impact, but then the lights are gone, and I'm on my own again, driving through the hills toward town with nobody behind me. I glance in my rearview, but the road is empty. I have no idea where they are. I'm going to make it. I'm going to get out of this.

Then I notice the front fender of another car beside me, its headlights turned off. They don't want to be seen. Their intentions are obvious. The car swerves out and then comes straight back at me. The sound of the fenders colliding is deafening. The back end of my car spins out of control, and I'm in a tailspin. When the car leaves the road, I brace myself for my impending death. The glass shatters and sends sharp shards into my face, and then the lights go out.

I'm alone now. Alone in a room with no sound and no light. The only reason I'm aware it's me is because I pinch myself and the sensation shimmers up my arm. Is this heaven, hell, or purgatory?

I'm aware she is here. I can sense her beside me. Her pigtails caress my face. She grabs my hand, holds it tight. She's as cold as ice. My face is wet with her tears. She's crying. I want to hold her, but my arms won't move. I'm crying too now. Crying because she is crying, and crying because I want to remember who she is, who I am. Her name dances on the tip of my tongue, but then it slips away again.

I shake with rage, so furious with myself for daring to forget, but then a light peeps through the darkness, moving across the ground, kissing my feet, then my ankles, my knees, my hips. Before long, I realize I'm in a large room with glass windows and a winding staircase. I search for her, yearn for her, but she's gone. The elusive young girl with the blonde hair.

When my senses start to return I remember this place is familiar to me. I sleep here. My mother too. It's my home. The home I share with him. A sound emanates from somewhere along the hallway and I realize he's here with me. My husband. The man who killed my best friend.

CHAPTER 39

CELL PHONE

THE LIGHT OUTSIDE is beginning to fade. That scares me, not because I'm afraid of the dark, but because I'm afraid of what he'll do to me when the sun disappears behind the horizon. I sit up, but my head is a pounding mess.

My hand is clenched tight, something hard and cold digging into the soft flesh of my palm. I peel my fingers apart and look down at the Redshoot key. I remember the blow to my head, the searing pain. My hand must have spasmed, gripping the key as I fell to the floor. I raise my other hand to the rear of my skull, touch the egg-shaped swelling that has formed. I wince as I run my finger over it. It's tender but I'll live. My hand comes away clean. No blood, no open wound. He's too smart for that.

My husband hit me, knocked me unconscious, and for some reason, brought me back here. What kind of a sicko is he? Mary Elisabeth is dead, probably buried somewhere that nobody will ever find her, and yet he kept me alive. Why is that? Am I worth something to him? Am I of value? Or is it simply because if he kills me, his alibi doesn't work? I suspect he'll tell the police I had another fainting episode, which would be believable considering what happened in Casa Conejo. He already has the lead detective in his pocket, after all. I'm merely a mess that needs tidying up.

I creep toward the kitchen, pour myself a glass of water, and swallow two extra-strength Tylenol. I have to lose this headache before it becomes a migraine I can't control. The pain is clouding my judgment. I listen out for him, my ears attuned to the corridor. I hope he still thinks I'm unconscious, that I'll be like lying on the sofa in a state of catatonia for a few hours.

I remember Mary Elisabeth's office, the blood on the cabinet. I was frustratingly mere seconds away from finding what was inside. He must have realized that, too, and so he panicked. He would never have acted so rashly if he hadn't. What is it he wants? Why try to kill me? Why not then kill me when he had a second chance?

I sit at the kitchen counter, wondering what I should do. I can't go to the police, that much is for certain, and Kaiden has proven himself to be less than trustworthy. Mary Elisabeth would have been my next port of call, but Wesley's gotten to her, too. I'm all out of options, all out of ideas. Unless I confront my husband head on, which would be crazy given he appears to be holding all the cards, I have nowhere left to go.

I sit with my head in my hands, pondering my desperate situation. What can I do? What can I do?

I recall my dream, the vivid images of my last moments before the crash. I was in a house, one that seemed to be familiar to me, but not this house. I was clearly afraid of whoever was standing at my door. I thought of the danger I was heading toward, but I wasn't afraid. Then I was in my car, being pursued by another vehicle, forcefully rammed off the road, which was exactly how the detective described it. Then she was with me, the little girl who I can't remember, but who I'm sure is important in some way. Perhaps this is it. Perhaps the dam that has been holding my memories back is starting to give a little, a tiny crack that will split the whole thing open, spilling out all my thoughts, my fears, my cherished moments. If I can pick at it a little, scrape away some of the mental concrete, then perhaps I can speed up the process. I have to try. It's all I have.

I remember Frank Duvall's note. It's tucked in my back pocket. The number, the little hand-scribbled sentence.

Call before it's too late.

Is it already too late? Have I given my husband too much time? Frank was so determined, so afraid. He's no saint—he admitted as much to my face—but he was trying to help me. I'm sure he was.

I find the little slip of paper and unfold it on the counter. I sip some more water, rub my fingers against my temples. My head is still pounding, my vision swimming. Am I in any fit state to make a call? What would I say? "Hi, this is Sierra Coleman. I think you might be able to help me?" What if the person on the other end of the line isn't as friendly as I hope? What if Frank's setting me up? What if he's given me a number that goes directly to my husband in an attempt to placate him in some way? I could be walking headlong into a trap.

I slide my phone toward me and look at it. If I don't make the call, I'll never be sure if Duvall is lying. If I do make the call, I could be revealing my hand. It's two sides of a loaded coin. Once more, It's like the whole world is drawing in on me, as if I'm in a dark hole with two ladders out that lead in opposite directions.

I read the number aloud, keeping my voice to a whisper.

805 654 2319

It's a Ventura County number, which means it has to be local. If this person really can help me, they have to be no more than a short drive away. That thought gives me hope. It gives me a light in the darkness. A friendly face. Someone who might be able to tell me something about who I am, about what could have happened to me. I can't let it slide. I have to try, even if everything could get a whole lot worse. The risk is worth the reward. Frank Duvall has given me that, a man who has nothing to gain from this, except perhaps revenge against the man who has been terrorizing him.

I unlock my phone, type in the number, and hit dial.

CHAPTER 40

VOICEMAIL

I SIT IN the darkness and listen to the call connect. I'm sure Wesley is going to pick up and come walking into the kitchen, the phone held against his ear, that look of unrelenting rage in his eyes.

He doesn't pick up, and he doesn't walk in. I get a ringtone that goes on for what seems like forever, and then voicemail.

"Hi," a woman says. She sounds a little older than me with an East Coast accent. "Thanks for calling the offices of Barbara Rashford, Real Estate Attorney. I'm not here right now, but don't worry, your call is really important to me. If you leave your name, your number, and what your call is about, I promise I'll call you right back as soon as I can. In the meantime, have a fabulous Ventura County day."

The machine beeps and I realize I'm breathing down the phone. I hang up as quickly as I can and push it away. Barbara Rashford, Real Estate Attorney? Why would Frank Duvall give me the number of somebody who sells properties? It's not like I can sell this house from underneath my husband. I'm pretty sure he'd have something to say about that.

I want to slam my fist into a wall. I want to scream. What was Frank thinking, giving me hope like that? Now I'm in an even more desperate situation than before. I have nobody. I'm all alone. Sure, I have my mom, but what can she do? I can't bring her in on this. I can't put her in danger? She has to be left in blissful ignorance. Wesley won't hurt her as long as she isn't a threat to him. He likes her and she likes him. That much is obvious. If she knew what he had done to me, what he's done to Mary Elisabeth and Max Cramer, she would want to do something about it, and that can only lead to a bad place.

I'm so angry, so enraged. I want to spit, kick, claw at my husband's face. I don't like this side of myself. It's alien to me. I try to push it away, bury it, but it keeps rising to the surface. My face is hot, my skin flushed. At least my headache is starting to subside.

I think of Bob, of the room at the back of the shop, the things he told me. I think of the Ruger, of the magazine full of shells. I think of what I would do if my husband came at me while I was carrying that thing. I'd pull the trigger, relish the loud retort, watch as the bullet left the gun. I gasp, raising my hands to my mouth. Could I do that? Would I kill a man in cold blood? Do I have it in me?

A door closes, and I realize my husband's on the move. If he realizes I'm in the kitchen with my phone and a telephone number written in a stranger's hand, his reaction will be less than positive. He's already aware I saw the bloodied handprint, and that I suspect he killed Mary Elisabeth. It wouldn't take much to push him over the edge.

The sound of footsteps resounds from the hallway. I hastily

fold the slip of paper, tuck it into my back pocket, and head back to the living room. Maybe if I can pretend to be unconscious, maybe he'll leave me be. I realize I have no way of knowing that. Lying down puts me at a disadvantage against him. If he's decided to kill me, I'll be presenting myself to him on a platter. No. I'm not going to submit to him. I'm going to fight, to resist him at all costs.

He's coming. He's whistling something. Something happy. That makes me hate him so much more.

I stop in the middle of the living room, trying to decide which way to go. Every footstep is like a bullet to my heart. It's like I'm in a cage. My mouth is dry and my headache has returned.

Outside, the stars have started to come out. It's pretty, like a scene from a movie, but the movie that's playing out inside this house is anything but. His breathing is hoarse and ragged, like a bull on steroids. He will crush me. He will obliterate me.

I make a decision without knowing it. I head to the cabinet, search for my keys. For one second, I think he's taken and hidden them. Wouldn't that be just like him? I start to panic as his footsteps grow closer. I can't outrun him. I've fainted, been hit by a car, and struck in the head. My body isn't up for the chase. I have to meet Bob, procure a gun, and ready myself for what comes next. Whether I can shoot the thing or not, I can't go into this next phase unarmed. I have too much to lose.

I search and search, tossing aside key after key, my fingers moving like chopsticks. Finally, I find them beneath my mother's little-lamb key fob. I can't believe I missed them. I grab them, tuck them in my pocket as Wesley nears the open door to the living room, and head toward the exit. I take one final look at the darkness leading to his office and then I slip out the front door, letting it close gently behind me as I make my escape.

CHAPTER 41

FRANTIC

THE FRONT DOOR opens as I gun the engine of the Camaro. I risk a glance in the rearview mirror and see him, standing in the doorway, a hulking silhouette. I'm too far away to pick out the expression on his face, but I can imagine it. I'm pleased the darkness blankets his features. I'm not sure I could face him.

Then I see something else. Something that makes my blood turn cold. It's the upstairs window, the room at the end of the hall. The light comes on, and my mother is standing there in her gown. She's looking outside, wondering what's going on. My husband looks up at her and I imagine him grinning, knowing if I go, I'm leaving her alone with him. He'll be relishing how that makes me feel. It's okay. I don't believe he'll hurt her. I'm almost sure he won't.

"Don't worry, Mom," I say as I pull away. "I'm coming back."

I head for the highway and breathe out. I won't be long. I'm going to meet Bob, buy the gun, and then come back. I'll be in a much better place, knowing I can defend myself, can defend my mom.

My head's a little clearer. I can think better. Maybe Mary Elisabeth's not dead. Maybe it wasn't her blood after all. I have no evidence to suggest it was her, only that it was in her house, and whoever hit me over the head didn't want me snooping around. I think about the attorney, Barbara Rashford. Maybe she isn't a dead end. Maybe she has something that in my scrambled state I can't picture. I'll call her again in the morning, find out what she has, if she has anything at all.

I'm starting to feel a little better about everything, but then the whooping burst of a police siren blares from behind me, followed by flashing red and blue lights.

My heart leaps in my throat. This can't be a coincidence. Wesley must have called them. I realize they want me to pull over, but I keep going, wondering what the hell I should do. What if they take me back to him? What if he's pinned the assault that took place in Mary Elisabeth's house on me? What if he's framing me for murder?

I put my foot on the floor and pull away from the police car. The car behind follows suit, trailed by the constant whine of the siren. The hillside flashes with whirring lights. My heart is like a machine gun in my chest. I'm so scared. Am I really in a police car chase? Is this what it has all come down to?

I take a right at the next intersection, almost running headlong into a big rig. The rear wheels of the Camaro cry out in protest, but I make the turn and put my foot down. The police car almost misses the junction and has to go around the back of the truck. By this time, I'm a little further away. I make a left and then a right, and now I'm heading toward I-23. If I can make it to the freeway, I have choices.

The police car is catching up to me, so I push it harder. Everything is going by so fast now. My mind can barely process everything in the darkness. I don't want to hit anybody. I don't want to cause another accident.

A coyote appears from out of nowhere and I jerk the wheel, almost losing control, but then I'm back in my lane and the coyote's gone, unaware it was almost a bloody smear on the window. A second police car is approaching from my right. I turn left, heading away from both of them. It doesn't matter. They're persistent. The night is filled with the wail of sirens.

I look down at my fuel gauge. The rental company didn't give me a full tank. I realize if I keep going at this speed, I'm going to run it dangerously close. I don't care. I have no choice. I can't be arrested. I can't allow myself to be walked back into my house where my husband waits like a movie villain, casually biding his time.

I take another left and then a right, and now I'm in the hills, the town of Thousand Oaks way off to the north, the ocean to the south. I keep going, but I don't have enough grunt in the engine to get away.

Both cars are perilously close to me now. I take another right, almost losing it completely at the bend, but I just about make it, swerving wildly to avoid a Station Wagon that was in my blind spot. The driver yells at me as the two cars miss each other by a whisker, and then I straighten up and keep going.

One of the police cars misses the turn, and the second skids through the dust, losing speed. I slam my hand down on the wheel.

"Yes!" I holler. "Yes, goddamn it!"

For a small moment in time, I decide being alive is actually worthwhile, that waking up from the coma wasn't a complete mistake. I've been so tired, so desperate, but right at this moment, right in the here and now, I'm so alive. If I can harness this, use this, perhaps I can find a way out, a way I can make things work.

I look up and the moon's hanging high in the sky, smiling down on me. Maybe she's looking out for me, rooting for the good guy, if a good guy actually exists. I start to laugh, as if these past few days have merely been one long joke. I open my window, raise my hand, and flip the night sky the bird.

"Fuck you, Wesley. Fuck you!"

The smile has barely left my face when the red and blue flashing lights come racing toward me, and two further sets approach from my rear. My heart sinks. I've got nowhere to go, just one long road surrounded by hills and scrub. I can't outrun them and I can't drive through them. Maybe this isn't my moment after all. Maybe there's no victory here.

As the car ahead blocks the road, and the two cars behind maneuver me so I'm hemmed in from either side, I stop the car, open the door, and raise my hands.

CHAPTER 42

ARRESTED

I SIT IN the back of the squad car with my hands cuffed, like I've been the criminal all along. I'm not even sure why the police came after me, although my reckless actions after that have given them a pretty good reason for my arrest.

"Where are you taking me?" I ask, watching as the houses swim past.

"You'll know soon enough."

"I'd rather know now."

They don't answer me. I guess they don't have to. They're the police and I've just led them a merry dance.

I'm relieved when the car turns away from Lake Sherwood and toward Thousand Oaks. Maybe I can beg my case when I'm in front of police officers who aren't on the payroll of my husband. He can't have bought the whole police department. At least, I hope he hasn't.

They take me from the car to the station, shoving me like

I'm a petty thief. I'm booked in, made to give my prints, and left in a room with one insanely bright light and a cold, metal table. My cuffs are removed but it gives me little comfort. This looks serious. Way more serious than I had expected.

I'm scared and thirsty. I'm hungry, too. I realize I haven't eaten since my meeting with Kaiden at lunchtime, and I barely touched the sandwich. So much has happened since then. The last thing I've been thinking about is my lack of sustenance.

I sit on that chair for what I guess must be an hour or more. At one point, I let my head rest on the table, allowing the coolness of the steel to lay flat against my cheek. It's soothing for a little while, but then my neck stiffens and my back throbs.

When the door opens, it's a relief. Another face. Then I realize who's entered, and it's like I'm trapped again.

"Hi, Sierra."

"Hi, Detective Wilson."

He closes the door and takes a seat. He hasn't shaved since yesterday, and he smells of greasy fries and cigarettes.

"Please, call me Brady."

I don't reply. I can't think of any words.

"The boys tell me you took off when they tried to pull you over."

I remain silent. I wonder whether I need a lawyer, but I don't want to incriminate myself.

"You know, resisting arrest is a felony, right?"

"Why would I be arrested?"

He smiles, glancing toward the door.

"You want a coffee? I want a coffee."

He stands and leaves the room. I remain seated, wondering what the hell is going on. As far as I'm aware, I haven't been charged with anything yet. Maybe this is some sick way for

Wesley to get back at me. Have me locked up here while he does whatever he's planning. The thought sickens me.

At last, the door opens and the detective appears with two Styrofoam cups. He's still got the stupid grin on his face. He places one in front of me and sits down, sipping from his drink while the steam envelopes his face.

"As I said yesterday," he says, wincing, "it's not as good as the stuff you serve at your house, but it's hot, and it's free."

I relent and take a sip. The bitterness is sharp against my throat.

"So you wanna tell me what you were doing out there?"

"You wanna tell me why your guys wanted to pull me over in the first place?"

He laughs. "Man, you're much more feisty today than you were yesterday."

"A lot's happened to me since yesterday."

He nods, takes another sip. "You could have made this a whole lot easier if you'd have just stopped the car."

I look up at the window as two female police officers walk by. I want to be on the other side of the glass. I want to have a conversation with someone who isn't allied with my husband.

"I have reason to believe the people in this precinct don't have my best interests at heart."

He leans forward. "Meaning?"

"Meaning you."

He frowns, setting his cup down. "Now you've got me all confused."

I try to decide what else I can tell him. If I let him know I saw him at my house, laughing and joking with Wesley, I'd give the whole game away. If I don't, I've got nothing here. I'm guessing I wasn't a good poker player in my life before the crash, because he reads my expression like a book.

The Lies We Tell

"You're keeping something from me."

"I don't trust you."

He nods. "Okay, I understand. You've recently survived a trauma, a serious trauma that caused you to lose your memory, and that's made you suspicious of everyone. I totally get that. Hell, I'd probably be acting exactly the same way if I was in your shoes."

"But you're not, are you?"

"No, I'm not, and that's a good thing."

I take another sip of the bitter coffee. "How do you figure that?"

"Because, whether you believe it or not, Sierra, I'm on your side."

He's a damn good actor because he almost had me believing him then. In fact, if I hadn't seen him cozying up to the man I suspect killed my best friend and a guy I'd shared drinks with, I'd be spilling my guts all over the table to him, believing him to be the answer to all my problems.

"Are you going to tell me why I was pulled over? Because if all we're going to do is sit here and chat over a cup of coffee, I can think of better places to be."

He laughs again, but this time it's tinged with something more serious.

"Okay, okay," he says, holding up his hands. "You got me. I should tell you what all this is about."

I'm relieved but anxious. This guy is Wesley's pal, and Wesley has been trying to buy his way onto the Mystic Spring development, but I have no proof of anything. If my husband has pinned anything on me, I have no way of countering it.

"Bob," he says. "Bob McAllister?"

I'm so stunned, I almost knock steaming hot coffee all over

the table. How can he know about Bob? Was I seen? If so, who saw me?

"I'm sorry. I don't know who that is."

He bites his bottom lip. "Now, you see, that's not true."

"Are you calling me a liar?"

"Well, now, I never said that, did I? I didn't say that. All I'm saying is, you might be confused."

I'm angry now. Furious. I've been chased all over the county by the Thousand Oaks Sheriff's Department, almost driven right off the road, and although I did meet with Bob McAllister to buy a handgun, the least I deserve is to be told how this guy knows that.

"I'm not confused. I told you I don't know that name, and I meant it."

The detective stands and looks out the window. He places one hand on the glass and taps it as if he's playing an imaginary drumbeat to a tune nobody else can hear.

"Then you're gonna have to tell that to Bob," he says. "Because a little over an hour ago he called me and told me you were in there today trying to convince him to sell you an unlicensed handgun."

This time the coffee cup does topple and everything inside spills out.

CHAPTER 43

SUSPICIONS

"YOU NEED TO level with me, Sierra," Brady says, as if we're old friends. I don't need to do anything, this is Bob's word against mine.

"I'm sorry," I say. "Do I need a lawyer?"

"Not if you don't want one."

I can't get the image of Brady drinking coffee with my husband out of my head. They're in it together. They have to be. This thing about the gun is just another way to tie me up in knots. For all I know, Bob's in on it too. Maybe the handgun Wilson claims to have found in my car was never really there in the first place. Maybe this is all an elaborate deception.

"If you're going to charge me with anything, detective, why don't you go ahead and do it."

He mops up the spilled coffee with a napkin. It's not a great job, and some of it slops onto the floor.

"This isn't about that," he continues, trying to prevent the caffeine from staining his crumpled shirt. "This is about me finding out what's going on with you."

He feigns compassion, but I'm not falling for it. "And why would you want to do that?"

"Because I'm worried about you."

Again with the words. This guy must think I'm an idiot. "You don't have to worry about me. I can look after myself."

"Sierra, less than two weeks ago, you were almost killed in what I'm starting to think was a deliberate attempt on your life. Since then, you've been seen at the scene of a homicide, caught trying to buy an unlicensed handgun, and been involved in a high-speed police chase."

I have to admit, when he puts it like that, it does sound kind of crazy. And that's only the half of it.

"What were you doing at my house today, detective?" I blurt my question out without thinking. "What were you doing meeting with my husband?"

If I'd hoped the direct approach was going to unsettle him, I'm sadly mistaken. He brushes it off with a shake of his head. "You saw me?"

"I did."

"And what do you think I was doing?"

"I don't know. You tell me."

He smiles. "Are you always this paranoid?"

I try not to let his question phase me. "I've had one hell of a week."

"Look," he says, sensing I'm in no mood for sarcastic comments. "I just came over to update you on our investigation. You weren't there, so I told your husband. Has he not passed any of this onto you?"

"We're not exactly speaking at the moment."

His mouth falls open. "Okay, I didn't know that."

The Lies We Tell 187

"Why would you? Unless, of course, you and he are friends."

"Why would I be friends with your husband? I met him for the first time at the hospital."

He seems sincere, but sincerity, I've learned, is cheaper than dime-store wine. "You looked pretty friendly when I saw you today."

"He offered me a coffee, which I accepted, and we had a good long chat. Hey, for what it's worth, he said some pretty nice things about you."

I bet he did, I think to myself. *I bet he laid it all on pretty thick.*

"He can be quite the charmer." I pick at a hangnail. "So what did you tell him?"

He folds his arms, stares at me long and hard. "That we managed to get some paint from the wreck, paint that doesn't belong to your vehicle. I've sent it off to the lab to get analyzed. We should have it back any day now."

His news sparks me to life. If he has paint from the other vehicle, then there's every chance he can match it to whoever rammed my car off the road. I think of Wesley's truck, the sky blue paint, the stark red lettering. "What color?"

"What?"

"The paint, what color is it?"

"I'm afraid I can't reveal any details until I get the analysis back from the lab."

"Oh, don't give me that bullshit, detective. This is my life here. Don't I deserve to know if somebody is trying to kill me?"

"Of course, you do. But only when we have something concrete."

"Is it blue?"

"As I said, I can't reveal—"

I stand, slamming my hands on the table harder than I'd

intended. "Blue, Brady! Is the paint you discovered on my car sky blue!"

"No!" he yells. "It's not."

I sit back down, deflated. I felt sure this was going to link Wesley to the murder attempt. It doesn't mean Wesley wasn't behind the wheel, but it does mean if he was, he was in another vehicle. I think about the car in my dream, about how the driver turned the headlights off.

"Sorry," he says. "I guess that's not the news you were hoping for."

I shake my head, chew my lip. Nothing is adding up the way it should.

"I have another question for you," he continues. "The homicide up at Casa Conejo. What were you doing there?"

"I knew him."

"You knew Max Cramer?"

I nod. "I met him the day before he was killed. In fact, I met him twice that day."

He ponders that little nugget. He's running scenarios through his mind, one of them being that I had something to do with Max's death.

"Did he say if you two knew each other before your accident?"

I'm not sure if I should tell him what I say next, but now it appears he isn't collaborating with my husband, I start to believe I can trust him after all. "Yes, but you can't tell any of this to Wesley."

"Whatever you tell me in here, Sierra, is entirely confidential."

"We hooked up. In a bar. Spent the night drinking shots and dancing."

He nods. "When?"

"A few days before my accident."

He mulls that second little grenade over. "Did your husband find out?"

I'd love to say yes. I'd love to say that Wesley and I argued about it before he headed out in his truck, returning shortly after Max had fallen to the ground with a half dozen knife wounds in his chest. "I don't know. Maybe."

He scratches his chin. "Interesting."

It is interesting, but it's hardly proof. "Did you find anything at the scene? Anything to link the murder to anybody?"

"I can't comment on that, Sierra. You know that."

I do, but it doesn't stop me from asking. Anyway, there's uncertainty in his eyes, an awkward way in which he's holding himself. He does know something, but he's not letting on.

"If this is in any way linked to my crash, Brady, you have to tell me."

He doesn't answer, but it doesn't matter. His silence speaks volumes.

CHAPTER 44

CONFUSION

"THERE'S SOMETHING ELSE," I say, thinking that I may as well tell the detective everything. I'm so far gone now, I have nothing left to lose.

His expression is unmoved. "Okay."

"It's about my friend, Mary Elisabeth."

"Mrs. Harper. The lady who lives two blocks down from you."

I nod. "She called me. Earlier today. I was in town with a friend."

"What friend?"

"You swear you won't tell anybody about this?"

He nods. "As I said, nothing in here gets disclosed outside of these walls."

"Kaiden Marshall."

His eyes narrow as he rifles through his mental files. "Should I know that name?"

"He was the nurse on duty the night I was admitted to hospital."

"And you were meeting with him because?"

"We've become friends. He was nice to me in the hospital, and he's been looking out for me."

I sense he realizes there's more to what I'm telling him than just the words that are leaving my mouth, but I leave it at that. This has nothing to do with the case. "Anyway, Mary Elisabeth called me and she sounded upset."

"Upset as in afraid?"

"I don't know. Maybe, maybe not. She wanted me to go over to her house as soon as I could."

"And when was this?"

"She called at lunchtime."

"And what did you do next?"

This is the part I didn't want to go into. The part where it took me several hours to travel the few miles between the coffee shop in Thousand Oaks and Lake Sherwood.

"I had some things to attend to."

"Such as?"

If he thinks I'm going to admit to meeting with Bob, he's got another thing coming. "Private things."

"I'm guessing this is your way of telling me you didn't get to your friend's house until a little later in the day."

He's got me, and not in a good way. "Right."

"So what time did you arrive."

"A little after five p.m."

He doesn't react, but I can read his mind. He's wondering what the hell was so important that it took me five hours to answer an urgent call from somebody I'd already professed to being my best friend.

"And what did you find when you got there?"

I swallow. "I knocked but nobody answered, and then I noticed the door was open. I went inside, but Mary Elisabeth wasn't home. The house looked fine. I couldn't see any signs of a break-in or anything."

"Okay. That's good."

"Right. Except, when I entered Mary Elisabeth's home office, which is located between the kitchen and the stairway, I noticed that a whole bunch of her paperwork had been scattered all over the office floor."

"Is Mrs. Harper a messy person?"

I shake my head. "And that's not all. There's a tall filing cabinet in the room, and on one of the drawers, there was a handprint. A bloodied handprint."

He leans forward, his eyes unblinking. "You're telling me you saw signs of somebody being assaulted in your best friend's house."

"I think so, yes."

He's animated now, rolling up his sleeves. "And where is Mrs. Harper now?"

"I don't know," I say.

"You haven't called her?"

"No."

"Why not?"

The egg-shaped swelling at the back of my head is throbbing, and I recall the heavy blunt object as it smashed into my skull. "Because somebody knocked me unconscious."

❄ ❄ ❄

I'm left in the room on my own while Brady goes out to make some calls. The way he looked at me was like a dagger in my heart, as if I'm the world's worst best friend. He doesn't need to say it. I'm already feeling guilty enough. In my head, I've only known Mary Elisabeth for a few days, but in reality, we've been friends since we were kids. I can't have any excuse for the way I abandoned her like that. I only hope she's okay, because if she isn't, I'm not sure I can handle the guilt.

I check my watch. It's late. I've been at the station for almost two hours. Wesley will be wondering where I am. I don't care. I just hope he doesn't take his anger out on my mother.

The door opens and Brady walks in. He looks different, as if he's been told to speed this up.

"I've called someone," he says. "They'll be here in a few minutes."

"Who?"

"You'll see."

His lack of transparency unnerves me. Up to this point, he's appeared as open as he can be. Now he's a closed book.

"I hope you haven't called my husband."

"And why's that?" He seems caustic, agitated. "What is it with you two, anyways?"

I can't tell him. What would I even say? I have no evidence to back up my suspicions. Anything I level against Wesley is circumstantial at best.

"Let's just say we haven't exactly hit it off."

"But you've been married to him for three years, right?"

"Apparently."

"And he pulled you from a burning wreck, didn't he?"

I turn away, trying to hide a sneer of contempt. This is why I can't say anything. To everybody else, Wesley is like the perfect guy, a hero who saved his wife from almost certain death.

Somebody taps the door and Brady stands to open it.

"Hi," he says. "Thanks for coming."

He opens it wide, revealing the one person I hadn't expected. The one person who I thought was either wounded or dead.

"Mary Elisabeth?" I leap up and go to her. "Are you okay?"

She frowns, laughs nervously. "Sure, Sea. I'm fine."

Something about her demeanor throws me off. Something casual. "But your house, the office?"

Brady offers her a seat which she takes. She's dressed in a red top and charcoal pants. Her red hair is clipped back. She looks up at the detective, flutters her eyelashes. I'm so happy she's here, so glad I don't have her murder on my conscience. Maybe that makes me selfish, but I'm genuinely pleased she's okay.

"I'm sorry," I say, grabbing one of her perfectly manicured hands. "Sorry it took me so long to get to you."

She looks down at our hands, and then back at me. There's something I'm not getting here.

"Do you want to tell Mrs. Coleman what you told me, Mrs. Harper?" Brady asks.

Mary Elisabeth nods slowly, pauses. "The detective says you came by at around five p.m., a few hours after I called you asking for you to meet me."

"That's right," I say. "That's why I'm apologizing. I got sidetracked. I didn't realize you were in trouble, but then I saw the blood, and then I knew. I would have searched for you, but I got hit on the head—"

"By an intruder," she says. "Apparently you were knocked unconscious."

"Right."

Mary Elisabeth looks across at Brady, and a moment of knowing passed between them that makes it seem like I'm the only lunatic in the asylum.

"Am I missing something here?" I ask, anxious and tired.

Mary Elisabeth shoots me a sympathetic smile.

"Oh, you poor dear," she says. "You must still be suffering from that terrible accident and the effects of the concussion."

I'm shaking now. What is she saying? "What are you talking about? I saw the blood, right before the intruder attacked me."

Mary Elisabeth leans forward, gripping my hands as if she's trying to save me. "Sierra, that can't be true because I've been at home. I've been working on an urgent article for the magazine ever since I called you this morning."

"I don't understand," I say, suddenly unsure of myself. "But I saw the blood. I saw the handprint."

"Sea, I promise you, you never came around. In fact, I haven't seen you since yesterday."

CHAPTER 45

HOSPITAL

I LEAVE THE police station with my head spinning. I had been so sure of what I had seen at Mary Elisabeth's house. I can't have imagined it, can I? Everything had seemed so real. The paperwork on the floor, the blood on the cabinet, the blow to the back of my head. I stand in the parking lot, searching for the egg-shaped swelling that's now no longer there. What am I becoming? I'm not in control of my own mind. How can I trust anything I see, anything I hear?

Brady let me go without cautioning me. He seemed more concerned about my state of mind than the chase I'd led his officers on, or the accusation from Bob McAllister that I'd tried to buy an unlicensed firearm from him. I left him with Mary Elisabeth, the pair of them watching me go as if I were an elderly relative. I've never been so embarrassed, never been so ashamed of myself.

My car is parked next to Brady's, no sign of the hairpin

turns I was pulling earlier, or the dust I was churning up from the winding roads. I had thought I was some sort of heroine, escaping the clutches of the evil authorities, when in fact I was a delusional woman on the verge of middle age who can't even remember the name of the school she attended, or her first high school crush. I feel so pathetic, so useless.

I get into the car and slowly bash my head against the steering wheel. I may as well give up now. Every turn I take, every door I open, I run into more trouble than if I'd just stayed put. Not for the first time, I wonder if I've had everything upside down and back to front. Aside from beating Frank Duvall to a pulp, what has my husband actually done to me to make me mistrust him? Yes, we've had our cross words, and yes, he's lost his temper, but haven't I been just as guilty of riling him up, going off on wild goose chases to find something I can't prove exists?

I consider going home and leveling with him, tell him how I've been feeling, and how his behavior has been unsettling me. Maybe I'll find something, some feelings that are still buried deep inside of me. Maybe my mother's right. Perhaps he's a good man, and I'm losing that by focusing on my own paranoia.

Something slips out of my pocket and falls onto the floor of the car. It's my phone. The activity unlocks the home screen, revealing the last number I dialed. It was my call to the office of Barbara Rashford, the real estate attorney. I realize I've never squared that circle. Frank Duvall had considered it important enough to approach me in the street.

I collect my phone and glare at it. Maybe, just maybe. It's almost midnight so she won't pick up, but I've got nothing to lose by leaving a message.

I dial the number and wait for the voicemail to kick in. When it does, I speak as calmly and rationally as I can. The police already think I'm losing it. I can't afford for anybody else to harbor the same suspicions.

"Hello, Barbara," I say. "This is Sierra Coleman. I was given your number by Councilman Frank Duvall. He seemed really keen for me to speak to you, so here I am, leaving you a message. If you could call me back when you get this, I'd be so grateful. I have a feeling you know something about me that perhaps I should also brought up to speed on. I'm hoping so anyway."

I leave my number and hang up, suspecting I've made another in a long line of mistakes. I glare at the phone again and another thought occurs to me. Perhaps it's another lapse of judgment, but I phone Kaiden. Despite his lies earlier in the day, I still believe he's the only really genuine person I know, and he has feelings for me, too. There's that little humdinger of a fact to consider. Heck, I've been contemplating my own feelings too. The ones that give me the impression I'm not the faithful kind.

I listen as the phone rings, hoping and praying he'll answer, that he'll tell me I'm not insane, and that if I say I saw blood in Mary Elisabeth's house, then of course that was what I saw. But he doesn't answer. The line rings out. I don't even have the opportunity to leave a message, not that I wanted to. What would I say?

Even so, I have to talk to him. I have to tell him everything that's happened since we last spoke. I need someone to rationalize my thoughts, my emotions. Mary Elisabeth's insistence that she had been in her office all day has thrown me way off. Why would she lie about that? She has nothing to gain from it. Maybe I'd gone straight home after my encounter with Frank Duvall and fallen asleep. Maybe it had all been some crazy nightmare. But if that were true, what had the hard lump on my head been?

Something I'd gained after being hit by the car just after I'd left Kaiden at the coffee shop? It's a possibility. I can't rule it out.

I start the engine and drive. If Kaiden isn't going to pick up his phone, I'm going to have to go to him.

The hospital is a 15-minute drive away. I arrive in the darkness, the moon overhead and a few street lights the only things guiding me. I shudder as I look up at the hospital sign. The last time I saw it, I was leaving after having been discharged. I didn't think I would be back so soon. At least this time I get to walk in.

I head to reception and ask where Kaiden Marshall works. The pretty young female tells me he usually mans the serious incidents ward. After she gives me directions, I thank her for her time and ride the elevator to the third floor. He'll be shocked to see me, but I don't care. Right now, he's the only person I can think about talking to.

I ask for him at the desk. This time it's an older man who helps me. He has white hair, the faint hint of a mustache. He looks up at me as if he's looking at his daughter. He looks disappointed when he tells me Kaiden didn't show up for work today.

"It's odd," he says. "He usually calls in if something comes up."

I'm not listening. I felt sure I'd find him here. I was so ready to unload on him, to get everything off my chest. I wanted the catharsis of it, the sounding board he would offer me.

"Maybe I'll go visit him at home," I say. "Check in on him."

"That's a good idea," he replies. "Tell him to give us a call."

I start to step away but then realize I have absolutely no idea where Kaiden lives.

"You don't... happen to have his address, do you?"

He eyes me with suspicion. I shoot him a lopsided grin, one that says, *come on, give a girl a break.* "It's just that we were meant to meet for dinner tonight, and he didn't show. I'm worried about him."

He checks his watch. "It's a little late for you to be checking on your friend's well-being isn't it."

"I guess," I reply. "But he would do the same for me."

His hard exterior softens.

"I'm not really supposed to do this," he says, before writing the address down and handing it to me. "Just don't tell anyone it was me who gave it to you."

I'm heading for the exit before he has a chance to reconsider. If my nurse in shining armor won't come to me, I'm going to have to go find him.

CHAPTER 46

RAGE

I GET BACK in the car. My phone rings before I have a chance to start the engine. It's Wesley's number. I consider not answering, but then I think about what I was considering earlier. Whether I'm the problem here. Whether I need to be less hostile to my husband.

"Hi," I say. "Everything okay?"

"Where are you?" He sounds calm, monotone.

"I'm in the car."

"Where?"

I stop myself from snapping at him. "Detective Wilson wanted to see me. I've been at the station for the last two hours."

"Don't bullshit me, Sierra."

His verbal attack leaves a bruise. Who the hell does he think he is? "Call him if you like. I'm sure he'll be only too happy to verify it." Why am I justifying my absence?

"Maybe I will. When are you coming home?"

"In a little while. I've just got something to take care of."

I can hear the sharp intake of breath and sense his anger beginning to swell. "It's almost one a.m., and you're trying to tell me you have something that can't wait until the morning."

"That's right. It can't."

"I want you home, right now. Right this second."

"Sorry, compadre," I say, my tone almost mocking him. "No can do."

I start the car and drive. I was wrong, or maybe I was right. Wesley is the misogynistic baboon I always knew he was.

"Sierra," he says. "Whatever you think is going on here, you're wrong. You're my wife, and you love me, even if you can't remember it."

I keep my eyes fixed on the highway, trying to zone out his voice. What does he know about how I feel? I'm the one who has been having to deal with a total loss of memory, a burgeoning paranoia, and a whole host of surprises.

"What are you talking about, Wesley? I'm fine."

"No. You're not. You're a long way from fine."

The restraint is evident in his voice. He's trying to control himself, stop himself from losing it.

"I'm running an errand. That's all. I'll be home before you know it."

"The detective told me that they found paint on your car, that they suspect somebody tried to ram you off the road."

It's the first time he's mentioned the cause of the crash. His directness surprises me.

"That's why I want you home, Sierra. That's why I want you by my side. If somebody wants to hurt you, I need you here where I can protect you." His voice cracks. I can't tell whether it's because he's emotional, or because he's struggling to keep his act together. "I couldn't bear the thought of you being hurt again. I just couldn't cope."

I grip the wheel, trying to focus. Maybe he's right. Maybe I shouldn't be roaming the streets after midnight, trying to find answers; but unless I do, I'll never know.

"I'm fine," I say. "I promise I'll be home soon. Don't wait up. Get some sleep. I'll see you in the morning."

There's a loud crunch, like the sound of a hand striking a wall. "You know, you always try to push me, Sierra. Always try to drive me to do things I don't want to do." The shift in him is palpable. "All I want is for you to do as I ask without question, but every time, every single damn time, you have to come back at me, show me how independent you are, how I can't control you."

"And is that what you want?" I ask. "To control me?"

"I didn't say that."

"But you implied it."

"Damn you, Sierra!" There's a louder crunch now, as if something's snapped in half. "You're pushing my buttons. You're pushing my goddamn buttons!"

Here's the real Wesley. Here's the guy I know. "Just take a moment, Wes. Just calm the hell down."

"Don't tell me to come down! Don't you dare tell me to calm down!"

He sounds like he's on the verge of erupting. I think about my mom who's probably sleeping upstairs. I have to do something to appease him.

"If you don't come back right now, then don't bother coming back at all. You hear me? If you don't come home to your husband, the man you married, then we're done, Sierra. You're not welcome here, and that goes for your mom, too!"

There it is, the thing I was worrying about, the moment he brings my mother into our little confrontation.

"Leave her out of this. She's got nothing to do with what's going on between you and me."

"Oh, right. But it's okay for me to put her up in the spare room, to feed her, give her a lifestyle she never had when your father was alive."

My blood boils. "Don't you dare speak about my dad like that?"

"Oh really? You're angry I've insulted your old man. Then tell me, Sierra, what was his name? What did he do for a living? What was his favorite TV show?"

The tears come then. Tears of anger, tears of upset, tears of pure, unabated frustration. "Fuck you, Wesley."

He laughs, but it's the kind of sound that bears no hint of happiness or humor. It's a laugh that says he's won, that his attack has left its mark. He's right, of course. I can feel the welt in my heart an inch deep.

"I'm telling you one last time, Sierra. You either come back here straight away, or you and Evie will be waking up in the morning with nothing but the clothes on your back and the money in your pockets."

He hangs up. I'm seething. My teeth are grinding together furiously, my hands slamming repeatedly onto the wheel. I won't let him win. He can't win. I've come too far and fought too hard. I will not be dictated to. I will not be controlled. I am stronger than that. I am better.

My thoughts turn to my mother. She's all alone in that house with a guy who's on the verge of violence. I can't leave her at that place. I can't. I approach the sign to Sandstone Peak which is in the direction of Kaiden's cabin, consider my options, and reluctantly decide to turn around. Lake Sherwood beckons.

CHAPTER 47

RENDEZVOUS

IT'S 2 A.M. and I'm sneaking around the streets like a cat burglar. If anybody were to look out the window, they'd call the cops on me without a moment's hesitation. The crazy-looking woman all hunched over, scouring the boundary of the Coleman residence.

All the lights are out. I guess Wesley's turned in for the night. I hope he's sleeping well, safe in the knowledge he managed to get to me.

My mom's window overlooks the pool. I stand on the edge of the water, looking up at the dark portal of glass that hangs overhead. She'll be asleep. I tried to call her but her phone's turned off. I suspect she's let the battery run dry. I stoop down and spy the small pebbles that line the border. I'm like a kid trying to wake up her friends.

I toss a stone at the glass and it clatters off the plaster, rebounding into the pool. It's only the slightest of noises, but I turn to the downstairs windows, expecting Wesley to be standing behind the glass, glaring at me. The darkness is a welcome relief.

I try again, and this time the pebble glances off the glass. I stand motionless, watching, waiting for my mom to appear. There's nothing. I try one more time, this time with a slightly larger stone. I hit the window square on making a much louder clang. I whirl to look at the downstairs window again, certain that Wesley will have heard me, but all's quiet.

When I turn my attention back to my mom's room, she's standing there looking down at me. I gesture for her to come down. Instead, she opens the window and leans out.

"Sierra, what the devil are you doing?"

"We need to leave, Mom. Grab some things and meet me by the car."

Her expression turns to one of horror. "Whatever for?"

"Now's not the time for questions. You'll have to trust me on this. It's not safe for you to stay here."

"Sierra, you sound ridiculous."

I've been trying to keep my voice down, but I hadn't expected my mom to be so belligerent. I glance back at the downstairs window again, and then back up at the bedroom. The longer this goes on, the greater the risk that somebody hears us.

"Look, Mom. Wesley, he's not who you think he is. Some things have happened, bad things, and unless we get out of here right now, I can't guarantee our safety."

My words appear to leave an impression because she closes the window. She's moving around, grabbing clothes, a suitcase, some shoes. She keeps peering out at me, maybe to check whether I'm still down here, perhaps to see whether I've changed my mind, whether this is all one big prank.

I slip deeper into the shadows, trying to conceal my presence from prying eyes. We don't have long. We have to get on the road as soon as possible.

I'll take my mother to Kaiden. She'll be safe at his house. I can talk to him about what our next steps are. The only thing I'm sure about is that we need to get away. I can't spend another night in this house with that crazy sonofabitch in the next room. Things have gone past the point of reconciliation.

My mom's disappeared from my view. I'm immediately anxious about her. What if Wesley's crept up on her? What if, right now, she's trapped in her room with him? What if he hurts her?

I eye the trellis that's attached to the wall and consider climbing it. I have no idea whether it will hold my weight, but I have to try. I can't stand here waiting for the inevitable to occur. I have to intervene.

Right as I place my foot on the first timber strut, my mom reappears. She has her phone in her hands. It obviously did have a charge. She'd just turned it off. I don't have a chance to consider why she would have done that, because she hits dial.

I grab my own phone and wait for it to ring. This is the smart move, the safer way to communicate. If we continue calling to each other through an open window, eventually my husband will catch us.

Something stirs inside me as I stand by the pool, waiting for my phone to ring. I look back up at the window. My mother's talking to somebody on the line, but that can't be. Who would she be calling if it isn't me? I'm the one standing here waiting to take her away.

She's animated, pointing at me. I shrug, meet her eyes. She looks away and that's when I realize she's done something stupid. The worst possible thing she could have done. My heart sinks into the pit of my stomach as the lights come on in the downstairs living room, and a hulk of a shadow heads toward the door.

I look up at her and she stares back at me. She looks sorry, full of regret. I turn as the front door opens and Wesley steps outside.

"Sierra!"

At first, I'm rooted to the spot, paralyzed by my mother's betrayal. Why would she do this? What does she think I've become?

Wesley's walking toward me now, the satisfaction evident in his smug grin.

I begin to move, my jog becoming a run. If he catches me, he'll hurt me. I'm sure of that. He watches as I start back to the car, but he doesn't hurry. He doesn't need to. He holds the upper hand in this exchange and he knows it.

I don't realize I'm crying until the tears slip down my cheeks. My chest is heaving. I'm so utterly alone and so completely afraid. He's done this to me. My husband. The world thinks he's the hero, the man who pulled me from a smoldering wreck, but in reality, he has been killing me slowly every day since I left the hospital. Maybe that's why he did it, to give himself the satisfaction of dismantling me slowly.

I reach for my car door as Wesley comes around the rear of his truck. I open it and slip inside, locking it behind me. He stands at the window, looking down at me. He doesn't try the door handle. He doesn't slam his fist into the window or scream at me to come back inside. He stands in the darkness, hands in his pockets, grinning as if he's won big at the blackjack table. He watches as I cry, reveling in the effect he has on me. It leaves me feeling tarnished, spoiled.

As I pull away, he stands there in silence. I know then that at some point in my future, I'm going to have to kill him.

CHAPTER 48

ABDUCTION

I HAVE NO idea where I'm going or what I'm planning. All I can think about is Wesley's smug grin and my mother standing at the window, her ear to the phone as she betrayed me to the man I now truly believe tried to kill me. It's close to 3 a.m. and I'm exhausted. My eyeballs feel like they're coated in sand. My hands are shaking. The remains of tears coat my cheeks and upper lip. I glance at myself in the rearview mirror. I look like a wreck, like the scorched car I was hauled out of.

I instinctively pull into the mall parking lot. It's almost entirely empty. I park in the middle of the wide space, figuring it gives me the best view of my surroundings. I'm still not sure whether my husband followed me. If he did, I don't want to be hemmed in. He now knows I was planning to leave him. That's not an act he'll forgive easily.

I open my phone without thinking. My mom hasn't called. There's no message. No apology. No reason for why she did what she did. It's okay. Her motive is clear. She thinks I'm going crazy. Everybody does. The police, Bob McAllister, Mary Elisabeth. Maybe I am. My mind is a scrambled mess of lies and mistruths.

I glare at my phone. Instagram is blinking at me. I open the app, knowing that it's a waste of time. I've already checked everything.

Aside from the video of Kaiden at The Blind Pony, everything else is a vanilla checklist of stock photos, emotionless smiles, and bland backgrounds. My last post looks new, as if it were uploaded recently, but the date stamp on it is way before my accident. It takes me by surprise. Did I miss it? Did I scroll over it, too eager to find something incriminating against my husband?

I press my palms into my eyes and look again. It's a young girl with light hair and hazel eyes. I realize without a second's hesitation that it's me. I look maybe eleven or twelve years old. I'm standing by a stream with the sun at my back. I'm looking up at somebody, somebody I obviously adore. A broad smile is painted on my face. My freckles reflect the sunlight. The river bank behind me is peppered with wild sage. I remember this place. The curve of the stream, the shrubs, the red earth.

It's Mystic Spring. I'm standing right where my husband plans to build over a hundred condos. I have a connection to that location. That's why I was mumbling its name, semi-conscious as I was wheeled into the hospital.

The photograph sends my senses spinning. What does it mean, and why has this image suddenly appeared on my social media account? If I had posted it before my accident, why hadn't I seen it until now? If I have a connection to Mystic Spring, would I have been unhappy about Wesley trying to buy his way onto a contract to build on the land? If I do have a connection with the place, what is it? My mom hasn't mentioned it to me. Neither has my best friend.

I'm so exhausted. My eyelids are heavy. They droop closed. I snap them open, peer into the shadows. I'm alone. Nobody is outside. My eyelids droop again, but this time I let them. The soft embrace of unconsciousness beckons.

I see her. She's with me again, but this time we're running along the stream. I have her hand in mine and I'm laughing. She's laughing too. It's a cool day. I feel the breeze. We pass a sign that reads "*Mystic Spring—The Hidden Jewel of the Valley.*" The paint is faded and flaking. It looks like the kind of billboard that appears in old movies. We skip beneath it, head toward a picnic blanket that's been laid out for us. We have sandwiches and lemonade. The girl with the blonde pigtails makes it to the blanket first. I'm out of breath. I stand at the bottom of the slope and look up at her, my hands on my hips. Now that her sad eyes have become full of so much happiness, I realize she's the most beautiful thing I've ever seen, the most precious. I want to climb the hill and take her into my arms. Hold her until my heart breaks. She's all I have left since that one tragic day, the one piece of him I got to keep, the lingering sense of him, the color of her hair, the way she smiles.

I don't realize we're being watched until it's too late. If I'd harbored any suspicions, if I'd had any clue of what was about to unfold, I would never have let her get so far ahead of me. I can't get to her in time, although I try with everything I have.

A dark shadow emerges from the trees, the black clothing, mask pulled over the unseen face. She doesn't realize what's happening. She's still laughing, holding up a sandwich as she takes a huge bite.

She must see something in my eyes, because her expression changes. She goes to turn, but an arm is already around her chest, hauling her to her feet. The sandwich tumbles from her fingers, sliced cheese and strips of cooked chicken spill onto the blanket.

She tries to scream, but a gloved hand draws across her mouth. She bites down hard, splitting the glove. Her attacker yells.

I'm closer now but not close enough. She's been pulled back toward the trail, back through the thick shrubs and gnarled branches. I can't let them take her into the darkness. I can't let them steal her from me. I cry out. It's a hoarse, bitter screech of rage and desperation. It echoes off the hills like a siren. An engine roars followed by the crunch of tires on gravel.

I fall to my knees, bellowing into the ground. She's gone. They've taken her. Those bastards have taken her.

I sense somebody close, somebody standing beside me. A tapping noise like old hot water pipes springing to life rattles beside me. I turn my head toward the sound, and suddenly the land around me starts to flitter and fade. Daylight bursts through the trees, peeling back the bark, boiling the stream water. The layers of my memory unfold like the pages of a book.

When I look up I'm confronted by a knuckle. A knuckle behind glass, a uniform, a life preserver, and a pair of dark eyes. The eyes look down on me, judge me, accuse me. I slip into myself, hoping and praying that this isn't the end.

CHAPTER 49

CALLBACK

"YOU CAN'T PARK here, ma'am."

The security guard's voice startles me. I'm still in a world where the little girl with blonde hair has been kidnapped and I'm buried in my own tortuous grief.

"I'm… I'm sorry," I say, trying to force the words through my ragged throat. "I must have fallen asleep."

"I can't hear you," he says, making the universal gesture for me to lower my window.

I oblige.

"I was apologizing. I didn't realize I was so tired."

It's morning. The sun is just cresting the trees. I shield my eyes, try to look as normal as possible.

"Well, be that as it may, ma'am, the sign over there is quite explicit."

I follow the line of his arm. A bright yellow sign with red

and black letters is nailed to a wooden post. It reads, *"No overnight parking. No exceptions. $1,000 fine."*

"Oh, my," I say. "I didn't see that."

"If I write you a ticket, you're going to have to pay those people," he says.

"I'll move on," I say. "I promise. I'll just go."

"It's a thousand bucks, lady."

"I understand that, but you see, I don't have it. My husband just kicked me out and he's left me with nothing." It's a half-truth, but it's close enough. I allow the glint of tears to dance in my eyes. It's manipulative, it's self-deprecating, but I can't be cited for parking illegally. I'm in enough trouble as it is.

He looks at the sign, glances at the ticket book in his hands, and then down at my face.

"You won't do it again?"

"No way, sir. I don't know what I was thinking, but I swear to you, this will never, ever happen again."

He shakes his head, hisses through his teeth. "You know, I can get into a lot of trouble for this."

I don't reply. I just look up at him. I don't blink. I just hope.

"Oh, what the heck. You seem like a nice lady who's in a tight spot. Go on, get outta here."

I start the engine.

"Thank you so much," I say as I roll away. "I won't forget this."

He blushes as I head for the exit. I drive aimlessly toward town, trying to shake myself awake. The dream is still in my head. I can't forget how I felt. It was so real. I'm sure it was another memory, another glimpse at my not too distant past.

My phone rings. The jangling noise startles me and I almost swerve into the oncoming traffic. I pull onto the side of the road and glare at the screen. I don't recognize the number. I consider not answering it, but something inside me tells me this could be important.

"Hello," I say. "Who is this?"

"Hello, Sierra Coleman? This is Barbara Rashford, Real Estate Attorney. You called me yesterday."

I shake my head. With everything that happened last night, I'd forgotten about the message I'd left.

"Right, yes. Thanks so much for calling me back."

"I must say, I wasn't sure whether to. Your message was a little confusing. You mentioned Frank Duvall gave you my number."

"That's right. He did. He told me you might have something important for me."

"And you said your name is Sierra Coleman?"

"That's right."

"Well, that's interesting to me, because I don't have a Sierra Coleman on my books."

I wonder if this going to be another dead end. The attorney really doesn't sound like she wants to help me.

"The only reason I called back is because I recognized this number."

I jerk in my seat. If she recognizes my phone number, that must mean I've been in contact with her before.

"Okay," I say, sounding more uncertain than I'd intended. "So what does that mean?"

"It means that either you have somebody else's phone, or you've recently changed your name, Sierra."

"Changed my name?"

"From Sierra Medina."

That name means something to me. It sounds so familiar. It's mine. Sierra Medina, not Coleman.

"And your voice is the same. Listen, I don't know what's going on here. Has… has something happened to you?"

The emotion wells inside me. I'm not Sierra Coleman, which means I'm not married to Wesley. If that's the case, then how much of anything can I believe? Is Mary Elisabeth my best friend? Is my mom really my mom?

I tell Barbara about the crash, about my total loss of memory. She listens without speaking. She gasps down the line repeatedly as I reveal what's happened to me since waking from the coma.

"You've been through a lot," she says. "Sierra, I'm so sorry."

"Don't be," I reply. "I just need to know the truth."

She pauses. "Well, firstly, you're Sierra Medina, the daughter of Henry Medina."

Henry Medina? Again, the name sparks something inside of me, a sadness.

"I know that name," I say. "Is he still alive?"

"I'm sorry to have to tell you this," the attorney replies, "but he passed a few months back. Heart attack. You were devastated. We all were."

I recall the man in the photograph smoking the Chesterfield, the image of my friends and I standing beside the Winnebago. More images return to me. My father walking me to school, flipping burgers on the grill, pitching me a ball. They're happy memories, filled with joy. Sadness enveloped me like a heavy shawl. I'm grieving all over again.

"Listen, Sierra," Barbara says. "Your father owned a chunk of land. It's located over in the—"

"Hidden Valley," I say. "Mystic Spring."

"You know of it."

"I mentioned it to my nurse in the hospital. I've been there, too."

"Okay, well then you'll know your father left that land to you in his will."

The Lies We Tell   217

"No, I had no idea." I'm reeling from the news, but at the same time, I sense things starting to click into place.

"Listen," she says. "I have to go to a meeting, but I can free my calendar this afternoon. Can you come in at, say, two p.m.?"

"Of course."

"Okay, good. That's great." She draws in a breath before adding, "Just take care of yourself, Sierra. I can help you through this. It's what your father would have wanted."

She hangs up and I'm left shell-shocked and speechless. Frank was right. The attorney did have important information for me. It's the one piece of the jigsaw that fits perfectly. I have something now, something I can use. The only problem is, it throws everything I thought I knew about myself up into the air. I can't trust any of the people who are close to me, with one exception. Kaiden. I have to go to him.

I pull out onto the highway and head toward Sandstone Peak.

CHAPTER 50

THE CABIN

I PASS THE valley where Mystic Spring is located on the way to Kaiden's cabin. I try to remember my father down there, working the land, the sweat rolling down his neck. His face is all I can think about; his smiling eyes, his auburn hair. I want to call him, to see him. He would protect me. If only he hadn't died. If only I could be with him one last time.

I drive into the hills, following the GPS as it takes me to a place that's nestled into a cut out in the mountains. It's set back, almost completely hidden. I drive the car up a dirt track, the car shuddering as it rolls over gravel and deep divots. The cabin is up ahead, a single-story place with a wraparound porch. I park the car and head to the front door. I almost don't notice the handwritten sign that hangs from the mailbox. It shocks me. I stop dead in my tracks. *Redshoot Cabin*.

I retrieve the key from my pocket, hold it up to the sign. It's the same handwriting. This is where this key belongs. Kaiden is involved with what's been happening to me. The web is closing in, but I'm more like the fly than the spider.

I approach the house with caution. I have no idea what's waiting for me inside. If Kaiden's a part of this, that makes him an enemy. The thought terrifies me. Kaiden, Wesley, Mary Elisabeth, my mom. I can't trust anything I've been told. It's all been an elaborate deception, a lie that's taken me down a dozen blind alleys.

I stand in front of the door, listening out for any sound. There's the constant staccato rhythm of a thousand cicadas and the haunting cry of a faraway Loon.

I try the door. but it's locked. I hold out the key, but it's not a match. This door is deadbolted.

I think about getting back in the car and driving to Barbara's office. Maybe I can just wait outside until she's ready for me. Maybe it's the safer option, the one where I don't end up wounded or dead, but now I'm here, I can't turn back. Kaiden was supposed to be my friend. He told me he had feelings for me. Was that just a lie, too? I can't decide how that makes me feel. Angry? Outraged? Disappointed?

I decide to try the backdoor. I creep along the porch, expecting somebody to leap out at me at any moment. I realize nobody is within a mile of the place. If Kaiden wanted to kill me, he could do it right here and nobody would ever know. It's the perfect location for a murder, cut off from the world, so remote my screams would go unnoticed.

I pass by a kitchen window and peer inside. Cups are stacked in the basin, a plate of half-eaten cinnamon bread is left abandoned on the table. Kaiden isn't inside.

I try the backdoor. The handle moves and the door gives just a little. I open it a crack, peer through the opening. A dark hallway lies beyond. A pair of muddied boots stands next to a bookcase. I open the door fully, taking care not to make any sound. I step inside. The wooden floor bows slightly beneath my shoes, lets out a little groan. If I was hoping to enter unnoticed, that notion soon evaporates.

"Kaiden!" I yell. "Kaiden, it's me. Sierra."

I don't receive an answer. I look inside the living room. A small sofa lies to my left, a TV, a coffee table made out of a sliced stump of oak. Along the right-hand wall is a bank of computer terminals, monitors, and countless cables.

"Kaiden, I know you were involved somehow. I have the key, the one I found at the crash site. I know it's to a lock that's located somewhere in this cabin."

Again, silence. My words echo off the cabin walls, answering me like the undead whisper of a hundred spirits.

Leave, Sierra, I hear my father say. *You don't need to be here.*

"I do, Dad. I have to know."

I spy a door to my left. It's located beneath the staircase. I go to it, open it. Cool, damp air comes rushing up at me. A set of steps leads downward into a dark hole. The basement. I don't want to go down there but I know I have to.

I glance behind me to make sure I'm not being followed. My mouth is so dry. My heart won't stop slamming into my chest. The fear is so visceral it paralyzes me. I look toward the back door. It's welcoming to me, like a doorway to another world. I shake my head. I can't take the easy way out. I've been chasing the truth for so long, I can't let it slip away from me.

I step into the darkness, fumble for a light switch. I eventually find one. It hangs from the ceiling overhead. I pull on the thin cord, hoping it won't snap. A tiny bulb erupts into life. The light is barely bright enough to illuminate the stairway. I peer down at the bottom. A tiny hallway stretches to the right and leads to another door.

I place my foot on the first step. The groan of the aging timber is accompanied by the sound of movement on the other side of the door. My heart catches in my chest. Somebody's in that room.

"Hello?" I call out.

"Hello?" The sound of a young girl's voice comes at me through a gap in the door. "Help me. Please, help me."

I race to the bottom, my fear now blotted out by the certainty that somebody is being held prisoner in the basement.

"I'm here to help you," I say.

"Please hurry. They'll be back soon. I know they will."

I try the door but it's locked. Of course, it is. I slam my shoulder into it but it doesn't move. It's solid, thick.

"I need to find a key," I say. "I'm going to go look for one."

"No! Don't leave me," the girl cries. "Please don't leave me here alone! I'm scared."

Her voice breaks my heart. I have no idea why Kaiden would do this. Why would he keep somebody in his basement? I picture him standing in the shadows of the bar, watching me on the stage. Maybe this is who he is. Maybe I had him all wrong.

"I need to find the key," I say. "Otherwise the door won't open."

Then I remember. The key in my pocket. The Redshoot key. This is what it's for. It's the key to this underground prison cell.

I retrieve it from my pocket and slip it into the lock. It's a perfect match. I'm about to turn it, to open this door and release whoever is being held captive, when somebody behind me speaks.

"Please don't do that," a woman says. "Don't make me do something I don't want to do."

I turn slowly and there she is. She's holding a gun to my

head, a Ruger SR22. Mary Elisabeth smiles as she steps into the hallway.

"You and I need to have a little talk, Sierra," she says. "There's some things I need you to understand."

CHAPTER 51

CONFESSION

"YOU'RE SUPPOSED TO be my best friend," I say. "Or is that all a lie, too?"

I stand against the wall, the barrel of the gun pointed directly between my eyes. I have no idea what's happening or what Mary Elisabeth has to do with all of this.

"No, I'm your best friend. Or, at least, I was until a few months back."

The look in her eyes is pure malice. Her immaculate persona has evaporated. She looks like a desperate woman, somebody who will do whatever it takes to get what she wants. I don't doubt her determination.

"So, what happened?"

"Everything happened, Sierra," she says. "Everything and nothing."

She's twitchy, as if she's barely holding it together.

"I know my name isn't Sierra Coleman," I say. "And I know I own the land at Mystic Spring."

"Congratulations," she snipes. "You win today's big prize."

"And I also know I'm not married to Wesley."

"Woah, that's three in a row. You've been doing your homework, Sierra. But then, you always were the smart one out of the two of us."

"I don't feel so smart," I say. "You're the one with the gun, and I'm the one in the basement with no way out."

She laughs, but the sound of it is cold and soulless. "You know how hard it is to be me, Sierra? You know what it's like to be a single woman in this town with no husband and no kids?"

"Is that what this is about?" I reply. "You want children? You want a husband? Are you and Kaiden in on this together?"

She laughs again. "Kaiden? The nurse?" She's mocking me, and she's enjoying it.

"Then what is it?"

"I met Wesley at a magazine launch event. You were there, too. Of course, you were. You were always the shining star of the company. Sierra Medina, award-winning journalist."

Her admission shocks me. I had no idea I had a successful career.

"Wesley's company sponsored the event, and so he was there, using that charm of his to make as many influential contacts as he could. Turns out, the only important contact he made that night was me." She sighs. "You know, he really understands how to look after a woman."

I'm startled. Mary Elisabeth and Wesley are an item.

"So why did he lie about being my husband?"

"That was my idea," she says, grinning churlishly. "I thought it would be ironic. Almost poetic."

"So you wanted me in the same house as the man you were sleeping with? That doesn't make sense."

"It does if you knew what we were trying to achieve," she

says, her face darkening. "If you knew what's waiting for us at the end of the rainbow."

I'm starting to lose what little control I have over my actions. This woman pretended to be my friend and tried to manipulate me into doing what she and Wesley wanted. This whole time, I've been questioning myself, second-guessing every suspicion I had, when all along, the person closest to me has been the architect of my downfall.

"I told him it wouldn't work," she continued. "This whole pretense, this charade. I knew you would never fall for it. You've never liked Wesley, so the notion of you thinking you were in love with him was never going to cut it."

"But you do? Love him, I mean?"

"Yes." Her mouth twitches. "Ever since we first met. You tried to warn me off him, tried to tell me he was no good for me, but what do you know? You haven't had to worry about the dating scene, about trying to validate yourself by being associated with a successful man. Wesley might not be perfect, but he looks after me."

"He's violent, Mary Elisabeth. He has a temper."

She blows air through her teeth. "He's not afraid to do what it takes to get what he wants, if that's what you mean. It's one of the things I like most about him."

"He beat the living crap out of a Thousand Oaks councilman."

She sneers. "Frank Duvall deserved what he got. He was lucky it wasn't far worse."

"You're condoning Wesley's behavior."

"I'm condoning somebody doing what they said they would do. You have any idea how much money Wes has paid that guy over the years?"

I can't believe she's justifying the use of violence to get

what she wants. This isn't the Mary Elisabeth I thought I knew. I look around the cabin, remember where we are.

"Who's behind the door?" I ask. "And why is she here, in this house?"

"Ha," Mary Elisabeth spits. "You want to know what that lover boy of yours has to do with all of this, don't you?"

"I want to know why we're in Kaiden Marshall's cabin, and why you have a young girl locked in the basement."

She cocks her head. "Oh, is poor Sierra sad that the person she likes is actually a bad guy."

Her words hurt me. It's true I thought Kaiden was on my side, that he was the one person I could rely on. Now it's like that was just another deception.

"He would turn up at the karaoke nights in The Blind Pony, every Friday night, waiting to catch a glimpse of us. He took a liking to you, actually. You shrugged him off. Said something about you not being ready to date again."

I wonder what she means by that. Dating again?

"I got to talking to him, started messaging him on Facebook. Turns out he's quite the tech wizard. Anyway, he needed money, and me and Wesley, well, let's just say we needed an extra body."

"So he was a hired hand?"

"Something like that."

"You paid him to help you with whatever the hell this is."

"As I said, he needed the money."

It's like somebody has reached in, grabbed my heart, and wrenched it from my chest.

"And where is he now?" I ask. "Why isn't he here?"

"He won't be bothering us again."

I recall the handprint in Mary Elisabeth's office, the lies she told Detective Brady Wilson.

"You killed him."

"He wanted to go to the police and confess everything. What choice did I have?"

Her confession is like a kick in the ribs. Kaiden's dead. I'll never get to talk to him ever again.

"Ouch," she sniggers. "Hurts doesn't it? Well, if it makes you feel any better, he only started feeling that way about this whole thing after he met you at the hospital. That was the one thing Wesley and I didn't factor in. That he might actually fall in love with you."

I'm shaking now. Sorrow grips me like a vice. "But it wasn't supposed to be him there. You called me."

"It's true. I was thinking about killing you, too. This whole thing had been going on for too long, and it was clear at the crash site that your memory wouldn't be lost forever. That was why I took you there, to see whether you would remember anything."

I try to pull myself together, to control my ravaged nerves. If I'd have shown up at her house when she'd wanted me to, I'd be dead. "And how did you plan to explain it all away? Kaiden's murder? How were you going to hide the truth from the police?"

"Well, that was the beauty of it. When I knocked you unconscious, some of his hair and blood may have accidentally found its way onto your clothes."

"You were going to pin it on me?"

"Why not? You weren't playing ball with Plan A, so I improvised."

I think about the detective, about how he already thought I was crazy, and then I think about Kaiden, bleeding out as I arrived at Mary Elisabeth's house. I could have saved him. I could have done something.

"You're evil," I say, but the insult doesn't faze her. If anything, she looks flattered.

CHAPTER 52

REUNITED

"HELP ME!" IT'S the girl's voice again. She's just behind the door, no more than two or three feet from me.

"I'm going to open that door and let her out," I say. "You don't need her. You have me."

"I don't think so," Mary Elisabeth replies. "The way I see it, I now have both of you."

"You can't win, you know that right? You can't get away with kidnapping. Somebody would have seen you. Somebody will point the police in this direction."

She shakes her head. There's that confidence again, that look of steely defiance. I realize she won't listen to me. It was what I thought when I entered her house. Mary Elisabeth is a woman who knows her place in the world and isn't afraid to defend it. "Nobody's coming, Sierra. After that little incident last night, the detective thinks you're on the verge of losing it. When he searches the house, he'll find some things in your room that incriminate you for everything. There's no going back from this. It's gone too far."

I want to cry, to scream. What have I ever done to these people? Why would they want to ruin me like this?

"You've already taken my past," I say. "You've robbed me of my memory, almost killed me. If we were friends, why would you do this to me?"

Her head jerks to the side. She looks distracted by her own thoughts. "I didn't have what you had when we were growing up, didn't have the meal ticket. I've had to scrape and steal to get where I am. I didn't have the education you had, the money, the loving father. I had to beg you to get me a job at the magazine, even though you were against it. After I got the post, you'd look out at me from your office as if you were the queen sitting high up in her palace, looking out over the poor people."

"So this is revenge," I say. "For what? For me being more successful than you? For me having a loving family?"

"For you being you, Sierra!" she yells. "For you being the beautiful, charming, perfect you!"

I can't listen to this. This woman is deranged, deluded. I can't remember the world she's painting for me, but so what? Just because she has an inferiority complex, doesn't excuse her for doing what she did. Corruption, lies, murder.

"I'm opening that door," I repeat. "And I'm letting that girl go. You have no right to keep her in there."

"You go anywhere near it and I'll shoot. Don't think I won't."

I eye the key. It's hanging from the lock mere inches from my hand. I could go for it, turn it quickly and let the girl out, but if I do that, Mary Elisabeth will likely shoot me, and shoot the little girl, too. The only way this ends peacefully is if I get my hands on the gun.

I move swiftly, striking Mary Elisabeth across the cheek before dropping my hands onto her weapon. She reacts by driving a knee into my abdomen, pushing me backward. We're face to face now, my hands gripping the gun, her other hand pulling my hair. We twist and turn as we slam into the walls. I try to wrench the gun from her grip but she's a lot stronger than she looks.

"Give it up," she says. "I'll never let you win."

"I don't want to win," I cry. "I just want to live."

She kicks me in my ankle and my leg gives out. I pull her down with me, and now we're on the floor, rolling around in the dust and grime.

She gets on top of me, her knees painfully gripping my sides. Her face is a ball of contempt. The hate in her eyes is like a dark chasm. I don't know why it has come to this, why she is so intent on doing me harm.

I swivel my hips, causing her to lose balance, and now she's on the ground and I'm on top of her. The gun is a thing between us. I use my fingers to try to pry her hand loose, but she swings a leg, and now we're rolling again. We're side by side, the gun at our waists. She snarls and spits, thrashing like a wild thing, and then the air is filled with the sound of a loud, ear-shattering bang. The sound resonates around the cabin like the crack of a snare drum.

I look down and see the blood. There's lots of it. It's spreading out from us, red like blackcurrant juice. It's on my clothes, in my hair. Spatters of it are on my arms, my neck. I leap up, checking myself. Mary Elisabeth doesn't move. Her eyes peer up at me unblinking. There's a hole in her chest where her heart should be.

"Oh God! Oh God!" I repeat, trying to wipe the blood away. Now I am a killer. I've murdered my best friend.

"Hello!" the girl cries. "Are you out there? Is anybody there? Please!"

Her voice startles me into action. I turn back to the door, grip the key with bloodied fingers. I turn it and wait for the lock to disengage.

The door starts to open, revealing a small room with a single bed, a toilet, and a bottle of water. The girl stands inside, dressed in the same clothes I saw in my dream, her hair in the same blonde pigtails, now a little frayed, a little greasy. She looks up at me, sees the blood all over my body.

For a moment, she thinks I'm hurt, but then she looks down at the body on the floor, the blood that's now running toward the open door. Her sad eyes are filled with tears, her cheeks grimy and soiled, but suddenly she's that girl again, the one who's running across the stream, drinking lemonade, laughing. She looks up and says the one word I don't expect, but a word that makes the horrors of the past week fade into nothing.

"Mom?"

CHAPTER 53

MEMORIES

SHE RUNS AT me and wraps her arms around my waist. I'm so shocked, I do the same. We hug as the tears come. She buries her face in my chest. It's like she'll never let me go. I kiss her head, smell the sweetness of her hair. She is the girl who's haunted my thoughts ever since the crash. She's never let me forget her. She's my daughter, a child I didn't know I had.

Something whirs in my head as if a motor has started turning, and suddenly I can see things that have been hidden from me. I remember being in the hospital, of holding this tiny, beautiful thing. A little hand wraps around my finger, two eyes peering up at me as if I'm the most wondrous, magical creature. The smell of her skin, the softness of her hair, the pull of emotion on my heart. I'll never be the same again, I'll never be as important as this tiny, miraculous gift. I remember a cake, a dozen pairs of tiny feet running around the house, my daughter laughing and giggling, cake frosting on her nose. I remember singing *Happy Birthday* to her, of the joy that overwhelms me as she opens her presents, hugging the toy doll as if it's a real, living thing. I remember her dressed in her school uniform on her first day, of the pride bursting through my chest. I remember walking her to the school gates, watching as she makes her way into class, the other kids joining her, another little girl holding her hand. I remember her playing in the garden, hiding behind a tree, making me chase her. I remember a husband, her father, a man with dark hair, a beard, his chocolate brown eyes. I remember him building a tree house, helping her climb inside, peering through the window at her, making her scream with laughter.

"I didn't think you were coming," the girl says, gripping me ever tighter. "I didn't think anybody was coming."

"I would never leave you," I say, but in truth, my mind is still being flooded with images and sounds. I reach for the little girl's name, trying to pluck it from a dusty, moth-ridden space buried under the wreck of my automobile and blackened shards of scorched asphalt. The love I have for her is leeching from me, pouring from my skin like sweat, soaking me in a downpour of emotion.

"But it's been so long," she says. "They kept me in here without telling me where I was or what was going to happen to me."

I want to tell her about the attempt on my life, of the mind-shredding amnesia that's kept me in a state of paranoia ever since I left the hospital. I want to tell her it wasn't my fault, that I would never have abandoned her like that, but I don't because it isn't what's important in this moment. She needs to know I'm here now, that I'll always be here.

I hold her as if I haven't seen her in years. In my mind, we've only just met, but then I remember a name. *Alaina*. I remember picking it from a book three months before the birth, of my husband and I sitting in our bedroom, eating popcorn from a carton, listening to cheesy eighties pop, and tossing names into the air like confetti. We discarded the ones that just weren't right for our princess-to-be, narrowed the list down to just two. He had wanted Alanis, I had wanted Leonie. We debated the merits of both before settling on a compromise. Alaina was the name that said everything we wanted it to say. We looked it up. It means sunrise. I couldn't think of a more fitting description for the bundle of happiness that's holding onto me as if I'm going to be wrenched away from her at any second.

"Nothing's going to happen to you, Alaina," I say, the name dripping from my tongue like honey. "I'll never let anything happen to you ever again."

In my mind, I'm transported to a time in my not too distant past, a memory that my brain has been suppressing, as if I've been afraid for it to resurface. I'm standing next to my husband when he takes the call, when we receive the news we've been dreading. He's been losing weight for months, his cheekbones now more prominent, his ribs jutting from his torso like the curved hull of a sunken ship. I'd been praying that our fears were just ridiculous, negative notions. It's in his face, the way he looks up at me, unable to meet my eyes. I go to him, hold him, tell him that no matter what it takes, however much it costs, we will get through this.

The treatment is long and painful, and it takes its toll. Zack, my husband, stands up to it like the oak of a man that he is, but it's one sucker punch after another, blow after blow, and eventually he succumbs to it. I remember standing by the hospital bed, the same hospital I was rushed to, his emaciated body like a skin-coated skeleton. We hold hands. I grip him so tightly, as if I can hold him back from falling into that dark chasm. When he eventually slips away, I collapse, a bundle of flesh and bone shrouded in a darkness that it takes me weeks to emerge from.

That sorrow rushes back at me now like an oncoming wall of torment. I'm crying. Alaina and I cry together. A husband I loved more than any man I had ever met, a daughter I cherished more than life itself. It's like I've taken some kind of mind-altering drug. So many emotions slamming into me at speed, battering me. I'm so happy, but I'm also so deeply saddened.

"They took me," Alaina says. "We were on Grandpop's land. Somebody rushed out of the woods. I tried to fight, Mom, I did, but they pushed me into the car."

I nod. I know. This was my dream, a memory that I'd managed to pull out of my subconscious while in a state of catatonia.

"Who was it?" I ask.

Alaina looks down at Mary Elisabeth's prone body and points. "Is she dead?"

I nod, still unable to process the fact that I've murdered another human being. Her unseeing eyes glare up at me, weighing and judging me. The executioner's noose tightens around my throat, but I don't care. Hate wells in my gut. This woman, this supposed friend, snatched my daughter away, knowing what it would do to me. The only question is, why?

There's a creaking, scraping noise from upstairs, the sound of a door opening. My body stiffens. I glance at my daughter and whisper in her ear.

"We need to be quiet."

CHAPTER 54

INTRUDER

THE FOOTSTEPS ARE in the hallway. My heart is in my throat, thick like a ball of hair. Alaina is at my side, gripping my arm. We climb the stairs, moving in unison. I dread the sound of a loose board or of us stumbling. The house is so silent, any tiny noise will reveal our location, and then we'll be trapped with no means of escape. We have to get out of the basement and hope the intruder isn't heading our way.

We take the next step and the next. Alaina is trembling against me, but she's holding it together. She is covered in dust and dirt, her clothes crumpled, but Mary Elisabeth has obviously been feeding her. She hasn't lost any weight and she still has her strength. Whatever my friend's intentions were, it wasn't to harm my daughter. It was to use her as leverage against me.

The door to the upstairs hallway stands ajar. A little light leaks through a slim gap, the promise of salvation. I yearn for it.

We still have a dozen steps to climb, each one of them with the potential of giving our position away.

I listen as the intruder moves around the house, opening doors, stepping into rooms. I picture Wesley upstairs, his face a mask of betrayal and outrage. He'll be searching for Mary Elisabeth. Maybe the two of them arrived together and he instructed her to come in and find out what I was up to while he checked out the perimeter. Perhaps, because Mary Elisabeth has been in here so long, he's decided to take matters into his own hands.

I want to scream up at him, to tell him what I've done, show him that I'm not the meek, downtrodden woman he wants me to be, to show him how strong I am, how defiant. I have a daughter to protect, a life to regain, and I will not let him win.

The basement door is close now. We've come so far, inched up step by step. Just three more steps await us. I go to place my foot on the next one, but I spot something wrong. A loose board.

I gesture to Alaina and she nods in reply. She can see it too. I adjust my leg and step over it, using the handrail to help me. Alaina follows suit. I'm so relieved that we narrowly avoided sending out a clear signal of our location.

I smile at Alaina and she smiles back. It's a shared victory. One that I'm so focused on, I don't spot the nail protruding from the second to last step until it's too late. My foot slips over it, presses down, and then it penetrates the sole of my flats and pierces the base of my foot, parting skin and flesh.

The pain is excruciating. I grip the handrail, try to stifle a scream. A grunt makes its way through, a biting, searing hiss of breath.

Alaina looks up at me, the alarm on her face threatening to spill from her lips. I look down at my stricken foot, at the place where I thought safety beckoned. I wait a moment for the pain to lessen a little. It's like somebody is holding a branding iron to my sole. I need to raise my leg in order to pull my foot free of the exposed nail. The thought makes me want to vomit.

Movement in the hallway again, this time much closer. I can't let Wesley find us like this with my foot literally nailed to the floor.

Terror grips me, overriding the pain. I slowly lift my leg, and now the pain has returned in all its mind-shattering glory. Alaina grips my hand, strokes my arm. I'm holding it together, but barely. The steel slips against my flesh, the warmth of the blood in my shoe. I try to blot out the image, knowing that the thought of it will only heighten my worsening sense of nausea.

At last, my foot is free. I place it down on a safe area, but I still have that searing, stabbing pain. I'm going to have to ignore it, to push it from my thoughts. I have far more pressing things to worry about, namely the homicidal maniac prowling the hallways of Redshoot Cabin.

I think about Kaiden and why he did what he did. He's not a bad person, but what Mary Elisabeth said wasn't a lie. She had nothing to gain from it. And there's the overriding truth that my daughter was kept prisoner in the basement of his house. Whichever way I slice it, everything adds up to Kaiden being one of them.

I step onto the small landing that leads out onto the main passageway. I peek through the gap in the doorway, wondering where Wesley is. He's normally so loud, so bullish. I guess that he's in the small dining room, but I have no way of knowing that. The hallway itself is clear. The front door is closed. I suspect he's locked it. He'll be very aware that it would be our first exit point. I open the basement door a fraction more, peer down the corridor. The kitchen beckons, as does the exit to the back porch. I decide that's the best way to go.

I turn to Alaina and gesture with my eyes. She nods her understanding.

I take a deep breath before stepping out into the passageway. Alaina follows close behind. I realize we're completely exposed now. If Wesley appears, he'll be on us immediately. I fight the urge to run down the hallway, drag Alaina behind me, and take our chance. I don't want to give him the satisfaction of getting the jump on us. Whichever way this plays out, we're getting away from here. That's the only truth I'm willing to accept.

We sneak along the wall. I keep one eye on the door to the living room, the other to the dining room. Everything has gone silent. I have no way of knowing where Wesley's lurking or what he's thinking. We need to get away.

I step into the kitchen, peer around the door. Shadows lurk in every corner, painting the woodwork, the floor, the ceiling. I wait for my eyes to adjust. I imagine Wesley looking inside, waiting for the right moment to strike. I hold Alaina close to me, gesturing toward the rear door. It's no more than fifteen feet away, so close I can imagine the sun on our faces. I think we can cross it in less than a few seconds.

I hold my hand up to signal for Alaina to get ready. When we move we need to move fast, and we can't stop. We have to get as much distance between us and Wesley as possible. I have no idea what I'll do next, whether we'll drive until we're hundreds of miles from here or head into town, but I'll worry about that as soon as we're safe. This is our moment. This is when I get my daughter and my life back.

I take a breath, count to three, and then we're running, dancing around the kitchen table, reaching for the door handle.

Alaina stumbles behind me, releasing her grip on my hand, and then she sprawls across the wooden floor, slamming into the kitchen cabinet.

I stop, bend down, and reach for her. She looks up at me, fear and terror in her eyes. I'm breathing hard, my body shaking.

Alaina starts to get to her feet, but it's too late. If Wesley's here, he now knows exactly where we are. I look up at the shadow monster filling the doorway and my blood turns to ice in my veins.

He's found us.

CHAPTER 55

PURSUIT

I DON'T WAIT for Wesley to reveal himself. I grab Alaina, lift her to her feet, and grab the back door in one swift motion. We rush outside, running across the back porch and down the steps to the backyard. The clouds are rolling in, casting everything in an inky gray. I don't look back but I can hear Wesley coming for us, his heavy boots on the timber boards, the stomp of his feet as he bounds down the steps.

"Mom!" Alaina cries. I can sense the terror in her. She's already been put through so much. Her young mind can only take so much more.

"Keep running, sweetheart!" I reply, but my voice is trembling. He has the advantage over us. He's so much bigger, so much stronger, but he won't win. He can't win.

The tree line is approaching and I welcome the comfort of the darkness and the leaf cover. It won't stop our pursuer, but it might slow him down. In here, we have a much better chance. We're smaller and more nimble.

Branches slap at us, thorny brambles tear at our clothes and skin. The ground is hard beneath us, like uneven concrete. The hole in my foot throbs like a sonofabitch, but I can't let it distract me. We have to lose him somehow.

He slams through the forest, slapping at the branches, snapping them as he continues his relentless pursuit. He won't stop until he has us both where he wants us. I can't let that happen. I've only just refound my precious daughter. Nothing can ever come between us again. I wish Zack was here. He would know what to do. He was always the one with the calm head and the logical thought process. He centered me, was able to control my reckless behavior. I realize that it's the first time I've been able to think of myself in the past tense. Before now, there was no past, just this horrifying, gut-wrenching present.

"Mom!" Alaina calls out again. "He's gaining on us."

My pulse is racing, my lungs burning with the exertion. I daren't look over my shoulder, can't look into his black, soulless eyes. If I do I'll be frozen to the spot out of sheer terror. I just have to keep us moving, to pray for a miracle.

"It's okay, baby," I say. "It's okay."

A path starts to form in front of us. The thick trees part like a tide withdrawing, and the ground starts to flatten. It's a man-made track. Weeds poke through the gravel like fingers protruding from the earth. I push us toward it, thinking it might lead to a public space, a road, maybe a park. Our best bet is to get somewhere where Wesley will be too afraid to confront us.

Alaina sees it too and she races ahead of me; she has the power of youth on her side. My chest is heaving, my lungs on the verge of bursting. I'm not sure how much longer I can keep this up.

The trail snakes to our left and up a slope. Alaina pulls me along, not realizing that my legs are now turning to jelly. I follow her, my calves now screaming at me for mercy.

"Come on, come on!"

It's only a shallow incline but it may as well be a mountain. Hard roots protrude from the ground like giant earthworms. I leap over them, but when my wounded foot hits the ground, the pain is like I've stepped onto hot coals. My leg almost gives way but I manage to hold it together somehow.

"Sierra!" a man's gruff voice cries out. "Stop!"

I ignore him, push his ridiculous words from my mind. He can't manipulate me anymore, can't worm his way into my psyche and control me like some kind of human-sized marionette. I'm no longer unaware of who I am or what I was. That part of his hoax has been shattered at least. I'm Sierra Medina, successful journalist, widowed wife of Zack Burton, daughter of Henry Medina, a loving mother to my daughter Alaina. Whatever power he imagined he had over me has been dissolved by the acidic burn of his lies.

We crest the hill and look at the path that runs downhill beside a stream. Alaina is already descending the slope and I go after her, trying not to stumble on the loose earth. A series of small boulders litter our way, along with a fallen tree that intersects the path at the point the stream curves away from us. Alaina dances around the rocks but I don't have her level of agility. I haphazardly swerve them, bashing my knee against one and almost running head-first into another.

Wesley is behind me. He's breathing heavily. The ground trembles with the hard slap of his feet. He's only seconds behind us, almost close enough to reach out and haul me back. I have to keep running, have to push through the pain barrier. There's a way out of this for us, I just don't know where it is or how far.

Alaina approaches the fallen tree, but she realizes before I do that we have no time to climb over it. We'll lose whatever precious lead we have. Instead, she turns to the water's edge, pauses for less than half a second, and then, in a blur of blonde hair and long limbs, she's in the stream, kicking through it as she rounds the tip of the fallen pine.

"Come on. This way!" she yells. "It's cold, but it's not too deep."

I have no option but to comply. She's already proven herself to be a smart cookie, so I don't pause to consider my options. I'm in the water with her now.

She's grossly undersold the temperature. It's not cold, it's absolutely freezing. I gasp as I grab the limbs of the tree and follow the line of it, splashing through the water as quickly as I can.

We get to the other side and approach the bank, but not before I hear Wesley in the stream behind us. He's realized Alaina was right. The trunk of the tree was too much of an obstacle. There's a loud splash and I figure he's tripped face-first into the water. I stifle a laugh. Maybe this is it. Perhaps this will give us the time we need to put some distance between us.

We climb onto dry land and turn to the path. It emerges onto a spot near to where I watched Wesley beat the councilman to a pulp. We're at Mystic Spring. The tragic comedy of it is bitter in my mouth. We're out in the open now, and I spot a road in the distance. We start to run to it, feeling every ounce of the promise of escape it provides us. Despite the pain, I don't think I've ever run this fast in my life. The wind is in my hair, a renewed strength in my legs. Maybe we can do it. Just maybe.

Then my wounded foot connects with a sharp rock, and the agony that fires along my calf and resonates through my hips sends me sprawling onto the gravel and dust. I'm a tangle of arms, legs, and scraped forehead. I lay in a heap, trying to regather myself, frantically scouring the woods for a sign of our pursuer. Alaina calls to me, and I hear Wesley stopping mere feet from my prone body. I roll onto my back and expect to be confronted with the face of the man who had once convinced me we were married.

Except when I look up, I realize it isn't Wesley that's been chasing us at all. It's the one person I didn't expect.

There, standing over me with a gun in his right hand, a grimace painted on his thin lips, is Detective Brady Wilson.

CHAPTER 56

GUNSHOT

"YOU KNOW," HE says, "this is exactly why I should stop smoking."

I kick backward, trying to get to my feet, attempting to draw myself away from what I perceive to be danger, but the pain in my ankle is even worse than the pain in my foot. I realize that I sprained it in the fall. If our chances of escape were slim before, they now look almost impossible.

"It's you."

"Yeah, it is, although I have to say our little run through the jungle there has almost killed me."

I peer up at him, waiting to see a shift in his demeanor. I don't know what to make of him showing up like this. I eye his gun, and he must notice because he slips it back into his holster. I wonder if that's just for show or if he really never intended to use it. Alaina is at my side, helping me to my feet. I stand upright, trying to shift my weight to my good foot. I keep my body between Alaina and the detective.

"Why are you all the way out here?" I ask.

"I might ask you the same question."

"I came to get my daughter."

"Yeah, I just found out about that little detail."

"Mom, who is this?" Alaina asks. "And why is he carrying a gun?"

"I'm a police officer," Brady replies. "I'm not here to hurt you. I came to help."

I can't decide whether to believe him or not. This all seems all too coincidental for it to be true.

"How did you know where we were?"

"I didn't," he replies, holding up his hands. "Look, I had a hunch that there was something about your story last night that I should look into."

I shake my head. "What part of it?"

"The part where you broke into your friend's house and found blood on the walls."

Alaina tugs at my hand. "Mom, what's he talking about?"

"I never broke in," I reply. "The door was open."

"Right," the detective approaches but I fight the urge to run. "Anyway, I went to check it out, just as a precaution. Sometimes in this job, the best lead is the one that literally slaps you in the face."

I suppress my desire to fire back a sarcastic jibe.

"I went over there, and just like you said, the house was empty and the door was unlocked. Sierra, I saw the papers all over the office floor and the blood on the walls."

"So now you know I'm not crazy."

"I never said you were."

"But that was how you made me feel when you bought into Mary Elizabeth's lies."

He nods. "Yeah, and I'm sorry. I shouldn't have doubted you like that."

I fight back the tears. It's the first time anybody has apologized to me since this whole crazy ride began. I'm not insane and I haven't been imagining things. Everything that's happened to me has been real, and the perpetrators have been getting away with playing a sick game of distraction and deviation.

"So what happened?" I ask.

"I got the CSI team to rush through some tests, and about an hour ago, they came back with a match."

I guess what he's about to say even before he says it, but when he confirms Mary Elisabeth's story, it makes me sick to my stomach.

"The blood belongs to Kaiden Marshall, the nurse that took care of you at the hospital."

It's like I've just lost someone important to me, someone I might even have feelings for, even though I now know he was on the payroll of the two people that tried to ruin my life.

"Mary Elisabeth shot him," I say. "She just told us."

"Right," the detective says again. He fingers the pack of Marlborough Reds in his pocket, his body fighting the urge to clamp one between his teeth and inhale. "And that brings me to the paint on the rear fender of that wreck you were pulled out of."

"A wreck!" Alaina cries beside me. "Mom, were you in some sort of accident?"

"I'm okay," I reassure her. "It was just a little incident. I'm almost entirely recovered now."

"Almost? What do you mean, almost?"

I avert my eyes from her gaze, fearful that she'll be able to read my thoughts.

"So where did the paint come from?" I ask, switching topics. "You've already told me it never came from Wesley's truck, so if not him, who?"

"The paint was from a brown Toyota Tacoma."

I think about what he's just told me. That vehicle, that color. I scour my gradually healing brain. I saw that truck not too long ago but I can't remember where. Then an image arrives in my mind's eye, two trucks in Mystic Spring, one with a damaged front fender.

"Frank Duvall," I say. "But why would he do that?"

"Already asked him," the detective says. "Seems like the councilman has a very large debt he has to repay Wesley Coleman, so large in fact he's willing to commit murder to clear the slate."

I recall the urgency in the councilman's face, the desperation. He knew what he'd done to me and he also knew what that meant for him. He was now in Wesley's pocket, on a leash that would never be broken. Giving me Barbara Rashford's telephone number was his way of atoning in some small way.

"So Wesley paid him to ram me off the road."

Alaina stiffens beside me. I can sense this is all too much for her young mind to cope with.

"Of sorts," the detective says. "Either way, your fake husband and I have some talking to do."

"Fake husband?" Alaina says. "Mom, I don't understand."

I'm fitting the pieces together bit by bit, but the problem is I still don't understand the motive. Why did Wesley and Mary Elisabeth want me out of the picture? It seems obvious that they tried to blackmail me by taking my daughter, but when that failed, they decided to try something more substantive and have me wiped off the face of the Earth. If they were willing to take such an unfathomable risk, there must have been an enormous benefit, something so large that they just couldn't stand by and let it fritter away.

I'm so preoccupied in my thoughts, I don't notice when the trees behind us part and someone steps out into the clearing with his arms held out in front of him. Alaina sees him first and she grabs me, pulling me to the ground as the loud retort echoes from the surrounding hills. Blood sprays the ground and I look up to see a hole in the detective's chest the size of a dime. The lights in his eyes go out almost instantly, and his hulking frame slams to the ground, sending dust and debris over our prone torsos.

As the blood trickles out from beneath him, I look up and spy the wafts of smoke billowing from Wesley Coleman's handgun.

CHAPTER 57

SURRENDER

"MOM, COME ON!" Alaina screams, and she helps me to my feet, dragging me back along the path.

I'm still in shock. Brady is dead. The detective who's been trying to help me is dead. Wesley killed him. If he's willing to kill a police officer, what other heinous acts is he willing to commit?

I catch sight of him as I spin to run down the rapidly descending slope. His face is pure hatred tinged with the desperate need to finish things. He has the unmistakable air of someone who knows things have gotten out of hand, but also realizes he has nothing left to lose. If I've been the catalyst for all of this, then I'm also the cause. I realize with a chilling sense of finality that the only way for him to find any kind of peace with this is to kill me once and for all, and that means he will have to kill my daughter too. That's not happening.

My leg is screaming at me to stop. My ankle is swollen to almost twice its size, and I'm pretty sure the hole in my foot is starting to become infected. My leg is hot and weak. I don't know how much further I can run, but I'll keep going until my body gives up on me. Any other option is inconceivable.

"Were they in it together?" Alaina asks through frantic breaths. "Aunt Mary and her boyfriend?"

I realize then that Alaina knew Mary Elisabeth and Wesley. Of course, she did. It's all coming back to me now: the nights when they would come over to my place for drinks, the questions about my dad, Wesley in a car outside Alaina's school when I collected her after class. Wesley's father was in the land business with mine, but they had some sort of disagreement, one that Wesley was trying to resolve for his own gain. They've been planning this for months, whatever *this* is. This isn't just some sort of random kidnapping followed by a murder attempt. This has been carefully plotted and thought through.

"I guess so," I say, trying to hold it all together.

"But why?"

"I don't know," I reply, but I guess we'll find out soon enough.

There's a loud crack and a bullet flies from a tree to our right. I look back and Wesley is taking aim again. He's either trying to hit us or he's trying to scare us. Either way, I don't plan on the two of us hanging around long enough to find out the answer to that question.

"This way," I say, and we dart into the bushes, trying to make ourselves less of a target.

Another bullet slams into a rock to our left, sending sharp shards of granite flying in all directions. I stumble through the undergrowth with my daughter holding me upright. I'm filled with despair as I realize I'm just slowing her down.

"You go," I say. "I can't keep up. It's me that he wants. Just get as far away from here as you can." I scramble around in my pocket and find the number to Barbara Rashford's office. "Call this lady. She'll know how to help you."

The tears start to come now. It's like I'm failing Alaina all over again. Losing her again, too. It's like somebody's reaching into my soul and setting it on fire.

"I'm not leaving you," she says.

"You have to."

"I don't care. I'm not."

Her bravery staggers me. She's so young but so mature. She's been through one hell of an ordeal but it doesn't seem to faze her. She's the adult here, the leader. She has her father in her, the way she holds herself, the slight dimples in her cheeks, that steely determination behind her stare.

"I'm coming for you, Sierra!" Wesley hollers. "And this time, I won't miss."

We push through the trees, scramble down another slope, and head back across the stream. It's much deeper here and the water comes up to our knees. It's a fast current too. For a moment, I think I'm going to lose my footing and get swept away by the water, but Alaina holds onto me.

"Just a little further," she says, but it's obvious she's just trying to buoy my spirits. Even if we make it to the other side, we still need to find somewhere to hide or somebody to help us.

The cold seeps into my bones. The shock of seeing the detective getting killed in cold blood, compounded by the actual freezing temperature of the spring water, is making my body temperature plummet. I come to the conclusion that we can't run away from this. We have to fight.

We scramble up the river bank and drive into the woodland, but I'm done with running.

"Get down in those bushes," I say to Alaina. "Don't come

out, even if something bad happens to me. You never come out. Do you hear me?"

"No," she says. "I'm not leaving your side."

"Alaina, I'm your mother and you'll do exactly as you're told."

The sternness of my voice shocks me and it shocks my daughter too. Tears well in her eyes as she makes her way into a dense area of scrubland. Before too long, I can't see her anymore. Perhaps that's a good thing. The sight of her hurt expression is almost too much for me to bear.

I search the area for something I can use. A rock, a flint, maybe even some metal. Wesley is approaching fast. I can see the outline of his huge bulk wading through the spring water. I can sense the anger in him too, watch as his free hand opens and closes, how the muscles in his neck twitch. He's imagining what he will do when he catches up with me, probably picturing the gun to my forehead, his finger depressing the trigger.

I spot it then. The sharp end of a snapped branch, the point of it like a medieval stake. I stoop to collect it and run a finger over the pointed edge. The weight of it is comforting in my hands. I think it could work.

I step behind a tree as he emerges from the water, the gun held out in front of him.

"You didn't think a little water was going to stop me, did you, Supernova? I thought you would have known me better than that by now. After all, we are married."

I feel his footsteps on the ground and watch in horror as his arm protrudes from around the tree. He doesn't know I'm here, not yet, and that means I have the jump on him. I grip the stake in my hands, grit my teeth, and summon every ounce of strength I have left.

I step out to the side of him and bring the sharp length of

The Lies We Tell

branch down toward him, meaning to slam it into his chest. He looks up at the last minute, and I cherish the alarm in his eyes and the panic in his reaction. He tries to move away, and it's enough to deflect my aim. The pointed tip strikes him in his right shoulder and shreds his shirt. It breaks the skin and embeds itself into muscle and tissue.

He cries out angrily, almost dropping the gun, but he manages to hold onto it. Realizing I've only wounded him, I begin to retreat, but he's regathering himself, pulling the makeshift weapon from his shoulder, and clutching the pistol with unsteady hands.

"Nice try," he hisses, his face now a twisted, gnarled ball of rage. "But now all you've managed to do is piss me off."

He aims the gun at my head and I prepare myself for the inevitable.

CHAPTER 58

REVENGE

"YOU KNOW, I'VE pieced it all together," I say, bluffing, but trying everything to distract him.

"You don't even know the half of it."

"I know you took my daughter," I reply. "Was that your idea or Mary Elisabeth's?"

His eyelid flickers. He's pondering whether to answer. "I figured taking the one thing you cared about the most would give me the most leverage."

"But it didn't work."

He exhales through his nose. "It would have if your friend allowed me to go through with what I was planning."

His words shake me to my core. He means he'd wanted to hurt my daughter.

"But, oh no, she says I can't hurt the girl, that we need to take good care of her." He shakes his head. "And that meant any leverage we had was completely worthless."

"So you went another way."

He laughs. "You could put it like that."

I glance into the bushes and catch a glimpse of Alaina's blonde pigtails. She's just a few feet from me, crouched behind a copse of bushes. I pray he hasn't seen her.

"You paid Frank Duvall to kill me."

His head snaps up as if I've slapped him across the face. "That sonofabitch owed me big time. You know, Frankie boy has a pretty nasty gambling addiction. I've told him time and time again to go see somebody about that."

The blood is oozing from his shoulder wound but he seems oblivious. He's so caught up in the moment, he barely realizes he's bleeding.

"So you offered to wipe the slate clean."

"Not quite. He was going to put in a good word for me with the others on the committee, see if he couldn't force through this development even though the one person with her name on the deed wasn't particularly happy about it."

It's the first time he's mentioned the Mystic Spring development, the first time he's even implied that he was bribing Duvall to gift him the lucrative deal. I press him on it.

"What do you mean, another way?"

"You know how much this land is worth, Sierra? You know how much your old man was sitting on all these years? You know how wealthy you could have been, if only he'd agreed to sell to my dad when he made him a very generous offer?"

I sense the final piece fall into place. Wesley didn't just want the development contract, he wanted the land, the contract, the whole thing. He wanted the ability to set his own price, and the only way he could do that was if I agreed to sell him what my father left me.

"But, oh no, old man Henry Medina was too stubborn for

his own good. When my dad passed, I made it my life's mission to get done what he couldn't."

"But then my dad passed, which meant you had to deal with me. I guess you thought that would be easy, right?"

His hand wavers on the gun. The pain in his shoulder is starting to affect his aim.

"I tried everything," he says. "Even got in with your best friend together to help me convince you."

I think of Mary Elisabeth lying on the ground, the pool of blood around her lifeless corpse. He tricked her into loving him for one reason only. To get his hands on what I had.

"We spent countless evenings with you, helping you get over your dad's death. We even organized a party for you to cheer you up."

I think about the photographs on my social media profile, of me standing with Wesley, of Mary Elisabeth by my side, drinking cocktails. That's what that was all for, to help create something that wasn't real.

"You manipulated her."

He shrugs. "I never said I was a good guy. Sometimes you have to ruffle a few feathers to get the chickens to lay."

I want to charge him, to claw at his face and eyes. Evil pours from him like an infectious disease.

"And when that didn't play out, you stole my daughter."

"Right, but even though we told you what would happen if you went to the police, if you didn't do as you were told, you decided to take matters into your own hands."

I remember the gun in the glove box. I must have known who was behind the kidnapping.

"You left a clue," I say.

"Not me. That imbecile, Marshall. I knew we should never

have brought him on board, but Mary Elisabeth said he could be bought, so that's what we did."

"But he left something behind."

"The key," he says with spite. "You found it out here where we snatched your daughter. You started making inquiries, and before long, you'd tracked down the cabin."

An unspeakable sadness gnaws away at me. I want to believe that leaving the key behind was Kaiden's way of leading me back to my daughter, but I don't know. Now he's dead, along with Mary Elisabeth, and I'm standing out here in the wilderness with a gun aimed at my forehead.

"So you had to act," I say. "Before I led the police straight to your door."

"It wasn't planned that way," he says, "but what choice did I have? You were onto us, which meant I only had one play left. Duvall didn't want to do it, but I made it real clear what would happen if he didn't."

"Except I didn't die."

"I knew he'd fuck it up," he says, "so I followed him, watched him clip you, watched as your car rolled three times before coming to rest at the side of the road."

"You could have left me there to die," I say. "What made you pull me free?"

"Goddam cops drove by, saw me looking beneath the car for signs of life and helped me pull you free," he says. "I had no choice but to act like the hero."

I think about the glass in my hair, the heat on my face, Wesley reaching in to grab me but the sneering look of desperation in his eyes. He didn't know at that point whether I was going to tell the police what had happened, so he concocted a lie.

"You told them you were my husband."

"That's right. The officers in charge didn't know you, and

I knew it would be a little while before they figured out who you really were. I acted so upset, so distraught, it was a damn Oscar-worthy performance. They just took what I said at face value. I figured that with your memory gone, I could get you to sign the deeds over to me. Hell, I even had fake marriage papers made up and got some guy in San Francisco to photoshop the wedding photos I showed you."

I'm shaking with rage now, at the sheer evilness of his plan. He had me tied up in so many knots, I was so lost, so alone. I thought I was losing my mind, that my suspicions that he wasn't all that he seemed were just some misguided notions brought on by my own burgeoning paranoia.

"You bastard."

"Hey," he says, shrugging. "It almost worked. Still could."

A thought occurs to me. "My mother."

"Yeah, right," he sneers. "Your mom."

"Except she isn't, right?"

Wesley twitches as if he's been slapped. "She wanted in on it. Thought she could help with the lie. Something about women believing other women more than they'll believe strange men."

"I don't understand."

"She was distraught when my dad died, blamed your dad for not signing the land over to him when he had the chance. They'd been best friends since kids, business partners, but your old man could never see the bigger picture. It was a lifelong ambition of my pop's, to develop this valley, make my family the kind of money he thought we deserved."

"Evie's your mom?"

"Evie Coleman. One and the same."

I can't believe I didn't see it before; the way she looked at Wesley, the way she talked affectionately about him. I've been so stupid, so naïve.

"You know I'm going to the police, right?" I say, trying to summon up some semblance of bravado. "There's no way you're getting away with this."

He sighs. "You're not walking away from this, Sierra. And neither is your little girl." My stomach flips as he steps forward and calls into the bushes. "I suggest you stand up, Alaina, unless you want me to put a bullet in your mom's face."

"She's gone," I say out of desperation. "By now, she would have made it to the road and probably been picked up by a passerby. I bet the police are on their way here as we speak."

"Don't take me for a fool, Sierra," he says, gesturing with the gun. "Alaina, you have three seconds and then your mommy here will be picking lead out of her teeth."

"No!" I yell, but Alaina is already standing. Her hands are up, her eyes flitting anxiously between Wesley and me.

"I'm sorry, Mom," she says, but I should be the one who's sorry. I led us both to this.

"I'm sorry," Wesley says, "but there's no way I can let you walk away from this. You know that, right?"

"No, wait," I say. "I'll sign the land over. You can have it. I don't want it."

"It's too late for that," he replies. "I don't know if you saw, but I shot a cop back there."

"Please," I say, my hands held out. "Kill me if you want, but not Alaina, not my baby girl." Tears stream down my cheeks as I hold my daughter close to me. It can't have come to this. It can't have.

"I'm sorry." There's a raw certainty in his eyes. "I can't leave any witnesses."

I hold Alaina, trying to shield her from him, but it's no use. I've failed in the one thing I'm supposed to be able to do as a mother, the one thing I promised Jake. I brace myself for the sound of the gun, for the impact of the bullet. I close my eyes.

There's a roar from the trees, and I look up as a man dives on top of Wesley. They roll onto the ground in a tangled ball of limbs. The gun spills from Wesley's grip and rolls into the bushes. Wesley tries to fight the man off, but although he appears to be bleeding badly, the stranger holds his own, punching Wesley in the face and trying to get his hands around his throat.

Alaina tries to pull me away, but I can't leave. I need to know what's happening. Wesley kicks out a leg and drives the man to the floor, and now he's on top, pummeling the stranger, but now I can see it's not a stranger at all. I cry out. The man with the hole in his chest is Kaiden. His skin is white, his eyes not quite there, but he's doing everything he can to save us. The only problem is, Wesley is too big for him, too strong. He's going to lose. I watch as fist after fist rains down on Kaiden. I stand motionless like a helpless victim. I can't be that, I won't be. Kaiden looks up at me through bloodied eyes and we share a moment of knowing. He didn't want this. He made mistakes. Saving us is his way of making amends. Now I need to do something for him.

The gun is cold in my hands, the grip like the scabbard of a sword.

I hold it up, trembling as I take aim. I don't have long. I have to act.

With my daughter at my back and the weight of my past life now bearing down on me, I pull the trigger.

EPILOGUE

THE AFTERMATH IS a blur to me.

The police arrived shortly after we called them and sealed off both scenes. I stood there, numb. I couldn't believe I killed two people, one of which was my best friend. I couldn't believe Brady was dead. He'd risked everything to help me and paid the ultimate price. Although I didn't trust him at first, now I realize I owe him so much.

Kaiden was taken to the hospital. He'd been shot in the chest, but thankfully the bullet exited through his shoulder. He'd been badly beaten and he'd lost a lot of blood, but thankfully he had the strength to pull through. I visited him in the hospital with Alaina every day. I hated him for what he did, but I felt sorry for him, too. He'd been manipulated into becoming involved, and then, when he'd tried to make it right, Mary Elisabeth had tried to kill him. He recalls visiting her at her house, of turning his back and then realizing she was holding a gun. He remembers the sound of the pistol firing, and then everything is blank. He woke up in the forest under a pile of dirt and leaves. Apparently, Mary Elisabeth had left him in the woods to be disposed of later. He'd managed to hot-wire a car and drive, bloodied and delirious, to his cabin, figuring that if anything was going to happen, it was going to happen there. I'll forever be thankful that he did. If he'd made a different decision, if he'd headed straight to the hospital, Alaina and I would be dead. The thought makes my body feel numb.

He told me all about the social media posts Wesley had made him create to help convince me about my life before. He'd been the one to delete what was there and add in only those pictures that Wesley and Mary Elisabeth had so carefully orchestrated at the fake party. He'd even blocked all my old contacts, made it seem as if I'd changed my number, preventing people I knew from messaging me. As far as everybody was concerned, I was out of town for a while on some sort of sabbatical. Mary Elisabeth had even helped perpetuate the lie at the magazine we both worked for.

When Kaiden realized what they'd planned to do with Alaina, he knew he needed to act. He visited Alaina frequently, bringing her food, water, and blankets. He'd even brought her books to read. I'd initially thought it had been Mary Elisabeth who had been caring for my daughter, but I was wrong. It had been Kaiden all along. He posted a few easter eggs onto my social media account without them knowing to help my memory along: the picture of Mary Elisabeth and I with my real father, the image of me at Mystic Spring, the video at The Blind Pony. He knew that if I saw him at the bar, it would lead me down a path, even if it meant exposing him as a liar. He knew he couldn't tell me directly, that if he did he would be killed, but he did what he could to lead me to the real truth.

Weeks later, we sit out in my garden in a house I now remember, watching as the sun starts to dip toward the horizon. Alaina is dressed in a pale blue summer dress. She looks so much like her father.

Kaiden's shoulder is still heavily strapped, but he's managed to regain some of his color. We're eating chicken salad and drinking homemade lemonade. At last, I feel like my life is close to what it was before; before Wesley and my best friend decided to delete my history from my mind.

"I'll go tomorrow," Kaiden says.

"You don't have to."

"Yes. I do," he replies.

We've been debating it for days. The police know Redshoot cabin belongs to Kaiden, but they have no proof that he had any involvement in what Wesley and Mary Elisabeth did to me. Kaiden wants to confess, Alaina and I don't want him to. I suspect he'll do it anyway. He's like that. Despite everything, he's a good man.

I've forgiven him. Alaina too. In fact, Alaina clings to Kaiden like he's an uncle she never knew she had. She will never forget his acts of kindness while she was imprisoned. I, for one, am glad he's around. Those feelings I suspected I had have grown since that fateful day in Mystic Spring. Maybe one day they'll even blossom. I promise myself not to push it. I'm a trauma victim, and that means my emotions are still all over the place. We'll take our time.

"When I'm out, we'll start again," he says. "Introduce ourselves properly."

"I'd like that." I smile.

He gets up and heads into the kitchen, carrying empty plates and bowls. I watch him leave. Alaina catches me looking and nudges me. She's no fool. She sees things in me I don't even see in myself.

I think about the project I'm planning at Mystic Spring in my father's name. The nature reserve that Max Cramer mentioned. It's going to be a place where families can go to witness the true wonders of the hills, educate what it is to be Californian. It was exactly what Wesley didn't want me to do, to use the land for what nature intended. If I have my way, it will be there forever, my father's everlasting legacy.

I don't notice the intruder standing in the trees, watching Alaina and I share a joke. In my mind, the terrors of the past few weeks are over. I've never been more wrong of anything in my whole life.

She shrieks as she lunges at me, her arm raised high over her immaculately coiffured hair, the blade glistening with the burnt orange of the slowly setting sun. I smell the unmistakable scent of lavender and peach blossom. I push Alaina away as the knife plunges into my shoulder and I fall to the ground with Evie Coleman on top of me, her eyes ablaze with hatred and vengeance.

I struggle against her, but my shoulder is burning from the stab wound. I slap at her hand, sending the knife flying, but it does nothing to prevent her assault. She slips her hands around my throat and squeezes. My larynx compress as my vision starts to blur.

"All he wanted was what was rightfully his!" she screams. "What your father denied us!"

I try to wriggle away, but she's so much stronger than she looks. It's clear in her eyes that she won't stop until my life has literally been squeezed from my body.

"And you killed him! You killed my sweet, sweet boy!"

I try to say that, *yes I did, but only because he was going to kill my daughter*, but by this point I'm barely there at all. My lungs are screaming for oxygen, my brain starved to the point of becoming nothing more than a vessel of empty thoughts.

Alaina is standing behind Evie. I try to tell her to run, to get away, but nothing comes out. Her blonde pigtails flutter in the breeze, and I wonder whether I'm dreaming again, whether

I'm back in a coma and Alaina is visiting me in my unconscious state.

Then I see the knife in her hand and I realize my daughter is done being a victim, and she's done watching her mother suffer. She brings the blade down into Evie's spine, and the older woman's eyes snap open as her mouth twists into an agonized grimace. Blood trickles from her ruby-red lips as she falls to the side, her hands like claws, her body lifeless.

I look up and watch as Kaiden comes running from the kitchen, but it's okay. I'm with Alaina and Alaina is with me. Nothing will ever change that ever again.